THE INHERITANCE

Recent Titles by Caroline Gray from Severn House

BLUE WATERS, BLACK DEPTHS
CROSSBOW
THE DAUGHTER
GOLDEN GIRL
MASQUERADE
SHADOW OF DEATH
SPARES
A WOMAN OF HER TIME
A CHILD OF FORTUNE

The Colonial Series

BOOK ONE: THE PROMISED LAND
BOOK TWO: THE PHOENIX
BOOK THREE: THE TORRENT
BOOK FOUR: THE INHERITANCE

THE INHERITANCE

Caroline Gray

This first world edition published in Great Britain 1999 by
SEVERN HOUSE PUBLISHERS LTD of
9–15 High Street, Sutton, Surrey SM1 1DF.
First published in the USA 2000 by
SEVERN HOUSE PUBLISHERS INC., of
595 Madison Avenue, New York, NY 10022.

British Library Cataloguing in Publication Data

Gray,   Caroline,   1930-
        The inheritance
        1.   Detective and mystery stories
        I.   Title
        823.9'14 [F]

        ISBN 0-7278-5463-1

Typeset by Palimpsest Book Production Ltd
Polmont, Stirlingshire, Scotland.
Printed and bound in Great Britain by
MPG Books Ltd, Bodmin, Cornwall.

Contents

There is a pleasure sure,
In being mad, which none but madmen know.
John Dryden

Part One

The Heiress

How pleasant it is to have money, heigh-ho!
How pleasant it is to have money.
Arthur Hugh Clough

One

The big Mercedes pulled up to the kerb and the uniformed doorman hurried across the pavement to open the door.

"Good morning, madam," he said.

"Good morning, Harris." Joanna Johannsson stepped out of the car, waited for the young man to join her. "There it is. Your future." She glanced at her son as she spoke. She sometimes found it difficult to believe that Raisul ben Hasim *was* her son, not only because he was so dark where she was so fair, but because at twenty he was so tall and powerfully built, while she remained a slight woman.

But even at forty-two, she remained beautiful enough to cause the passers-by to hesitate, and look again. No doubt the mink coat had something to do with it. But Joanna Johannsson had always worn a mink, from the days she had been Joanna Edge, the city whizz-kid who had used her looks and her allure to turn a bankrupt shipping company into a viable and successful business, back in the sixties before animal rights activists had become over-aggressive. She did not consider that changing attitudes should affect her lifestyle. No one was ever going to throw paint at Joanna Johannsson, accompanied as she always was by at least one large man. And surrounded by an aura of tragedy and high adventure, she thought, as she accepted her briefcase from her new chauffeur, Deardon. Deardon had been left in no doubt that the man he had replaced, Charlie Hatch, had died defending his mistress, and that he might be expected to do the same.

She wondered if she would ever achieve such a total

empathy with this man as she had shared with Charlie. Harris was holding the door for her and she swept inside, to be greeted by the various receptionists and telephonists, and the interior guard. All were pleased to see her, even if they saw her every day of the working week: Joanna Johannsson was a good person for whom to work.

Raisul followed somewhat diffidently. He had been to the offices of Caribee Shipping before, of course, but always as a visitor, the son of the Chairperson and Managing Director. This was his first visit as an executive . . . and all these people knew it. The elevator was waiting, and Joanna faced her son as it sped upwards. "Well?"

"Excited, I guess. What do I do?"

"You begin by familiarising yourself with every aspect of the business, from weather to shipbuilding. We have a new ship on the stocks now. I want you to go up to the Clyde and inspect her, and bring me back a detailed report on what you have seen, what you like, and what you don't like."

Raisul gulped. "Today?"

Joanna smiled. "No, Monday. You have today and tomorrow to have a look around the office. I'll have Nicola take you round. Don't be afraid to ask questions. That's the only way to learn."

"Do I see you at all?"

The lift came to a halt. "I'm always here." She stepped out, and her secretary was waiting to take her coat. Nicola Outridge was relatively new; a handsome young woman, she had only been in the job just over a year, but had fitted in very well with Joanna's rather sudden way of doing things. "You've met Raisul," Joanna commented.

"Of course. Welcome to Caribee Shipping, Mr . . ." Nicola's eyes fluttered behind her horn-rimmed spectacles.

"In the office, Raisul will be known as Mr Edge," Joanna said.

"Of course," Nicola said again. She knew that the boy was not the late Howard Edge's child. Howard Edge had been the

4

entrepreneur and ladies' man – and, incidentally, shipowner – who had swept Joanna Grain from the demi-monde into which she had been sinking following the murder of her police inspector father in far off British Guiana – as Guyana had then been known – and having installed her as his mistress, had then divorced his wife to marry her. Even in her teens Joanna had been irresistible.

Then Howard Edge had drowned, and the twenty-year-old immigrant – she had actually been born in British Guiana of English parents – had found herself an heiress to an all but bankrupt business empire. Nicola also knew that to resuscitate Caribee Shipping, Joanna Edge had had to undertake some very unusual financial wheeler-dealing. Which had involved marrying one of her admirers and supporters, Prince Hasim of Qadir. This young man's father.

Tragedy had always hung close on Joanna's heels, and Prince Hasim had been murdered by emissaries of his half-brother, determined to make sure he never contested the throne of Qadir. But Raisul had always been considered heir to the Caribee throne, even more so than his older half-sister Helen, Joanna's daughter by Howard Edge. But Helen . . . "Miss Edge coming in today?" Nicola asked.

"I imagine so." Joanna sat behind her desk, where Nicola had just placed her open diary.

"You're lunching with Mr Johannsson," Nicola said. "Le Caprice, at one."

Joanna nodded. Her fourth and last marriage was as unusual as any of the others. Michael Johannsson had so many business interests that he often slept in town, although he always weekended at Caribee House in Berkshire with his wife. But during the week he enjoyed occasionally meeting up with her as if they were merely lovers, rather than husband and wife. Michael was in many ways a man of mystery, Joanna reflected. She knew very little of his background, save that he had been born and lived most of his life in Canada, that he had been a widower and that he was a multi-millionaire. That in the strangest of circumstances he had plucked her from a prison cell, forgiven her many sins, married her, and placed his millions at her disposal – this had been all that she had really wanted to know about him.

No doubt she could be described as self-centred, but her apparent non-interest in his previous life seemed to please him.

"Tell Deardon to have the car ready at a quarter to," she said. "Mr Young in?"

"Yes, ma'am."

"Ask him to join me. Now, Nicola, I would like you to take Mr Edge on a tour of the building." She smiled at the nervous Raisul, hovering in the doorway. "Show him everything, and tell him anything he wants to know."

"Of course, Mrs Johannsson. Just let me make those calls first, Mr Edge." She ushered Raisul out and closed the office door.

Joanna took off her navy blue jacket and hung it in the wardrobe beside the mink; she wore a crisp white shirt with her navy blue skirt. She surveyed herself in the wall mirror: she used little make-up, as she still possessed a flawless complexion to go with the neatly chiselled features that had turned so many heads, but she liked to be sure that her yellow hair, which she kept long but wore in a tight bun when in the office, was not drifting about, as it had a tendency to do. She sat behind her desk and sifted through her mail, then got up again, as she always did, and stood in front of the huge chart of the world that occupied the entire inner wall. Marked on the chart by flags were the positions of every one of the six Caribee Shipping freighters, en route, discharging, or loading. The door behind her opened, and closed again. "All correct?" she asked, without turning her head.

"Shipping-wise," Peter Young said. This was another daily routine, partly so that they could see each other at least once

6

a day. But his reply was not the usual reassuring acknowl-edgement.

Peter Young had been Operations Manager and Company Secretary for Howard Edge, when both had been relatively young men. He had been appalled to find himself employed by a twenty-year-old girl whom many had regarded as little better than a whore. But dislike and distrust had soon changed to admiration and even love, although he had never attempted to do anything about the latter. In 1986 he was in his middle sixties, and still her most devoted admirer, since he felt that she also valued him. He had lost his job, in company with most of the Caribee senior staff, when Joanna's lifestyle had involved her in a prison sentence back in the seventies. But when she had got out, and so remarkably been set back on her feet by Michael Johannsson, regaining control of the company, her first act had been to recall Peter Young to his old position. Of course, he knew he could never equal a man like Johannsson, but just being close to his idol was satisfying enough.

Joanna returned behind her desk. "This has got to be about the best year we've had," she remarked. "If the government could get to grips with inflation, now, we wouldn't have a care in the world."

Peter sat opposite. "The low exchange rate rather suits us though. Ah . . ." he took off his glasses and polished them.

"Give." Joanna knew immediately when he had something on his mind.

"I was hoping you would tell me," Peter said.

Joanna frowned. "I have no idea what you are talking about." But she did, and felt a sudden constriction in her chest.

"She hasn't been in touch?" Peter asked.

"For God's sake, Peter," Joanna snapped. "No, she hasn't been in touch. She didn't come home last night. But then, she often doesn't come home nights. What are you saying, that Helen is in some kind of trouble?"

"Helen has been arrested on a drugs charge."

"A drugs charge? Why wasn't I informed earlier?"

"Because she didn't want you to know. She has been charged under her married name of Moore. I wouldn't have known about it had not Harry Sedgling, her solicitor, called me. Strictly on the QT. She's out on bail, but Harry felt someone should let you know. Unofficially. It could be quite serious. She's accused of peddling heroin."

"In the name of God . . ." Joanna sat back and drove her hands into her hair, destroying her hitherto immaculate coiffeur and bringing golden strands drifting down on to her shoulders as her bun collapsed.

"I know," Peter said. "She's good-looking, heir to a fortune . . . what does she need to peddle heroin for? But it could mean a custodial sentence."

"Tell Sedgling I wish to see him. Now. Where is Helen?"

"He wouldn't tell me."

"Well, he'll have to tell me. Get him."

"Right away." Peter stood up, then hesitated. "Jo . . . Helen is twenty-two."

"She's still my daughter," Joanna said.

So that was what Nicola had had in mind when she had asked, so innocently, if Helen was coming in. The wretched girl. Joanna got up and prowled around the office. But what had she expected? Of all the poor little rich girls in the world, Helen had to be the poorest, in terms of emotional instability. She had never known her real father, only a succession of surrogates. Then she had been left at the mercy of a surrogate mother while her own mother had gone to prison – for life had been the sentence.

Had it just been for one year, then that would have been sufficiently humiliating and traumatic for a teenage girl who had always considered her mother an indestructible driving force, leaping from success to success. That the life sentence had turned out to be only seven years, thanks to Michael Johannsson, should have been a bonus, but it had come too late for Helen, already living like a down and out in Brixton, subjected to a horrendous assault during the riots.

Joanna had done everything possible to rehabilitate her, kept her out at Caribee House, nurtured her back to at least physical strength, and introduced her to business as a Caribee executive. She had thought she was winning, until that disastrous voyage three years ago. It had seemed such a good idea, to send the girl on a long voyage on a Caribee ship, to Australia and back, not just as a passenger, but as a supernumary acting for her mother. It had all been going so well, until the ship had been hijacked by Indonesian revolutionaries. That had been an inside job, engineered by one of her own captains, Dennis Moore. But no one had known that then. Helen had responded magnificently, regaining control of the ship virtually single-handed, and had been touted in the media as the ultimate heroine . . . there had even been talk of a movie, although that had fallen through.

But she had also fallen in love with the other apparent hero of the operation, Dennis Moore, had married him over her mother's misgivings, and embarked on a tragic course that had ended in Moore's death. So it was back to square one when it came to emotional traumas. Once again, constant counselling and a great deal of tender loving care.

But it is not possible to keep a high-spirited and attractive young woman locked up in a country house, without resorting to law. That was something Joanna would never do after her own experiences. Helen was a beautiful young widow with a sensational past. Men wanted to be seen with her. Surely, Joanna had reckoned, out of the dozens who had come knocking on her door, she would find someone suitable? And yet, instead, she had wound up pushing drugs? She couldn't believe it.

She telephoned Michael and told him the news.

"Damn," he said. "Do you want to cancel lunch?"

"No. I'm looking forward to that. I just wanted you to know in advance."

"Anything I can do?"

He always said that, and if it was possible he did it, too. Theirs was, she supposed, a unique relationship. She had actually been sent to prison for killing Michael's son. It had been an accident, self-defence to an attempted rape. But the police had thought otherwise, having found evidence that Sean Connor was planning to blackmail her. They had charged her with a skilfully planned and committed murder, and they had won their case, less, she was certain, because their evidence had been overwhelming, than because she was the woman everyone hated to love, and therefore loved to hate: the ultimate success story, the phoenix who had risen from the ashes more than once, to triumph. How the City had smiled as she was put away.

Michael had rescued her from prison. Even the most hard-ened parole board had been unable to resist her application when it turned out she was going to marry the father of the man whom she had killed. No matter that Michael and Sean had long been estranged, that Michael had known just what a thug his son had turned out to be. It had been the utterly romantic concept that had won the day. Thus, again, the phoenix triumphant. Michael, recently widowed, had put all his millions at her disposal to buy back Caribee Shipping. He had put himself at her disposal to achieve everything she wanted. He had even put her sexual freedom at her disposal, a grant she had only ever taken advantage of once, and bitterly regretted it. His own support had never wavered.

But Helen was a personal problem, which even his millions and ebullient personality could not solve. Besides, Helen was the only subject on which they had ever really differed. Helen had not taken to her somewhat authoritarian stepfather; Michael had felt that Joanna was far too indulgent to the girl, while recognising and appearing to understand that Helen had lived an exceptionally traumatic life. "Just let me talk about it," she said.

William Grain came in. He was Joanna's younger brother,

10

another of her faithful supporters through thick and thin. Fair-haired and good-looking, he had actually stopped one of the bullets intended for Prince Hasim, and had never fully recovered – he moved slowly and awkwardly. But his loyalty had never wavered, and he was vice-chairman of the firm.

"I suppose you've heard the news?" Joanna asked.

"It's filtering through. What are you going to do?"

"I'm not sure what I can do. But it'll have to be something."

"You can't let Helen go to jail, Jo. That'll . . ." he bit his lip.

"Just drive her round the bend," Joanna agreed. "I know that, Willie. Like I said, it'll have to be something."

"If there is anything I can do . . . or Norma . . ."

"I'll let you know," Joanna said.

Sedgling arrived at half-past eleven. By then Nicola had finished showing Raisul the ropes, and had left him in a private office ensconced with piles of shipping material to be read.

"You knew about Helen's arrest, didn't you?" Joanna asked the young woman.

Nicola flushed. "Mr Young took the call in my office. But I didn't know if you knew, and the boy . . . Mr Edge."

"You're my secretary, Nicola," Joanna said. "Secrets we can do without. Show Mr Sedgling in."

The solicitor was nervous, a not uncommon misfortune for men confronted with Joanna Johannsson; a little man with a furtive manner, he seemed mesmerised by her dangling earrings as much as by her still untidy hair.

"Where is she?" Joanna demanded.

"She went to an hotel. She said she wanted a bath and a lie down."

"Which hotel?"

"The Royal Edward."

That figured. The only surprise was that it hadn't been the Savoy. "And has she any explanation for what she did?"

"I think she was high herself at the time. She was at this pub, with some friends . . ."

"Friends?"

"Well, that's what she said they were. And they were doing drugs, light stuff, and she offered a packet to a girl who had just joined the party, and who turned out to be an undercover policewoman."

"She was set up. I never knew she'd ever touched heroin."

"She says she didn't know the packet contained heroin. But . . ."

"But what?"

"That's what they all say, Mrs Johannsson."

"I am not supposed to know anything about it, I understand."

"Those were Helen's instructions. She *is* my client, you know."

"But you will take your instructions from me." She gave him a cold smile. "After all, you will be submitting your account to me, won't you?"

"Will I?"

"Sedgling, Helen may come across as a wealthy woman, but her money starts here. Who paid her bail?"

"Well . . . I did."

"And I'm sure you'll put the interest on the bill. Now I am telling you what I want done. I wish you to insist that she have a medical examination, right away, to establish whether or not she has a habit."

"The police had her examined by one of their people, and they say there is no trace of any needlework. I can have her tested for non-intravenous use, but somehow I don't think we'll find anything."

"Thank God for that. I'm sure I would have noticed something. But it's vital we have our own independent medical opinion."

"It's not all good news, Mrs Johannsson."

"Speak."

"Well, from a police point of view, the fact that she doesn't do drugs herself, but that she offered them for sale, suggests that she's a pusher. Most pushers have more sense than to use their own stuff."

"Helen has absolutely no reason to push drugs for money."

"Of course. But if the case comes to court, with her background, and, ah . . ."

"And my background? Is that what you were going to say?"

"Well, Mrs Johannsson . . ."

"Oh, get out," Joanna said. "Have her examined, from head to toe. I want a full report on my desk tomorrow morning. And suggest it might be a good idea for her to come home and tell her mum about it. Don't tell her I already know."

"I'll do whatever I can." Sedgling got to his feet, more nervously than ever.

"And find out what you need to do to keep this out of court," Joanna added.

Sedgling nodded, somewhat dolefully, and left the room. Nicola hovered in the doorway. "There are some calls . . ."

"I'm not speaking with anyone this morning," Joanna said. "I'm going out to lunch with my husband. Is Deardon waiting?"

"Yes, ma'am." Nicola could tell when her employer was in a very bad mood.

Joanna peered at herself in the mirror. "God, what a mess."

"May I assist you, ma'am?" Nicola fussed, tucking a stray wisp here, another there, re-creating the bun.

"That'll have to do. I don't know when I'll be back." Joanna put on her jacket, and Nicola held her mink for her. "Or if I'll be back, today."

"Yes, ma'am."

"What do we do for lunch?" Raisul appeared just as Joanna was leaving.

"Mostly you lunch at the office."

13

"With you?"

"Not today. I have a date. Lunch with Nicola. She'll send out for a sandwich and a bottle of beer. I'll see you later."

The door closed, and Raisul looked at Nicola. "Looks as if we have a date too," she said. "I'll order those sandwiches."

He remained standing in the doorway as she went into her office and sat at her desk, one knee crossed over the other. He saw that she showed a lot of shapely black tight-encased leg, while the rest of her, in her black skirt and white shirt, completed a very attractive picture, with her neatly dressed shoulder-length black hair and her pert features. Even the spectacles she wore around the office were attractive. He wondered how old she was. Older than himself, certainly. And then he wondered why he wondered. She was Mother's secretary. But then she was, or she could be, his secretary also, in the course of time.

He was suddenly randy. Girls had not been important at university; he had only been up for one year, for a crash course in business studies, and he had spent his spare time training for the athletics team. In any event, he had always regarded the female sex, as it operated in Great Britain, with considerable suspicion. Even if his right to the title had been renounced, he was still Prince Raisul of Qadir. They all knew that, as they all knew he was the son of a woman who had been convicted of a sensational murder in which kinky sex had been involved. He could never be sure that any of them were interested in him, rather than in what he was. But his own feelings for them were equally equivocal. He had an English mother and had been brought up as an English gentleman. But his father had *owned* women. Raisul was not at all sure that Father had not even owned Joanna; he had been only a small boy when Father had been gunned down. He knew, deep in his heart, that his desires were also centred upon owning. Did one own one's secretary? Not in England in 1986. But at least one employed her.

Having ordered the sandwiches, Nicola replaced the phone.

14

"When you look at me like that you make me nervous," she remarked.

"Why?"

"Because you look so . . . so terribly Arab." She bit her lip. "I shouldn't have said that."

"I'll take it as a compliment," he said.

Joanna rode down in the lift. Now she was seething, less at Helen's stupidity than at the point Sedgling had made. Helen was the daughter of a highflyer who was also a convicted murderess. Therefore, in the eyes of the tabloid press, and by extension the public and thus the police, she had to be capable of every crime known to man – or woman. It was so unfair.

The maitre d' smiled at her; she was one of his favourite customers, even when she looked as if she'd been dragged through a hedge backwards. "Mr Johannsson has not yet arrived, Mrs Johannsson. Will you wait?"

"At the table."

"Of course, madam." He relieved her of her coat, then escorted her through the tables, and she smiled at the people she recognised. He held her chair for her. "An aperitif?"

"Brandy and ginger. Make it a double."

"Of course, madam." He flicked his fingers, and one of his wine waiters hurried over. "I'll leave these." He placed the menus on the table beside her.

Joanna idly opened the folder and glanced down the list. She was less looking at the choices of food than avoiding questing eyes, wondering how many people in the room knew of her domestic problems. None at the moment, most likely. But they all would soon enough, when the media remembered that Helen Moore was Joanna Johannsson's daughter. She looked up with a bright smile as the maitre d' returned, then frowned as she saw that he was carrying a telephone. Oh, no, she thought.

"It appears to be urgent, madam," he said, placing the phone on the table.

Joanna picked it up. "Yes?"

"Mrs Johannsson? Reynolds here." John Reynolds was her husband's PA.

Joanna gave a little sigh of relief: she had assumed the call was to do with Helen. "Don't tell me; he can't make lunch."

She heard Reynolds gulp at the end of the line. "Mrs Johannsson, Mr Johannsson has been taken ill."

"Ill? How ill?"

"I'm afraid he's dead, Mrs Johannsson."

Joanna stared at the phone. Only dimly did she heard what Reynolds was saying: "It must have been a heart attack. He was just leaving to meet you, and he suddenly clutched his chest, and then collapsed. We did everything we could, Mrs Johannsson, had a doctor here in five minutes . . . but he could not be revived." He paused. "Mrs Johannsson? Are you there?"

"Where is my husband now?" she asked.

"He has been taken to hospital. But . . ."

"He's dead," she said. "Which hospital?"

"St George's."

"Thank you, Reynolds." She replaced the phone. "You'll have to cancel lunch, Antoine."

He had been hovering and had heard her end of the conversation. "Oh, Mrs Johannsson, I am so terribly sorry."

"Thank you. Would you call my car? I'll wait in the bar."

Antoine escorted her through the tables, found her a seat, hesitated, clearly wondering if she was going to be all right, gave his barman a meaningful glance, and himself hurried for the street door. Behind him the noise level in the restaurant grew; if perhaps they did not know exactly what had happened, they knew *something* had happened. "Would you like a drink, Mrs Johannsson?" asked the barman.

She shook her head. As she normally breakfasted on orange juice and coffee, the brandy she had just drunk was sitting on a very empty stomach. Besides, she felt sick. More in her head than in her gut for the time being, but she knew the two were going to come together at some time, probably quite soon.

16

Antoine hurried back, carrying her mink. "The car is waiting, Mrs Johannsson."

Joanna sank into the back. "St George's Hospital."

Deardon did not speak until he was safely in a traffic stream. "Something wrong, madam?"

"Mr Johannsson is dead." Again there was a brief silence. Mr Johannson is dead, Joanna thought. My husband is dead. Something she should be used to, as Michael was her third husband to die suddenly. How did one get used to husbands dying suddenly? But where Howard had drowned, virtually before her eyes, and Hasim had been shot down, definitely before her eyes, Michael had just died. Why? He was only sixty-one.

"I am most terribly sorry, madam," Deardon said at last. He was her employee rather than Michael's. But he had to worry about the future.

Anxious nurses, a nervous young doctor. "You do not have to see him, if you do not wish to, Mrs Johannsson," the doctor said. "The body has been identified."

"I wish to see him," Joanna said.

He went up in the lift with her. "He was a very big man," he remarked. "And heavy. I suppose . . . had he had heart trouble before?"

"No," Joanna said. The lift stopped, and she was taken to the room where Michael lay. He looked absolutely relaxed, no trace of strain or pain on his face. They had closed his eyes. "What happens now?"

"I'm afraid there will have to be an autopsy. Sudden death, you see."

"You said it was a heart attack."

"We are fairly certain that it was. But the law requires . . ."

"Oh, quite. And then?"

"You may go ahead with the funeral arrangements. The autopsy will be carried out this afternoon. And supposing the cause of death *was* heart failure, your husband's body will be yours to dispose of."

"Thank you." She left the room, the doctor hovering, undoubtedly concerned that there were no tears or visible signs of distress.

"Do you . . . need anything?" he asked.

She glanced at him. "Not right now," she said.

She was still numbed. Michael had been going to be the very last man in her life. Of course she had always known that because of the nineteen-year difference in their ages, he would almost certainly die first, but it was not something she had considered for at least another ten years. Now, presumably, life had to go on. She would have to take over Michael's business as well as her own, she supposed. She had no idea what was involved, but presumably he had efficient managers and accountants. Reynolds would be able to tell her about that. Then she would have to . . . his family! She knew nothing about his family, or even if he had one. She knew his first wife had died of cancer, and she knew how his son had died. He had never mentioned any other family in all the eight years they had been married.

And she, so busily reconstructing her own life, had never thought to ask. Only Michael had mattered. Certainly no other relative had ever intruded into their lives. But he had to have other kin. Well, all she could do would be to put a notice of death in all the leading papers, in Canada, where his main business enterprises were located, as well as in England. She needed to make a list of everything that should be done.

"Where are we going, madam?" Deardon asked.

She hadn't thought of that. But she wanted to be alone. "Home."

They drove out of town, hummed along the A4 towards Heathrow and Windsor; the turn-off was just beyond the royal town. Caribee House was situated close enough to Ascot for the shouts of the punters to be heard during the week. But in May that was still a few weeks off. They were at the house before she had even realised so much time had passed. The barking retrievers surrounded the car, and their mistress, with joyous exuberance; she wasn't generally home in the middle of the afternoon.

"Is everything all right, madam?" asked Parks the butler.

"No," Joanna said. "I am going up to my room, Parks. I do not wish to receive any telephone calls."

"Of course, madam." Over the years Parks had learned to take all unusual events in his stride, certainly where his mistress was involved.

"Is Mrs Montgomery in?" she asked. Matilda Montgomery was Joanna's older sister, a wreck of a woman since her husband's violent death some years ago; Joanna had given her a wing of the huge, rambling mansion built by Howard Edge's grandfather as a home, even if the two sisters had never really got on. They lived separate lives as much as possible – Matilda also had two children, and like Joanna's, these were now grown up and fending for themselves – but Joanna knew that this was something into which Matilda would be anxious to get involved – and to enjoy it.

"Mrs Montgomery is out, madam."

"Good. I do not wish to be disturbed, Parks. But I would like a plate of sandwiches."

"And a bottle of Bollinger, madam?" He was anticipating her usual wish.

"Why not?" Joanna asked. It was what Michael would have recommended.

Joanna showered, ate, drank, and fell into a deep sleep. When she awoke it was past five. She picked up the phone. "Have there been any calls, Parks?"

"Quite a few, madam."

"Tell me."

"Mr William. Mr Raisul. Mr Young. Miss Outridge. Mr Andrews. Mr Lustrum. And Mrs Montgomery has returned and wishes to see you as soon as you wake up."

But nothing from Helen, Joanna thought grimly. "I'll take

them in order. But don't tell Mrs Montgomery I've woken, yet."

"Jo?" William's voice was fraught. "My God, Jo, I'm most terribly sorry."

"Thank you. At least it seems to have happened so suddenly that there could only have been a second's pain."

"Is there anything you want me to do?"

"Yes. Handle the funeral arrangements. Nothing elaborate."

"I'll get on to it right away. When do we . . . ?"

"They're chopping him about now," Joanna said. "Just to make sure he wasn't poisoned or something. The body will be available tomorrow."

"Right. And . . . ah . . . ?"

"He is to be cremated," Joanna said. "On Monday. At the crematorium in Windsor. I want it kept very simple and with as few people as possible. Donations can go to a heart foundation."

"Right. Would you like Norma to come down for a day or two?"

Norma Grain was William's wife, a sweet woman but not really good at coping with grief. "I'll manage," Joanna said.

"Mum!" Raisul's voice was equally fraught. "Oh, Mum."

"Where are you?"

"At the office. I didn't know what to do."

"So you did the right thing. You can come home now, though. I've sent Deardon back for you."

"Oh . . . right."

Joanna raised her eyebrows. "Don't you want to come home?"

"Well, of course I do. Just as soon as I can." He had never been able to lie convincingly.

"Whenever you're ready," she told him. "Put me through to Nicola."

*　　　*　　　*

20

"I'm terribly sorry, Mrs Johannsson," Nicola said.

"Thank you, Nicola. I'm trusting you to field all the calls that come in until Tuesday. Make a list, and I will personally write to them all."

"Of course. There's just this one that sounded rather urgent . . . a Mr Lustrum."

"He's on my list down here," Joanna said. "I'm not sure I know him."

"He says he's Mr Johannsson's solicitor."

"Oh, right. I imagine he wants to arrange a reading of the Will. I'll speak with him from here. And Nicola, arrange all the necessary notices for the papers. They'll have to be in the Canadian papers as well."

"Right away, Mrs Johannsson. Do you wish to vet them before I send them out?"

"I suppose I'd better. Draft one and fax it to me here, will you? Now put me through to Mr Young."

"Joanna," Peter said. "My God, what a shock."

"Yes," Joanna said.

"Will you be coming in, tomorrow?"

"I don't think so, Peter. I'll be in on Monday, but right now I need to take it in. On second thoughts, I won't be in on Monday. I've fixed the funeral for Monday."

"Are you all right?" Her voice had cracked for just a moment.

"I'm all right, Peter."

"It's just that there are one or two problems."

Joanna frowned. "To do with Michael's death?"

"I'm afraid so. I've had Andrews on the phone . . ."

Joanna looked down her list. "He's been trying to get me, too." Barry Andrews was Area Manager of her bank. He was an old friend, who had faithfully supported her through some dodgy periods, but he was inclined to be anxious.

"It's to do with the new ship," Peter said. "He was terribly apologetic, raising the matter so soon after Michael's death, but the fact is that the borrowing was secured by Michael's personal endorsement, so that with his death that security no longer exists."

"That really is jumping the gun," Joanna said. "Call him back and tell him to put it on hold until the Will is read. I have no idea what's in it, but there should be an awful lot of cash lying about."

"Ah . . . yes," Peter agreed.

"I'll see you on Monday," Joanna said. "At the funeral."

Raisul looked across his mother's desk, at Nicola. "How do you reckon she's really taking it?" Nicola asked.

"You know Mother. She takes everything in her stride. Or she appears to. I imagine she's pretty upset. She wants me to go out there."

"Then you should. I'll just finish up here."

"I don't want to go home, right now," Raisul said. Nicola had already turned to the door; now she turned back. She didn't speak, just looked at him. "I . . ." he knew he was flushing. "I've so enjoyed today. You know . . ."

"Being the boss," she said.

"Is that wrong?"

"Not at all. I'd feel the same way. If I was the boss."

"Would you have dinner with me?"

"What about your mum?"

"She'll be all right. Helen will be there. They can weep on each other's shoulders, if they want to. It really isn't my scene."

"You'd rather weep on my shoulder," Nicola suggested.

"I think I'd rather like that."

"You are a very forward young man," Nicola said severely. "Just how old are you, anyway?"

"Twenty. And you?"

"A gentleman," Nicola pointed out, "never asks a lady her age. Where were you thinking of eating?"

"I don't know. I've only ever eaten at the Savoy, in London."

"Presumably with your mum. I don't think that would be a good idea. Listen, you can come home with me, and I'll boil you an egg or something."

Joanna dialled the last number. She had never met Lustrum: there had been no reason to. "Mr Lustrum? Joanna Johannsson."

"Mrs Johannsson! My most profound sympathy. I'm afraid we're all in a state of shock, here. Mr Johannsson had given no sign of any illness."

"He hadn't to me, either," Joanna said.

"Tragic," Lustrum said. "So tragic. As I say, my most profound sympathy."

"Thank you," Joanna said. "Was that what you wanted to say to me?"

"Ah, no. The Will. Would next Wednesday be satisfactory?"

"Does it have to wait that long?"

"Well, as I am sure you know, Mrs Johannsson, Kelly is a difficult person to get hold of, and . . ."

"I'm sorry," Joanna said. "You've lost me. Who is Kelly?"

There was a brief silence on the other end of the phone. Then Lustrum said, "Kelly Johannsson, Mrs Johannsson. Mr Johannsson's daughter. Your stepdaughter," he added for good measure.

"My . . . ?"

"You've never met?"

"I have never heard of this person, Mr Lustrum."

"Good God! I beg your pardon. Well . . . I know she disapproved of her father's re-marriage, of course, to . . . well . . ."

"To the woman who killed her brother," Joanna said.

Her head was spinning. Michael, she knew, had been estranged from Sean for years; Sean had even taken his

23

mother's maiden name. Although Michael, being Michael, had continued to pay his son a handsome allowance. But he had never mentioned that he also had a daughter! Who had disapproved of her father's second marriage. Understandably. But in eight years he had never made any attempt to bring about a reconciliation. Now . . . she supposed she would have to look after the girl, or woman, or whatever. At least financially.

"Are you there, Mrs Johannsson?" Lustrum asked.

"Yes," she said. "And have you succeeded in getting hold of Miss Johannsson?"

"I think we shall be able to track her down. There is a New York address and a telephone number amongst Mr Johannsson's papers. But as I say, I doubt we will get her over here before the middle of next week."

"I'm afraid I will need to have things sorted out before then," Joanna said. "Business waits for no man, and no woman either, as I am sure you appreciate, Mr Lustrum. I would like the Will read on Tuesday, please. A note can be taken of whatever bequest has been made to Miss Johannsson, and she can be informed in due course. Or when she arrives."

"Ah . . ." Lustrum hesitated. "I don't think you are quite aware of the position, Mrs Johannsson?"

"What position, Mr Lustrum?"

"Well, I should not be telling you this before the actual reading, but I think you should know that Miss Johannsson is Mr Johannsson's sole beneficiary."

Two

"Would you repeat that, please," Joanna said. Once again her brain was in a spin.

"I have of course seen the Will," Lustrum said. "It was originally drawn up in Canada, but a copy was given to me by Mr Johannsson personally, and he asked me to read it, and re-write it to obtain under English law, as he had removed his domicile to Great Britain. He and his daughter were very close during his wife's . . . I mean his first wife's . . . final illness, and immediately afterwards. That is what he told me, you understand. They had always been close. As he was estranged from his son, before Sean's, ah . . . unfortunate death, it was natural for him to make Kelly sole heiress. Then he, ah, encountered you, Mrs Johannsson, and determined to marry you. As I understood it from Mr Johannsson, Kelly was furious at that decision . . . but surely you know all of this?"

"I have told you," Joanna said. "I never even knew Mr Johannsson had a daughter."

"But . . . you were married to him for seven years, and you had been, ah . . . engaged for a year before that."

"Yes," Joanna said grimly. "We were inclined to respect each other's privacy. May I ask when this Will was drawn up?"

"Ah . . . nine years ago."

"And Mr Johannsson never considered altering it, after his second marriage?"

"I'm sure he did, Mrs Johannsson. However, he never

25

actually did. Of course, he could not have expected to die so suddenly and at such a relatively early age."

"Yes," Joanna said. "Well, I suppose we do have to wait for the chief beneficiary . . . did you say she was the *sole* beneficiary?"

"There some other bequests, of course, but these are all somewhat minor, compared with the bulk of the estate."

"And of course, as the Will was drawn up nine years ago, there is no mention of my name at all."

"Ah . . . I'm afraid not."

"Then I do not see there is any point in my attending the reading, Mr Lustrum. However, I would like to meet this Kelly, whenever she arrives."

Joanna replaced the phone and lay back, hands beneath her head. She had never felt in a position to importune Michael with details about his fortune, about his family, about his intentions – she had always waited for him to tell her as he chose. And he hadn't chosen. She knew how deeply he had grieved the death of his first wife. That he had rescued her, Joanna, from the pit of despair had been sufficient. That his millions had been behind her had been sufficient for the City. If those millions were no longer behind her . . .

But there was no necessity to panic. She might be faced with problems she had not anticipated, but her entire life had been composed of those. On the other hand . . . she called Caribee Shipping, but Peter Young had already left. So she called him at his flat, where he had just arrived. "Can you come out and see me?" she asked. "Tomorrow morning? I'll need everything concerning the financing of the Company, present margins, trading figures, the lot."

"Have we trouble?"

"I hope not. I'll expect you at ten." She hung up, had a shower, and dressed for dinner. She always wore a long dress in the evenings, simply because she liked a complete change from the day. Tonight she wore black and pearls, as she was in mourning.

Parks waited with a tray of champagne. "Just yourself for dinner, madam?"

"Isn't Mr Raisul back yet?"

"Not yet, madam."

Joanna went into the study, called Caribee Shipping again. The night watchman answered. "No, madam, Mr Raisul isn't here. He left some time ago."

"Where is Deardon?"

"Mr Deardon should be on his way back to you, madam. Mr Raisul dismissed him and said he would find his own way home when he was ready."

Joanna put down her glass. Who'd have children? Raisul had undoubtedly gone off to meet up with some of his friends. Damn him. But he could take care of himself. Helen was the one in trouble. And she didn't even know Michael was dead, yet. "Tell cook to put dinner on hold, Parks," she said. "And let me know the moment Deardon returns." She went upstairs to change again.

"What do you think?" Nicola asked.

"Very nice." Raisul looked around the small lounge, neatly but inexpensively furnished.

"It only has one bedroom," Nicola said. "Your mother pays well, but not that well. Anyway, there's only one of me."

"Don't you have a boyfriend?"

"Not this minute, no."

He glanced at her. "I'm glad you refused the Savoy. I don't really have much money. Although I suppose they'd let me sign, or something."

"You mean you don't have any cards, either?"

"Mother says I'm too young."

"I imagine she's right." Nicola opened the fridge and took out a large bottle of cider. "That's the house tipple. You pour."

She checked the larder. "Hm. Low on eggs. I think our best bet is sardines on toast. Okay?"

"Anything you say." He filled two glasses, held one out. "You really are being a treat."

Nicola sipped, subjecting him to one of her long stares, and he stretched out his hand and lifted her glasses from her nose. "You're just as pretty with as without."

"And you say the nicest things. Are you sure you're only twenty?"

"Does that rule me out?"

She sat down, crossed her legs. "Age is a man-made invention. It's all in the mind. Were you close to your stepfather?"

He placed the glasses on the table, sat beside her. "No. He was interested only in Mother. I didn't come here to talk about him."

"I just wanted to be sure about that," she said. "Would you like to eat now, or later?"

"Later." He leaned forward and kissed her on the mouth, which opened for him. His hand slid over her shirt, feeling the brassière beneath the material.

She got her mouth free. "Like I said, very forward. We don't really know each other."

He unbuttoned her shirt. "We have known each other for over a year. Ever since you started working for Mother."

"You mean we have said 'hello' on the half-a-dozen occasions you have come to the office. Or are you going to pretend you fell in love with me at first sight?"

The shirt was unbuttoned down to her waistband; he pulled it out of her skirt to reach the last two buttons. "You know how it is, you look at people on more than one level. Level one, you are my mother's secretary. Don't look twice. Level two, you are a most attractive woman. One has to look twice. But you're still my mother's secretary. Level three . . ."

She made no objection as he slid the shirt from her shoulders. "You suddenly reckoned I was available," she said.

"I hoped you were."

"You need to unbutton the sleeves," she pointed out.

"Oh." He did so, and the shirt came right off.

"If your mother finds out about this, I won't be her secretary any more," Nicola remarked, as he brought her against him to fumble behind her back for the clip to her brassière.

"Then I'll hire you as *my* secretary instead."

The brassière came away, and he could look at her breasts. Then he touched them, tentatively, as if he were exploring uncharted territory. He might know what he wanted, Nicola thought, but his approach remained juvenile. She wondered what he was going to be like, and suddenly knew she was going to have the time of her life, because he would need to be shown, so much. And he would want to be shown.

And afterwards? That depended on a great number of things. But this boy might well be her future. She let him fondle her for a few moments, then stood up to let her skirt fall to the floor, followed by her tights and knickers.

"Shall I come in with you, madam?" Deardon asked.

"No. But park close by. I may need you later," Joanna said, and went into the hotel lobby. "You have a Mrs Moore staying here," she said to the receptionist.

"Yes, madam, but she is not to be disturbed."

"Give me her room number."

"My instructions are clear, madam." But he was eyeing the mink coat with some apprehension.

"I am her mother," Joanna said. "And if you do not give me her room number I shall call the police."

He gulped. "Two-oh-five."

"Thank you," Joanna said. "And if you have any idea of calling her to tell her I'm on my way up, forget it. I will have you fired." The clerk gulped again.

The lobby was empty; most of the guests were in the dining room, from where there came the rumble of conversation and the clatter of plates. Joanna rode up in the lift, walked along the corridor. She was wearing high heels but the carpet was soft and quiet. She knocked on the door of two hundred and five, needing to do so three more times before she got a reply: "Who is it?"

"Mum."

There was another silence, then Helen said. "Just leave me alone, Mother, please."

"I will leave you alone, Helen, I promise. As soon as I have established that you are all right. I have something important to tell you."

The latch turned and the door swung in. Helen wore bra and panties; the rest of her clothes were thrown carelessly over a chair. She was taller than her mother, had the same full figure and straight yellow hair, at this moment drifting untidily down her back. Her features were blunt rather than chiselled, but still intensely attractive.

Joanna closed the door behind herself.

"See?" Helen asked. "I'm all right. How did you find me? Oh, I suppose that creep of a lawyer has been to see you. The bastard. Well, that's it. He's fired."

"Helen," Joanna said, "you could be in serious trouble."

Helen sat on the bed, hands dangling between her legs. "It was a set-up. I didn't know it was heroin; I thought it was ecstasy. And I didn't know that bitch was an under-cover cop."

"Let's hope we can make that stick in court," Joanna said, wandering about the room, which was as stark as any hotel bedroom. "Have you had an examination?"

"If you mean have I had a beastly quack pawing me about and taking a urine sample, yes I have. Was that your idea?"

"It was necessary. Get dressed."

"To go where?"

"Home."

"Forget it. I'm happy here. You said you'd leave me alone."

"So I'm breaking my word. I'm good at that. If you stay here on your own you'll go potty and do something stupid. Come along."

"Give me one good reason."

"I've already given you one. Now I'll give you two more. The first is that I wish to keep an eye on you. I'm your last line of defence."

"I can take care of myself."

"I don't think you can, in this instance. They are going to link your misdemeanour to my background, and declare that you have to be guilty just because you're my daughter."

"Thanks very much."

"There's no point in being stupid about it. You *are* my daughter. As they are going to pursue that line anyway, the best thing we can do is meet it together. Not miles apart."

"Give me the other reason," Helen suggested.

"I need a shoulder to cry on. Michael's dead."

"Michael . . . ?"

"He apparently had a massive heart attack and just dropped."

"Oh, my God! Did you know he had heart trouble?"

"I don't think *he* knew he had heart trouble. But there it is. I'm a little shook up."

"Oh, Mum!" Helen ran to her, hugged her. "I'm so very sorry."

"Why? You never liked him."

"Okay, I didn't. But you did. You loved him, for God's sake. You don't think . . ." she stared at her mother, mouth open.

"No," Joanna lied, definitely. "I don't think the little he knew about this business would have triggered it. It just happened. Will you come home?"

"Of course." Helen dragged on her clothes. "What are you going to do?"

"There's nothing I can do, save carry on. But there may be problems."

"Tell me."

"I will, when we get home. Deardon's waiting."

They went downstairs, and Joanna paid the bill with a card. She was just signing the slip when Helen muttered, "Shit!"

Joanna looked up and watched the man entering the lobby. He was quite young, middle twenties, she estimated, and quite good looking in a long-haired untidy fashion, matched by his torn jeans and shirt and trainers. "Gotcha!" he announced. "I've been looking for you the whole shitting day."

"So you've found me," Helen said. "Hello and goodbye."

She made to step past him, and he grasped her arm. "Not so fast, honey doll. We need to talk."

"We don't," Helen said. "Would you mind letting me go?"

"In there." He pushed her towards the Residents' Lounge.

"Mother!" Helen said.

Joanna looked at the clerk, who was looking anxious.

"You're her mother?" asked the intruder.

"Yes," Joanna said. "And if you don't let my daughter go, I'll have your guts for garters."

He regarded the mink. "Lady Muck," he remarked. "I'm not going to hurt the doll unless I have to. Just bugger off."

Joanna went to the door and on to the steps. "Motherrr!" Helen called as she was pushed into the empty lounge.

"Madam?" Deardon had parked very close, and seen Joanna emerge.

"Come in here a moment, will you," Joanna said. Deardon came up the steps, and nodded to the now terrified clerk, who was telephoning. "In here," Joanna said, leading the chauffeur to the door to the lounge, where Helen had been forced into a chair, and the young man was bending over her, speaking very intensely.

"Mother!" Helen said, looking past him. "Thank God!"

The young man looked up. "I told you to make yourself scarce, lady."

"And I told you I was going to have your guts for garters," Joanna reminded him. "He's all yours, Deardon."

The chauffeur stepped past her, and the young man straightened. "Out," Deardon commanded.

The young man licked his lips, then suddenly reached behind him. "He's got a knife!" Helen shouted.

The young man brought his arm forward, blithely unaware that Joanna had insisted that all her chauffeurs be trained in unarmed combat. Deardon caught the arm, half-turned the man, and used his other hand in a chopping blow. The knife fell to the floor and the young man went with it, kneeling and hugging his arm. "You've broken my wrist," he moaned.

"Probably not," Deardon said. "I didn't hit you hard enough."

"What's going on?" An assistant manager had arrived, summoned by the desk clerk.

"This thug was assaulting my daughter," Joanna explained. "My chauffeur just disarmed him."

"Do you wish me to call the police?" the manager asked.

"I don't think that will be necessary," Joanna said. "We'll leave. Perhaps you could look after his arm." She led Deardon and Helen out of the hotel. "Was he a friend of yours?" she asked.

"Not any more," Helen said.

"But he was with you last night."

Helen sighed. "I guess."

"Seems to me we have a lot to talk about," Joanna said.

"Mr Raisul called, madam," Parks said.

"Oh, yes? To say what?"

"That he is spending the night with a friend, madam."

"The wretch," Helen commented.

"Oh, it's understandable," Joanna said. "It's been an unsettling day. Did Mr Raisul say which friend, Parks?"

"No, madam."

"Well, Miss Helen and I will eat. Something light." She accepted a glass of champagne. "Now," she said to Helen, "tell me about that lout. I'm surprised you didn't clobber him."

Helen had proved, when she had been involved in the hijacking of the *Caribee Express*, that she was capable of clobbering anyone, even the general of a revolutionary army. She shrugged. "I guess I'm not feeling a hundred per cent. Geoff was scared I might have given his name to the police."

"And had you? Given his name to the police?"

"No. I didn't give any names."

"Which probably makes you even more guilty in their eyes. But we should be able to sort it out. Are you sleeping with this Geoff?"

"Well . . ." Helen flushed. "A couple of one-night stands."

"I hope you were wearing something."

"He doesn't have Aids."

"That's what they all say. You understand this case is bound to attract the media, just because of who you are?"

"You mean, whose daughter I am," Helen said, with a touch of bitterness.

"Joanna!" Matilda screamed, rushing into the bedroom with arms outstretched. "I didn't know you were back. Oh, Joanna! I just saw it on the news. You poor dear girl!" She enveloped her sister in a bear hug.

Once upon a time Matilda had been the more striking of the sisters, taller than Joanna, and she had a fuller figure to go with the tumbling golden hair, except that hers curled where Joanna's was straight. A strong woman, with a black belt in karate, in their early days Joanna had even employed her as a bodyguard. But she had allowed drink and disappointment – composed mainly of jealousy at her sibling's success – to get to her, and now she was overweight in every direction, from huge breasts to thick thighs.

Joanna extricated herself. "Thank you, Tilly."

"You're so calm. You're always so calm. Sometimes I think you're made of ice."

"I'm melting fast," Joanna said. "I just have a lot of things to sort out."

"Of course you do, darling. If there is anything I can do to help . . ."

"I'll let you know," Joanna said. "Right now I want an early night."

Raisul decided that waking up beside a most attractive woman, who had just given him her all, was one of life's great pleasures. Even if she wasn't actually there; with his eyes half-open he could watch her moving about the room, going to the bathroom, listen to the shower, wait for her to return, draping the towel over a chair. "Wakey-wakey," she said.

"I am awake."

She switched on the light, and he could savour her slightly plump figure, her lush, curling black hair, both on her head and her groin, her heavy breasts and strong thighs . . . had that really all been his?

She sat on the bed beside him, and he caught her round the waist to nuzzle her navel. "We haven't the time for that," she said. "Listen. We'll breakfast, and then I'll leave. I'll check in at the office early; there's some correspondence to be done. You stay here." She ran her finger over his chin. "You can use my razor. Then get dressed and come in at the usual time. Okay?"

"I think I'm in love with you."

She kissed him. "As I said last night, you say the sweetest things. I think we want to keep us very private for a while."

"Can I come back here tonight?"

"Of course you can't, Raisul. You mustn't. Tonight you go home with your mother, and you spend the weekend out there as well."

"But . . . when can we see each other again?"

"We'll fix something up for next week."

"Next week?" His voice was almost a wail. "I'm supposed to be going up to Scotland, to inspect the new ship."

"It'll be better for the wait," Nicola said, and stood up.

He held her hand. "Don't dress until after breakfast."

"Why not?"

"I just want to keep looking at you, naked. I want to remember you always, naked."

She stooped to kiss him again.

What have I got myself into? Nicola wondered, as she walked along the street towards Caribee Shipping. She had had affairs before. As a pretty girl she hadn't been able to avoid them, hadn't wished to . . . and had always been disappointed. Somewhere out there, she had no doubt there was a man who would fulfill all her requirements, but she hadn't met him yet. She remembered with more fondness than that reserved for any of the men the weekend she had spent in the West Country with an old school friend, Sally Mottram. Perhaps because of the guilt. But Sally certainly wasn't a lesbian, however ambidextrous she might feel from time to time. She was married and a mother.

So back to the men. Raisul had a lot of the qualifications she sought, and would have a lot more as he grew up. He was also in the typical throes of a first affair; he had confessed that to her. She thought it possible that she could attach him very firmly, but she was a sensible young woman, and realised there were endless pitfalls down that path. One was his age, twenty to her twenty-seven. Another was connected to that: once he had discovered women, and discovered that women were available, he would wish to stray. The third was his mother, quite the most formidable woman Nicola had ever met. And her boss!

But at the same time, she couldn't just tell Raisul, 'You've had your fun, now be a good fellow and push off.' Because he was also her boss, in real terms. It had all seemed such a good idea, last night.

"Peter!" Joanna had the quality of making everyone feel that he, or she, was the most important person in the world, at that moment. Although Peter Young prided himself that from time to time he *was* the most important person in her world.

For a widow of less than twenty-four hours she looked in very good shape, wearing black pants and a white shirt, and with her hair in a pony tail. If this was widows' weed, he reckoned every woman should be a widow all the time. Of course, she was experienced at being a widow. But it was never something she had enjoyed, or endured, for very long. Not for the first time, he wondered if . . . but now was not the time for that, he reminded himself, as she led him into the study, which was more of a small library, the book-lined walls making it a most cosy room.

"Shut the door," she told him. He obeyed, took the indicated seat in front of the desk, placing the briefcase on his knees. "I assume you had to collect all that data from the office," Joanna said.

"I came straight from there."

"Was Raisul in?"

"He came in at nine."

"How did he look?"

"On top of the world. Why?"

"It's just that he didn't come home last night. He was out with his pals, I imagine. I don't blame him; it was a pretty stressful day. But I'm glad he turned up. And the other good news is that Helen has come home. Now tell me, do you know a solicitor named Lustrum?"

"Lustrum, Lustrum and Wilde. Quite big."

"Apparently they are Michael's solicitors. I had a call from one of the Lustrums yesterday," Joanna said, and gave him the gist of the conversation.

"Shit," he muttered when she finished.

"Absolutely. Put me in the picture."

Peter spread papers on the desk. "The trading figures are good. The only problem is the two new ships, the replacement for *Caribee Express* and the one still on the stocks. As I said on the phone yesterday, and as you will remember, Michael guaranteed the cost, which was twelve million, give or take a few. It was to be repaid out of earnings, but with Michael's endorsement neither the bank nor us were hurrying. Just servicing the interest has been taking up most of our profits. There is still ten and a half million outstanding. And again as I said yesterday, no longer secured, unless the endorsement is renewed. And of course the new ship is not yet complete, and thus not earning."

"You've spoken with Barry?"

"Oh, yes. He's quite happy to wait for a reading of the Will. He just wanted to remind us of the situation. As he doesn't know the contents of the Will, he is supposing that you will pay off the loan immediately."

"And when he finds out that I can't? Will he call?"

"I imagine he will do everything in his power not to call. But his superiors may force his hand, at least to require a refinancing. Banks don't like to have big unsecured loans floating around for more than a brief period."

"Well, of course, we don't know that this Kelly won't agree to continue the endorsement," Joanna said optimistically. "What about re-financing, if it comes to that?"

"With credit as tight, and as expensive as it is at the moment? Prospects would be poor."

"Are you telling me we may have to sell the new ship?"

"As you say, Jo, we must hope it won't come to that. But there is another, and perhaps more worrying aspect of the situation."

"Can there be?"

"The shareholdings. As you will remember, when Michael refinanced the company it was capitalised in one hundred thousand shares of ten pounds each face value, to give a total of one million pounds. He just wanted a valuation; if you take in the four ships trading and Caribee Shipping itself, the company is worth fifty million in real terms. But as you must recall, the shares were split into blocks. He very generously gave me five thousand, and Raisul and Helen two and a half thousand each. Of the remaining ninety, you hold fifty per cent, and Michael retained forty per cent. Now, if that forty per cent is included in the bequest to this Kelly, well, that's a sizeable chunk of the equity."

"But I will still have a majority."

"Of course, especially with the support of myself and the children."

"Mm," Joanna commented. "The children. As you say, Peter, there are a lot of imponderables. There's the yard looking for money, too. Barry isn't going to quibble about another quarter of a million, is he?"

"Right now, no. But I think we need to be absolutely straight with him, as soon as possible."

"Yes. You'd better set up a meeting for Monday morning. Maybe Jonathan should sit in too." Jonathan Prim was her stockbroker. "Damn," she said. "I keep forgetting. Monday is the funeral. Listen, tell Barry if he cares to attend, I'll have a word with him afterwards."

"And Jonathan?"

"I can't have a business conference on the day of my husband's funeral. Put Jonathan down for later in the week. By then I'll hope to have Barry sorted out."

Peter nodded, stood up, and sat down again. "I know now is not the time, Jo, but if there is anything I can do to help . . ." he flushed. "I'm not just thinking about the business."

"I know, Peter. And I'm so very grateful. But as you say, now is not the time. I do need to think, about so many things. I'll see you next week."

He stood up again. "I'll be there."

The door closed, and a few minutes later she heard the growl of his car engine. Dear Peter. He so wanted to get close, had done so for years. So why not, at last? She needed a man about the house; there had always been one, since she had been a teenager. Not every one had been a success – when she thought of Dick Orton, who above all others she had supposed would be her surest support and lover. Peter was absolutely reliable – as a company secretary. No doubt he would be equally totally reliable as a husband, as well. But in bed? Joanna had never had any illusions about herself. When she felt erotic, she *was* erotic, with a total abandon that would shock many men – and had often done so.

So much to think about, and so much to do. Beginning at home. Helen was utterly contrite, less for what she had done than for the timing of when she had done it, however inadvertently. That was a plus. But there remained the threat of the court case hanging over her, and thus over them all. Court cases were things Joanna could do without. While Raisul . . . he came home that Friday evening, looking at once pleased and distracted. "So tell me how it went at the office," Joanna said, sitting beside him in the drawing room.

"Oh, great. I'm going to enjoy it. Even if there is an air of crisis."

Joanna explained the situation, as she had already to Helen. "Crikey," Raisul commented. "Can this female really upset the applecart?"

"She can give it a bumpy ride, if she wants to."

"And you think she'll want to? Can't you contest the Will? You're Michael's widow."

"Yes, I suppose I can contest it. But it could be a very long drawn out and sticky business. I need a solution now. At least to the endorsement and share situation. I think our best bet is to wait and see how she turns out."

"But you're not optimistic."

"The only thing I know about her, relayed via the solicitor, is that she was against her father's marriage to me. So against it that he never allowed even the mention of her to enter our lives."

"But he still left her everything. Isn't that odd?"

"I think it is. But then, Michael was an odd man. If he hadn't been, he wouldn't have come after me while I was in prison."

"Do we know how old this woman is?"

"No. I imagine she was younger than Sean. Sean was in his later twenties when he died. So he would have been past forty now. She'll be in her thirties, I should think."

"Still old enough to be a hard-bitten businesswoman," Raisul remarked.

Jonna raised her eyebrows. "Like me, you mean?"

Raisul flushed. "I didn't mean that. When does the dragon appear?"

"Some time next week," Joanna said. "The reading of the Will is on Wednesday. She'll be here for that."

"Right. Do you still want me to go up to Glasgow on Monday? Wouldn't it be better to wait until after the reading?"

Joanna shook her head. "No one must have the slightest inkling that we may be in a crisis situation. But you can't go on Monday. That's the funeral, and I have to sort one or two things out. You'll go up on Tuesday. Exuding confidence, Raisul."

"You bet. Tuesday. Right."

It was so pleasant to have dinner with just Helen and Raisul. No one spoke much, but then no one had to. Both the children were well aware that Joanna, for all her determined smile and the way she was carrying on as if nothing had happened, was deeply affected by Michael's death. If she had never loved him with the passion she had expended on Howard Edge or Prince Hasim, he had still been the very solid rock on which she had built the second half of her life, both emotionally and financially. And she was very well aware that neither of the children had ever really taken to him.

William telephoned to say that the cremation had been arranged for Monday morning. "Do you want the casket brought down before then?"

"Definitely not," Joanna said. She had slept in this house with Howard Edge's body lying in its coffin on the billiards table, and it was not an experience she ever wished to repeat. "They can bring it down on Monday. But it'll come to the house first."

She went to bed early, but slept badly. She contemplated taking a sleeping pill, and decided against it. She wanted a clear head tomorrow, and into the foreseeable future. So she lay awake, staring into the darkness, remembering . . . and considering. Why had Michael never told her he had a daughter? Was it because this Kelly was every bit as vicious as his son Sean had been? There was a terrifying prospect.

Or had they really quarrelled that badly over his decision to marry the woman convicted of Sean's murder? In that case, how come he had left his entire estate to her? There were of course several quite acceptable reasons for that – despite the supposed quarrel. He had set her, Joanna, up in business again, and left her, but for that ten million plus stone around her neck, totally financially secure. As he had not expected to die so suddenly, he must have assumed that long before he did die she would have paid off the loan and his endorsement would no longer matter, so that whatever happened to him Caribee Shipping would go from strength to strength. It was quite reasonable for him to wish to keep the bulk of his fortune in the mainstream of his family.

Less acceptable was the thought that he might have decided against changing his Will because he did not altogether trust his second wife, or accept that their marriage would necessarily last. He had married her because she was a beautiful woman whom he, knowing his son, had been sure had been wrongfully convicted. She had, in effect, been one of his projects, the resuscitation of outraged innocence; that it had cost him a few millions to buy her and set her up had not been relevant to a man who had so many to play with. But he had known all of her background, her tempestuous love affairs, her no less turbulent ambition. He had told her from the beginning that, as he was nineteen years older than she and no longer as sexually active as he had once been, she was free to have an open marriage, provided she told him about the affairs.

She had been vaguely shocked by that, but her life at that moment had been in such a turmoil, and so much in his hands, that she had regarded the offer only as a gesture of affection, had never stopped to think that it might be another of his projects, in which she was the main player, whose antics amused him. On the one occasion she had taken advantage of his offer, arising out of the horrific events that had surrounded the hijacking of *Caribee Express*, it had turned out catastrophically.

He had been as good as his word, never reproached her, accepted what had happened in such a generous manner she had sworn never to stray again, and she had kept *her* word. But had he secretly resented it, determined to make her pay for it, while all the time keeping a major part of his own life a complete secret? She would not have been human did she not resent that.

If he had kept his daughter a secret throughout their marriage, what else had he kept secret? But that was surely two o'clock in the morning thinking, when the human spirit is at its lowest ebb.

Joanna awoke with a start, surprised that she had slept, and found Helen sitting on the foot of her bed. Helen was fond of before breakfast chats. "Did you know that Raisul has a girlfriend?" she asked.

Joanna sat up and rang for her breakfast. "I assume you are pulling my leg."

"Shouldn't he have a girlfriend? He's not gay, is he?"

"Not so far as I know. But he's never shown any great interest in girls. He's never brought one home to dinner."

"Ah, but that is the ultimate. Bringing a girl home to meet mother indicates serious intent."

"And you don't think he's serious. Thank God for that. How do you know he has a girlfriend, anyway?"

"I just heard him on the phone downstairs. You don't generally ring a girl at seven in the morning unless you have something pretty intimate to say."

"And what did he have to say? Or did he spot you prowling about?"

"No, he didn't. He had his back to the door. But he was

saying that he didn't have to go up to Scotland on Monday after all, so they could get together that evening."

"Eavesdropping is a detestable habit," Joanna remarked. And frowned. "He spent Thursday night out. He said he was spending it with a friend."

Helen grinned. "I reckon he did."

"I meant with a male friend."

"I think it's a much better idea for him to sleep with a female friend," Helen said. "You going to ask him about it?"

"Certainly not," Joanna said. "As you say, if it's serious, he'll bring her home to meet mother. Or at least tell me about it. If it's a one-night stand, I don't really want to know."

"Two nights," Helen said. "At the very least."

Helen went to the triple garage, where her Ford Fiesta was parked, beside Raisul's Morgan and the Mercedes. Deardon was polishing the big car, but he stopped to watch her approach. He had taken off his cap and jacket, which seemed to make his splendid physique even more attractive. "I never did thank you," Helen said.

"Thank me for what, Miss?"

"For coming to my rescue, on Thursday night."

"That was a pleasure, Miss."

"Was it really? It's nice to have someone like you around, Deardon."

"I'm always here, Miss."

They gazed at each other, and Helen realised she was flushing. As was he. Deardon! The chauffeur! She got into her car and drove away.

Joanna breakfasted, bathed and dressed, and went for a canter on her gelding, Aries, followed by the enthusiastic dogs. Her restlessness was growing with every minute. There was so much to be done, and so little she could do until she found out the attitude of this young woman, who was fast assuming the proportions of a mental tornado, waiting to pounce. Whereas

Kelly was probably just a mixed-up young woman. By the time she returned home, both Helen and Raisul had taken themselves off, where Parks did not know; they had each taken their own car. But Raisul had apparently had a tennis racket.

Deardon and the Mercedes were waiting at the front steps, just in case she wanted to go somewhere as well, but she had no desire to leave the house before Monday. She sat in the drawing room and drank champagne, as she invariably did in the middle of the morning when at home, and now she kept visualising the casket in which Michael was lying disintegrating, waiting for the consuming heat of the crematorium which would complete his destruction.

Morbidity. If she was going to think like that, she might as well have had the body brought down already. She simply had to get over it. It was rather annoying of the children to take themselves off and leave her to brood by herself. She reckoned she had always given them too much freedom. But what can you do when you are whisked off to prison, officially for the rest of your life? That episode had ended any hopes of a proper mother-daughter or mother-son relationship. She reckoned she should congratulate herself on having re-created the family, however much she had to put up with a certain amount of selfish individualism. That was better. Positive thinking. And of course the hijacking episode had brought them closer together, reminded the children of the guts and determination and sheer courage that had taken their mother to the top, some of which had brushed off on them. Not that it had done much for Helen's stability. That was just as worrying as the business crisis. But she had always tended to put business first. That was where she had let her children down.

She listened to the growl of a car engine in the drive, and the dogs barking. Someone had come home. She got up, walked about the room; the drawing room did not face the drive, but instead looked out on the lawns and gardens at the rear of the house. She stood at the French windows, gazing at the flowers, listening to doors being opened, presumably by

Parks, to muttered voices, and realised that it was not, after all, either Helen or Raisul coming home. She turned to face the double doors as they were opened by Parks. "If you'll excuse me, madam," the butler said. "There is someone here wishes to speak with you."

"Hi, Stepmother," said a soft but surprisingly deep voice.

Three

Joanna stared at the young woman. She was tall, strongly built, with handsome rather than pretty features, wavy auburn hair which she wore loose, and a heavy suntan which had left her face a mass of freckles. She wore jeans and a shirt, a windcheater and thongs. "I'm Kelly Johannsson," she said in that attractively deep voice. "You know about me?"

Joanna got her breath back. "I know about you. Please come in."

Kelly Johannsson slowly advanced into the room, looking around her, and then at Joanna. "This is really something," she remarked. "Say, I thought those dogs were gonna eat me alive."

"They're retrievers," Joanna explained. "Noisy, but quite harmless, really. Thank you, Parks."

Parks had remained standing in the doorway, awaiting possible instructions as to what was to be done with the visitor. Now he withdrew, closing the doors.

"*You* are really something," Kelly commented. "Dad sent me photos, but photos never really do anyone justice, do they?"

"I suppose not," Joanna said. "Would you like a glass of champagne?"

"Is that what you're drinking? I'd love a glass of champagne. Did you know I was coming?"

"We were expecting you some time next week." Joanna poured, held out the glass.

"What do I say?" Kelly asked.

"Cheers will do. Nice to meet you."

47

"Cheers. Nice to meet *you*, at last. That guy Lustrum telephoned me yesterday with the news. So I hopped on a plane last night and came right over. Landed two hours ago. So I came here." She sipped, gave a little shudder. "Seemed a good idea for us to meet."

"I think it is an excellent idea. Where are you staying?"

"Well . . ."

"Have you any luggage?"

"My gear is in the hall."

"Well of course you must stay here." Joanna rang the bell. There were a million and one things she needed to find out . . . this girl had heard the news and just hopped on a plane across the Atlantic – did that mean she was already a wealthy woman? She didn't look it, but her hair was clean and her nails, if unvarnished, looked cared for. And *she* couldn't have asked for a better start to their relationship. Nor did the girl look in any way hostile. "Parks," she said, "ask Mrs Beckett to prepare the Blue Room for Miss Johannsson. And take her, ah, gear up, will you?"

"Miss Johannsson," Parks said, trying to get things straight.

"Thank you, Parks." He withdrew, again closing the doors. "I imagine you'd like a bath and a change of clothes," Joanna said. "Just give them ten minutes to straighten things out."

"You really want me to stay here?"

"Of course I do. We're family, aren't we?"

"I guess we are."

"And we have a lot to talk about, I would say."

"Oh, sure. I'm looking forward to that."

"Well, finish your drink and we'll go up."

Kelly drained her glass and put it down. "There's the taxi," she said. "I guess he's still waiting."

"I'll see to it." Joanna opened the doors and led her up the stairs.

"Some house," Kelly remarked, gazing at the gilded ceiling, the paintings; they were actually all prints. "Is it yours?"

"Yes," Joanna said. "It was built by my first husband's grandfather."

"And you've had a lot of those," Kelly said. "Husbands, I mean."

Joanna half checked, then continued to the top of the stairs. "A few," she agreed. She led Kelly along the wide upper hall to the Blue Room, which Parks was just leaving, He opened the door for them and Joanna stood back to let the girl enter. "Would you settle the taxi, Parks?" Joanna said. "There is cash in the desk drawer in the study."

"Right away, madam." Parks hurried for the stairs.

"Wowee," Kelly commented. "It really is blue. Even the sheets."

Which were at that moment being turned down by Mrs Beckett, a short, stout, no nonsense middle-aged woman, who regarded the somewhat untidy young woman with distaste. "This is my stepdaughter, Kelly," Joanna explained.

"Pleased to meet you, Miss," Mrs Beckett said, and glanced, ostentatiously, at the battered kitbag Parks had placed on the case rack.

"Hi!" Kelly held out her hand, and when Mrs Beckett responded, slapped the outstretched palm. "Great to be here."

Mrs Beckett looked at Joanna in alarm.

"Thank you, Mrs Beckett," Joanna said.

Kelly opened the double doors on to the balcony overlooking the drive. "Heck," she said. "Standing here I feel like the Queen, or something."

"It is an attractive view," Joanna agreed, and went into the bathroom, which was also decorated in blue. "I think you'll find everything you need." Kelly stood at her shoulder, apparently speechless as she gazed at the appointments. "If you wish anything that isn't here," Joanna said, "just ring the bell and Mrs Beckett will fetch it for you."

"I've never had servants before," Kelly said, half to herself. "Well, there was this nurse Mom had towards the end, but you'd hardly call her a servant."

"I suppose not," Joanna said, and was tempted to point out that she didn't have servants now, either: the servants were hers. "I am sorry about your mother."

Kelly glanced at her, and Joanna had an odd sensation of an icy hand running up and down her spine. "Yeah," Kelly said. "It was sad."

"Well," Joanna said. "You have a bath. And a lie down, if you like. Come down whenever you're ready. Lunch isn't for another couple of hours. I'll be in the drawing room."

Joanna closed the door behind herself, leaned against it for several seconds, found she was breathing quite heavily. Obviously Kelly had taken the death of her mother very hard. Equally obviously she would resent the woman who had taken her mother's place, quite apart from the Sean business. But the only hostility she had so far revealed had been in that single glance. And that hadn't been just hostile. It had been . . . she didn't know *what* it had been, but she had only felt that experience once or twice before in her life; the last time had been three years previously, when she had been diving to the wreck of the *Caribee Express* off Borneo, and had been attacked by a shark. She would never forget those eyes.

She went into the study, looked up Lustrum's home number, and called him there. "Philip is in the garden," the woman said, disapprovingly. "It is Saturday, you know. Is it important?"

"To me," Joanna said. "Tell him Joanna Johannsson needs to speak with him."

She waited, fingers tapping on the desk. "Mrs Johannsson?" He was faintly breathless. "Is there something the matter?"

"Just when were you expecting Kelly Johannsson to arrive, Mr Lustrum?"

"Ah . . . I telephoned her at the number left by Mr Johannsson in his papers. New York. That was yesterday afternoon. Morning her time."

"How did she take the news of his death?"

"Much better than I expected. She was quite calm."

"Do you know, or did you form any impression, of how old she is?"

"I'm afraid not, Mrs Johannsson."

"And did she say when she was coming over?"

"No, she didn't. I told her we were reading the Will on Tuesday, and that Mr Johannsson would be interred on Monday, but she didn't make much of a reply to that, either. So I asked her to call me when her plans were finalised. I haven't heard back from her yet, but I imagine she'll try to get here for the funeral."

"Miss Johannsson is at this moment sitting in a bath in one of my spare rooms, Mr Lustrum."

"Ah . . . I don't understand."

"She caught a flight out of New York last night."

"Good heavens! And she came to you?"

"She seemed to think it was the natural thing to do. I agree with her."

"Ah . . . yes. And . . ."

"All is sunshine at the moment, Mr Lustrum. But I think I am entitled to know, in advance of Wednesday . . . did you tell her she is in line for the bulk of her father's estate?"

"No, I didn't, Mrs Johannsson. But don't you suppose she already knew? From her father?"

"Perhaps," Joanna said thoughtfully. "OK, Mr Lustrum. I just thought I'd put you in the picture."

"Would you like me to come out?" Lustrum asked.

"I can manage, thank you. You go back to your garden." Joanna replaced the phone, brooded at the wall. Was she being paranoid? Wouldn't she have done the same thing, jumped on a plane the moment she heard of her father's death? And then gone to probably the only address she had in England? If it hadn't been for that look . . . She picked up the phone again. "Willie?"

"Oh, hi, Sis. All well?"

"I haven't the faintest idea," Joanna said. "I need some detective work, fast."

"Tell me." He listened as Joanna related what had happened so far that morning, omitting the glance. "So?" William asked. "Maybe she's not the avenging angel suggested by Lustrum."

"She's not like anything suggested by Lustrum, Willie. Not least in the way she looks and the fact that she's a good dozen years younger than I had expected. I need to know a lot more about her. Like where she was when her mother died, and just how her mother died . . ."

"I thought it was cancer?"

"That's what Michael said, yes. But it's turning out that so much of what Michael said, or didn't say, bears no relation to the truth I'd like to be sure. I also wish to know just what Kelly has been doing the last seven years."

"I'll get on to it. It may take a little time . . ."

"Time is what I haven't got, Willie. I need to know all of these things before she and I get to talking business. Certainly before next Tuesday. It shouldn't be all that difficult. Michael was a big man in Canadian business. There are certain to be a lot of people over there, especially in Vancouver, who are, or were, familiar with his personal life. Don't we have an agent in Vancouver?"

"We do. Are you saying that in seven years of marriage you learned nothing of your husband's previous lifestyle?"

"It never occurred to me to probe. We sort of mutually agreed that our respective pasts should be buried. But now this Kelly business . . ."

"Don't you think she might spill all the beans if you just ask her?"

"I intend to do that. But it has to be handled carefully, and I need to know if what she tells me is the truth or lies. Right?"

"Right," William said. "I'll get on to it right away."

Joanna felt better, as she always did when she was acting positively. She listened to another car engine, got up and went into the hall to greet Raisul, who was just laying his tennis racket on the table. He looked splendidly bronzed and fit. But also quite disconcerted; his face was flushed.

"Do you know what I just saw?" he inquired.

"I shouldn't think I can, unless you tell me," Joanna said. "But it can keep. Now listen, we have a houseguest."

"That's it," Raisul said.

"What?"

"I just saw her."

"Oh. Right. Well . . ." Joanna frowned. "Where did you see her?"

"Standing on the balcony of the Blue Room."

Joanna nodded. "That's where I put her. She's just having a bath and changing her clothes . . ."

"She's done that," Raisul said. "Although I wouldn't say she's changed her clothes."

"Just what do you mean?"

"She was standing there, Mother, on the balcony, starkers."

"Oh, good lord," Joanna commented.

"And is she built," Raisul said, and looked past his mother. "Well, hello."

Joanna turned, not at all sure what she was going to see, but Kelly was again fully dressed, as before in jeans and a shirt and thongs. It was difficult to tell if they were clean clothes or if she had put on her previous gear; she at least looked, and smelt, clean, and she had washed her hair, which was damply tied up with a ribbon.

"Hi," she said. "You'll be Raisul."

"That's me. Ah . . ."

"This is your stepsister, Kelly," Joanna said.

"You were driving that little open car, just now," Kelly said.

"Well, yes . . ." he flushed again. "You took me by surprise."

"Because this isn't actually a nudist camp," Joanna said, tartly.

"Oh, I'm so sorry," Kelly said. "I hope I didn't offend you, Raisul."

"Not at all," Raisul said, avoiding his mother's eye. "I feel like a drink." He led the way into the drawing room, where the champagne bottle still waited in its ice bucket. Parks had brought in fresh glasses, and these Raisul filled. "Welcome to Caribee House," he said. "To England, in fact." Never had Joanna seen anyone so quickly and obviously smitten.

"Thank you," Kelly said. "It's great to be here."

"I think you want to go and get changed for lunch," Joanna suggested.

"I'll be right back." Raisul hurried from the room.

"Cute," Kelly remarked. "How old is he?"

She was certainly direct. But two could play at that game. "Raisul is twenty," Joanna said. "How old are you?"

Kelly was wandering around the room, looking at the ornaments, as before at the pictures. "Twenty-four. But you knew that. Didn't you?"

"No, I didn't." Joanna sat on the settee, patted the space beside her. "Come and sit down." Kelly obeyed, one leg carelessly thrown over the other. "I have to tell you that I didn't even know you existed," Joanna said. "Until Lustrum told me. After your father's death."

"Dad never mentioned me in all those years? Oh, he was deep."

"According to Lustrum," Joanna went on, "as it was told him by your father, you opted out when he decided to marry me, and you had a quarrel. Isn't that right?"

"Now, why should I want to do something like that?" Kelly asked, eyes enormous. "I've been dying to meet you for years, but Dad wouldn't let me."

Joanna felt like scratching her head. "You mean you *weren't* opposed to our marriage?"

"I thought it was brilliant. The old gink needed a woman."

"Then why was he so determined to keep us apart that he never even mentioned you?"

Kelly grinned. "You'll have to ask him. Oops, you can't, can you?"

Joanna drank champagne; this was going to require patience. "But he obviously told you about me, and about Raisul, and Helen."

"Helen. She's your daughter, right?"

"Yes. She's out right now. So you know about all of us."

"Yeah, well, Dad used to write, and sometimes he'd come out and visit."

"In Canada, Vancouver. That's where you lived, wasn't it?"

"Until Mom died." Joanna braced herself, but there was no frightening glance this time. "Then Dad decided to come and live over here. To marry you, I guess." She gave a little giggle. "So I was left to do my own thing."

"Wait a moment," Joanna said. "If you are twenty-four now, seven years ago, when your father and I got married, you would have been seventeen. You mean he just walked away from a seventeen-year-old daughter?"

"Yeah. He was a bastard."

Joanna was beginning to agree with her. "What did you do?"

Kelly shrugged. "This and that. He kept me funded."

So that's how she had the money to pay for her air fare, Joanna thought. "I'm sure he did. You poor girl." She put her arm round Kelly's shoulders. "I am so terribly sorry."

"Water under the bridge," Kelly said. "But I'm glad you're sorry." To Joanna's amazement, she kissed her on the lips.

Joanna remained absolutely still for a few seconds, while Kelly's tongue stroked, then she gently freed herself. "Some more champagne," she said, and got up. What in the name of God do I do now? she wondered. And how do I handle the inheritance angle? But she simply had to find out where she stood. She refilled their glasses, and this time sat in a chair facing the settee. "You do know that your father was a very wealthy man?"

"Oh, sure. Millions and millions. That's what he always said."

"You never discussed money with him?"

"I never discussed anything with him."

"I see. But you do realise that you are in line for a considerable inheritance?"

"Am I? Wowee! I'll drink to that. How much?"

The question came like a pistol shot. She might come across as somewhat fey, Joanna thought, but there was nothing the matter with her brain. "The whole estate."

Kelly slowly put down her glass. "Say again?"

"That's what Lustrum tells me. Your father left his entire estate to you."

Kelly stared at her, then gave a shriek of laughter. "The old bastard! He must've been nuts. And I came over here looking for a hand-out from you."

Chance would be a fine thing, Joanna thought. "I think Michael was very fond of you," she said. "And maybe regretted cutting you out of his life, so to speak."

"Big deal," Kelly said. "When you say, the entire estate, how many zeroes are we talking about?"

"I think one could say seven, with quite a large figure in front."

"Wowee," Kelly said again. "And how much do you get?"

"I get nothing."

"Say again?"

"Your father set me up in business again after I came out of prison. I suppose he felt that was enough."

"The bastard," Kelly said again.

"There are of course some overlapping items," Joanna said, carefully. "But I am sure we can clear those."

"Sure," Kelly said.

Waves of relief flooded Joanna's system. It had all really been so simple. "Well," she said, "the funeral is on Monday morning. You'll want to attend that."

"No," Kelly said. Joanna raised her eyebrows. "I don't like funerals," Kelly said. "They make me feel real bad."

"Oh. Right. It's up to you. What I was going to say was,

after the funeral, say Tuesday, if you'd care to come into the office with me, we can sort things out then."

"Sure, if that turns you on. Lustrum said something about the Will being read on Wednesday."

"Yes. We didn't expect you to come across so quickly. Would you like it brought forward?"

"You bet. I mean, you and I can't get down to the nitty gritty until we both know exactly where we stand, eh?"

Once again Joanna was taken aback by the sudden change from careless compliance to pinpoint acumen; she was also disturbed by the indication that Kelly perhaps knew more about her father's business affairs and their relations with Caribee Shipping than she had supposed. "I'll give Lustrum a ring," she said, "and confirm that we'd prefer to have the Will read Tuesday morning."

"What's wrong with Monday afternoon?"

"Ah . . . well, so soon after the funeral might . . ."

"Make people talk? They always do. Let's go for Monday afternoon."

"I'll talk to Lustrum," Joanna agreed. "Here's Helen."

"As our new relative would say, wowee," Helen remarked, joining her mother in Joanna's bedroom after lunch.

"She is a little far out," Joanna agreed.

"But friendly."

"So far. I can't help feeling that there are some brick walls behind that pleasant façade. What's she doing now?"

"Walking the grounds."

"You'd think she'd be suffering from jet-lag. And where is Raisul?"

"Walking the grounds."

Joanna went to the window. "You won't see them," Helen said. "They went into the wood."

"Shit!"

"What's bothering you? She's old enough . . ."

"Certainly not to be his mother. Do you know he saw

57

her in the nude, standing on her balcony, when he came home?"

"Lucky him. She must've been something."

"Don't you start," Joanna said. "He got quite obviously turned on."

"Well," Helen said, "if she's taken him walking, after that, isn't it a step in the right direction, from our point of view?"

Helen thought Mother was taking the appearance of this possible cuckoo in the nest very calmly. But then, Mother took most things calmly, and by all accounts she had had to face some fairly horrendous situations in the past.

She had even taken the hijacking of one of her ships, and the kidnapping of her only daughter, calmly. At least on the surface. She had merely caught a flight to Singapore and sorted the whole thing out. *She* had been a vital part of that operation. In fact, she had been in at the beginning and at the end, having accumulated and lost a husband along the way.

Dennis Moore had been a rat. Her entire life had been a business of accumulating rats. Harry Dean. Dennis Moore. And now Geoff Best. Why? She knew she was an extremely good-looking woman, not to say beautiful. So she attracted men. Surely at some stage she had to attract a decent, *nice* man, who would also be a turn-on. If she didn't she was going to go nuts. Many people thought she already was.

She went outside to inhale the afternoon air. The Mercedes waited at the foot of the steps, and Deardon was polishing the bonnet. Today he was wearing full uniform, including his cap. "You can put it away again," Helen said. "I'm pretty sure she isn't going anywhere, today."

"Thank you, Miss. By the way, I've polished out that scratch on your car."

"Scratch? Shit, I'd forgotten about that. Parked too close to a wall."

"Happens all the time, Miss."

"But not to you, eh? Anyway, thanks a million." She grinned. "Seems I'm always thanking you for something."

"It's my pleasure, Miss."

Why did he have to be a chauffeur? Or more importantly, her mother's chauffeur?

"What a lovely place," Kelly remarked, strolling through the trees that bordered the back of the property. "How many acres are there?"

"Seven and a bit," Raisul said.

"And your mother owns it all? It wasn't part ownership with my dad, or something?"

"Not so far as I know. Your dad bought it for her. I mean, she had owned it before, but she lost it when she went to prison." He glanced at her. "I suppose you know about that?"

"Some."

"Well, when she came back out, and they got together, your dad bought it back for her. You'll have to ask her the exact terms."

"Real romantic." Kelly continued walking until she came to the stream that rushed between the trees. "Say, that's absolutely beautiful. How deep is it?"

"Maybe four feet in the middle."

"You ever bathed in it?"

Raisul grinned. "When I was a kid."

"Long time ago, huh? This place is growing on me. It makes me feel, well . . . free."

"That's how we want you to feel," Raisusl said. "Free."

"You know about me?" Kelly kicked off her thongs.

"I never even heard of you until a couple of days ago."

"So tell me what you think of your step-sister." She took off her shirt; she wasn't wearing a brassière.

Raisul swallowed. "I think you're just tremendous."

"I reckon you're tremendous too." She dropped her jeans; she wasn't wearing knickers, either.

Raisul wondered if she had flown the Atlantic like that. "Ah . . . there are gardeners. Two, in fact."

"But this isn't the garden," she pointed out. "Anyway, it'll give them a kick." She stepped down from the bank and waded into the water while he stared at her gently moving buttocks; they were about the only part of her body not smothered in freckles. When she was thigh deep, she turned. "Cold . . . Aren't you going to join me?"

Raisul looked left and right. But there was no one about, and she had been quite right when she had said that the gardeners had no business out here. But he had never been naked in the open air before. And certainly not in the company of a beautiful woman. Or any woman, for that matter. He wondered what Mother would say, and decided against wondering. Then he wondered what Nicola would say. But Nicola couldn't compare. And in any event, like Mother, there was no need for her ever to find out. But this woman was his sister. Of course, she was not: she was his *step*-sister. There was no blood between them.

"You don't have to, chicken," Kelly said, stooping to scoop water over her shoulders.

"I want to," Raisul said, undressing as fast as he could, while she watched him, quizzically, only her head visible to suggest that she might be sitting on the bottom. He found that a peculiarly evocative thought, leapt into the water beside her, and knelt.

"It's not a very big one," she remarked. "Shouldn't you have a big one? Haven't you got Arab blood?"

"I am half-Arab," he said proudly. And gasped as her hands came through the water to hold him. Nicola hadn't done that.

"Then you should have a big one," she told him. "But it's growing. Would you like to fuck me?"

"To . . . we've only just met."

"That's the best time," she said, apparently seriously, her fingers busy. "We haven't had the time to dislike each other."

"Ah . . . gosh," he gasped.

Kelly released him, rubbed her hands together in the water. "That was quick. And you never touched me."

"I'd like to."

"So what's keeping you?"

He ran his hands over her shoulders and breasts, stroked her cold-hard nipples. "You are . . . I don't know."

"Say the first thing that comes into your mind."

"Tremendous."

"You said that already. But I like it." She stood up, letting his hands drag down her thighs. "You got a steady?"

"Not exactly."

"But you're not a virgin, right?"

"Of course not."

"Don't take offence." She climbed up the bank, spread her jeans, and sat on them, her back against a tree, one leg up. She was irresistible. He climbed out beside her. "Was your dad really an Arab? I can't see your mom in bed with an Arab." She giggled. "I can't see your mom in bed with anyone, least of all my dad."

"My father was an Arab prince," Raisul said. "He was Mother's second husband."

"So you're royalty. I've never been fucked by royalty. You simply have to come in there." She regarded him. "I reckon you'll make it again, pretty soon. That's what so great about youth."

"Don't you think, well . . . it'd be more private at the house?"

"With all those servants roaming around? Not to mention your mother and sister. No way. Anyway, we can't go back till we've dried a little. We've no towels."

"Heck. I hadn't thought of that."

"So come here," she said, sliding down the tree until she was lying on the grass. "And we'll dry each other with a little friction."

Joanna knocked before she entered the Blue Room.

"Come in," Kelly shouted. "I'm in the shower." Joanna closed the door behind herself. The girl seemed to have a water fixation. But that was no bad thing if it meant she was that clean. "What's up?" Kelly emerged from the bathroom, naked, towelling vigorously.

Joanna sat down, crossing her legs. "I thought I should let you know that we usually dress for dinner."

"I wasn't planning on coming down like this."

"I meant we normally, well, put on something dressy. I'm not necessarily talking about black tie or long gown, but Raisul always wears a tie, and Helen and I wear at least cocktail dresses." She paused, because Kelly was regarding her with one of those quizzical expressions. "You do have a dress?"

"Never wear them."

"Ah. Well, you'll find they're quite usual in England. And often necessary. We'll go shopping on Monday . . ."

"Before or after the funeral?"

"Damn! I'd forgotten the funeral. We'll go out early. There's quite a reasonable dress shop in the village. That suit you?"

"Sounds terrific. And tonight?"

"Well, tonight you can wear your own usual gear. We'll make an exception, and for tomorrow." She watched Kelly dress with growing consternation. "Don't you use underwear?"

"Never saw the need," Kelly said.

"Ah . . . maybe we'll buy you some lingerie as well," Joanna said, wondering just how they were going to get through Sunday. "I can lend you some of mine to go on with."

"Wouldn't work," Kelly said. "Your tits are bigger than mine, and . . ."

"So is my waist," Joanna said, a trifle ruefully. "Helen is more your size."

"Listen," Kelly said. "Don't bother. I'm happy without."

"I didn't mean to importune," Joanna got up and went to the door. "Did Raisul show you the grounds, this afternoon?"

"Some of them. He's a sweet kid. But then, he'd have to be, with you as mother and an Arab prince as father."

She does lay it on, Joanna thought. But she had to be humoured, in everything, until Caribee's finances were sorted out. "You say the nicest things. You were gone a very long time."

"Well, we had to wait to dry."

"Eh?"

"After our dip," Kelly explained. "We didn't have towels, so we had to sit on the bank and wait to dry. That's why I was having a hot shower, just now. We got quite chilled."

"Of course," Joanna said, in preference to 'Jesus Christ!' "May I ask where you dipped?"

"In that cute little stream you have."

"Where else. Well, come down whenever you're ready, and have an aperitif."

"Say again?"

"A drink before dinner," Joanna said.

Raisul did not come down until the dinner gong went, and he carefully avoided his mother's eye throughout the meal. She had wanted to speak to him earlier, but his bedroom door had been locked. More than ever she was wondering how she was going to handle this situation. She desperately needed to keep on good terms with this girl, at least for the immediate future. But she couldn't have her take over their lives, teach them an entirely new set of mores . . . of which she could not possibly approve.

"Tell me about being hijacked," Kelly said brightly, to Helen. "I mean, one reads about planes, but a whole ship . . . wowee."

"It wasn't fun," Helen said.

"But you shot a lot of them. I remember reading about it."

"It was them or me," Helen said.

"I've never shot anyone in my life," Kelly said, apparently with genuine regret.

"It's not something to make a habit of," Joanna said.

"And then you got married, but the guy turned out to be a baddy," Kelly said.

"Yes," Helen agreed, quietly.

Joanna glanced at her daughter. One never knew what was going on in Helen's mind, when she might be about to explode. "It's not something we talk about," she said.

"There I go," Kelly said. "Putting my foot in my mouth again. I apologise."

"Forget it," Helen said.

Kelly kept the conversation bubbling throughout the meal, but strictly on the subject of the English half of the family. Joanna tried to turn things round. "I've been meaning to ask you," she said. "Of course I'm putting the notices of your father's death in all the leading Canadian papers. But you're now living in New York, aren't you? Should I put a notice in *The Times*, as well?"

"I wouldn't bother," Kelly said.

"Ah . . . right. But what about your other kin? Your cousins, or aunts and uncles? I feel I should write them personally."

"There aren't any."

"You mean you have no relatives at all?" Helen asked.

"Not right now." Kelly grinned. "Save you guys."

"You poor dear," Joanna said. "Of course we're your kin. Now and always."

Joanna at last got Raisul alone after dinner, by sending the two girls off to the billiards room to play snooker. "Just what happened this afternoon?"

"We went for a walk," Raisul said, a trifle sulkily.

"And a dip, as I understand."

"We went into the water, yes."

"And then had to hang about waiting to dry. What did you do during that period?"

Raisul flushed. "Heck, Mother, she wanted it."

"And you obliged. Your own stepsister."

"We're not actually related."

"That's not the point. She's our guest, and our responsibility. And her father has only been dead forty-eight hours."

"She *wanted* it, Mother."

"And you're the great big stud willing to oblige. What about this woman you've been seeing in London?"

"Well . . ." Raisul's flush deepened. "How'd you know about that?"

"You'd be surprised what I know. I have no objection to your sowing some wild oats. However, let me make something perfectly clear. I am not running a brothel, and I am not into incest. Even half incest. You do not, *not*, do what she wants, again. Do I make myself perfectly clear?"

He glared at her, the flush slowly fading. "I'm an adult."

"In the eyes of the law, yes. In my eyes, you're an adult when you start showing a sense of responsibility."

"Oh, Mother . . ."

"It's up to you," Joanna said. "I'd prefer not to speak with Kelly on the subject. Certainly not right now. If you force me to, I will have to ask her to move out. And I think that would be very bad for her, and bad for the family."

"And perhaps very bad for your finances," he snapped.

Joanna's head jerked, and she all but slapped his face. "Yes," she said. "It could be very bad for my finances. Which you need to remember are *your* finances as well. So you go to bed, and you lock your door, and you don't open it under any circumstances before tomorrow morning."

"We normally go to church on Sundays," Joanna said at breakfast. She had no idea whether or not Kelly had attempted to make contact with Raisul during the night; they all looked bright enough this morning.

"Sorry," Kelly said. "Count me out. Churches give me the wobblies. Anyway, I've nothing to wear, right?"

"I could probably find you something," Helen suggested.

"I said no," Kelly repeated.

"Ah . . . right . . ." Joanna hesitated.

"I'm not very keen on church this morning, as a matter of fact," Helen said, aware that her mother didn't want to leave Kelly alone in the house.

"Then Raisul and I will go," Joanna said.

Raisul opened his mouth and then closed it again.

Joanna went upstairs, bathed and dressed, and predictably was joined by Helen before she was finished. "What exactly am I guarding?" she asked. "The family silver?"

"Of course not. It's just that . . . I feel she is so unpredictable."

"Did she have Raisul?"

"She had Raisul for tea. And if we're not careful, she's going to have him for lunch, breakfast and dinner, as well."

"I don't see what she sees in him, frankly."

"Spoken like a sister. I'm not sure what she sees in any of us. But it's something."

"You're sure you're not being a little paranoid? She's a kid who's just lost her dad, and is adrift in a pretty horrendous world. She just craves affection."

"I'm sure you're right. And I'm prepared to give her all the affection she craves. But she isn't right for Raisul. As for being a kid, she's older than you are. Just keep her company, and be nice to her, and we'll be back in a couple of hours."

Helen got dressed, deliberately in shirt and jeans to match Kelly's, and went downstairs to sit on the terrace and wave Joanna and Raisul away. Raisul was not looking pleased; he'd have preferred to be at home himself.

"You're a pretty close-knit family, huh?" said Kelly as she sat beside her.

"We have reason to be."

"Sure." Kelly began playing with things, and Helen realised she was rolling.

"Do you mind?" she said.

"Don't you want a drag?"

"No," Helen said. "Not right this minute."

"Bit early, eh?" Kelly completed the joint with deft fingers.

"Listen," Helen said. "If my mother finds you smoking grass in this house there'll be hell to pay."

"Just the one," Kelly said, and struck a match. She inhaled, then held the weed out toward Helen, who hesitated, then shook her head. "Don't be a wet."

"I'm on a charge right this minute."

"For this? That's a joke."

"For peddling heroin."

Kelly's eyes were enormous. "You got some of that?"

"No. And I didn't know what I was doing. I thought it was Ecstasy. Then there was this bitch of an undercover cop . . . it's a mess. Mum will sort it out, I know. But right now . . ."

"Some lady, your mom." Kelly took several deep drags. "Tough. You were raped, once, right?"

"If it's any business of yours, yes. More than once. It was a gang-bang."

"Shit! I've never been raped. Not even by one guy. And then the hijack. And you saw your dad die too, right?"

"No. You're thinking of my stepfather, Prince Hasim. Raisul's father. But I wasn't there when he was shot. My dad died before I was born."

"Some life." Kelly lay back with her eyes shut, still slowly inhaling. "You need some of this stuff, I reckon. I saw my mom die."

"I'm sorry. Cancer, was it? That must have been terrible."

"Cancer," Kelly said, half to herself. "That's what they said. Because Dad told them to. Oh, she had cancer . . ."

Helen was frowning. "You mean it wasn't cancer that actually killed her?"

"My dad was like your mom. People said what he told them to, put what he told them to on death certificates. I guess that's why they got on so well together. What time do they come back from church?"

"Another hour or so. Then how did your mother die?"

67

It was her turn to be on the end of a cold stare. "That gives us time to go upstairs and have a quick roll in the sack." Kelly put out the cigarette and stood up.

"I hope you're not serious," Helen said.

"Sure I am. I get randy every day about this time, and it's more fun with someone else."

"And the sex doesn't matter? I thought you were into my brother?"

Kelly giggled. "You mean he was into me. He's kind of young. Needs to be shown. But he's coming along. Now *you*, I reckon, know it all."

"No, I don't," Helen said. "Only one side of it. If you really are desperate, run along and play with yourself. I'll wait for you to come back." Mother had said to humour her, but there was a limit.

"You don't want to make me mad," Kelly said. "I get real mean when I'm mad."

"So do I," Helen said. They stared at each other, and were distracted by the roar of a motorbike engine, coming up the drive at speed. "Geoff," Helen said. She had never been so happy to see anyone in her life before . . . and she had never expected to be glad to see Geoff again.

"Friend of yours?" Kelly asked.

"In a manner of speaking."

The motorbike came to a scraping halt at the foot of the steps, scattering gravel.

"Hiya, doll," Geoff said. "The dragon about?"

"The dragon is in church."

"There's good news. But I thought she might be." Geoff took off his helmet.

"Good-looking, too," Kelly murmured.

"Well, hi," Geoff said, coming up the steps. "I don't think we've met."

"My stepsister, Kelly," Helen said.

"Nice work, if you can get it," Kelly remarked.

"I didn't know you had a stepsister," Geoff said.

68

"Neither did I, till yesterday," Helen said.

He looked confused.

"I'm a bundle of surprises," Kelly said. "You and she an item?"

"Well . . ." Geoff looked at Helen.

"Definitely not," Helen said. "How many knives do you have on you today, Geoff?"

"Just the one," Geoff said.

"Listen," Kelly said. "Why don't you run along and play with *yourself*, honey doll? This Geoff and I are going to have a little chat."

"I thought the vicar was rather sweet," Joanna said, as Deardon drove Raisul and herself back from church.

"Yucky," Raisul commented.

"Sweet," Joanna insisted. "Michael was a much respected man in this neighbourhood."

"Money will get you everywhere, and everything," Raisul observed.

"You are starting to annoy me," Joanna said.

"I'm sorry, Mom."

"Mom?"

"Well . . . look, would you like me to get out of your hair?"

"Doing what?"

"I could go up to town for the afternoon."

"To see your friend?"

Raisul glanced at her. "Could be."

"Tell me about her."

"Her?"

"I know it's a her, Raisul. I'm not mad, really. I just like to know what my children are doing."

"Let me get to know her better, and I'll tell you."

"That's fair enough." Joanna reflected that any her was better than Kelly. "What is that?" They were into the drive, and she was looking at the parked motorbike.

"Haven't a clue," Raisul said. "But it's a nice machine."

Joanna had never let him have a motorbike; she regarded them as dangerous.

Deardon braked before the steps. "It belongs to the young man, madam."

"What young man?"

"The young man at the hotel in London, madam. The man with the knife. That bike was parked outside the hotel."

"Good God! And he's here?" Joanna got out. "Of all the nerve."

"Would you like me to drive over it, madam?" Deardon asked. "My foot could slip on the brake."

The man was fast becoming a treasure. "Leave it for the time being," Joanna said. "He'll need it to leave. But stick around, Deardon."

"Of course, madam."

"Just what is all this about?" Raisul asked.

Joanna led him into the house. "If Deardon is right, that bike belongs to a rather unpleasant character with whom Helen has been knocking about. Did you know she's on a drugs charge?"

"Helen? Holy smoke."

"At least partly because of that lout. Parks."

"Madam?" As always when she came in, Parks was carrying a tray with a bottle of champagne and some glasses.

"Where is Miss Helen?"

"In her room, I believe, madam."

Joanna took a glass and drank. Raisul also took a glass, and she pointed at him. "Just one, if you really are intending to drive this afternoon." She turned back to Parks. "And Miss Johannsson?"

"I believe she went for a walk, madam. With the young gentleman."

"If you mistook him for a gentleman, Parks, you need spectacles."

"Let me get this straight," Raisul said. "Kelly . . . Miss Johannsson . . . has gone for a walk with some man?"

"Yes, sir."

"God damn it." He put down his glass.

"Just simmer down," Joanna said. "You don't own her. And this fellow has a habit of producing knives. You just stay indoors."

"I'm going to break his fucking neck," Raisul said, and ran out of the front door.

Joanna went to the door behind him, biting her lip, watched him disappear round the side of the house.

"Something wrong, madam?" Deardon asked, getting out of the Mercedes.

Joanna hesitated. She really didn't want Raisul to be nursemaided; the boy was in an odd enough frame of mind as it was. And he was certainly bigger than the Geoff she remembered from the other night. But as for the knife . . . yet surely he wouldn't go driving on a Sunday, obviously intending to meet up with Helen, carrying a knife?

"Just hang about," she said, and looked up as another car came down the drive. William's Toyota. At least she was gathering a lot of support. "Well, hi," she said. "What brings you down here?"

One look at her brother's face as he got out of the car was sufficient to tell her it was nothing good. "We need to talk," he said, coming up the steps.

"In the study." She led the way.

"Where's Miss Johannsson?" he asked.

"Walking in the grounds, surrounded by male admirers. She's like a bitch on heat. She *is* a bitch on heat."

"You'll have to explain that."

"It would take too long. You look bothered." She sat behind her desk.

William carefully closed the door. "Yesterday morning, as soon as I had spoken with you, I put a call through to Evans, our agent in Vancouver. That's where Michael used to live, right?"

"Right." Joanna's heartbeat quickened.

"I told him it was urgent, and he said he'd get on to it right

71

away. Well, he certainly did that. You know it's still night over there. He called me an hour ago. He'd worked all day and into the night, looking up newspaper reports, calling old friends . . ."

"And?"

"Mrs Johannsson, the first Mrs Johannsson, actually committed suicide."

"What?"

"Oh, she had cancer, and was dying. She knew this; she'd been given three months to live. So one day when she was alone in the house, she poured herself a hot bath, got into it, and . . ."

"Oh, my God!" Joanna said. "No wonder Michael would never speak of it."

"I'm not quite finished," William said.

"What else?"

"She didn't cut her wrists, Jo. In the time-honoured fashion. She had a large cut-throat razor, and did just that."

"You're not serious."

"I'm afraid I am. One gigantic slash."

Joanna stared at him. She just could not envisage anyone doing that, no matter how desperate. "That poor kid," she said. "I suppose she knows what really happened."

"Kelly discovered the body, Jo."

Joanna clasped both hands to her neck. "What did she do?"

"She seems to have gone berserk, tried to drag her mother from the bath – Mrs Johannsson was apparently dead by then – and she actually did manage to tumble her out on to the floor. Then, covered in blood and water, Kelly ran out on to the street, screaming."

"That poor, poor kid."

"She was quietened down," William said, "and Michael sent for . . . he was out of town on business. But Kelly had gone completely round the bend."

Joanna frowned at him. "So what happened to her?"

"She was certified insane, and sent to a mental hospital."

Four

"I don't understand," Joanna said. "Kelly was sent to a madhouse, eight years ago . . . and she's here? And lives in New York?"

William nodded. "I'm finding out about that, but Evans will need more time. He's going out to the mental institution where she was confined this afternoon, and will come back to us the moment he finds out anything further. But I thought I should let you know right away."

"But if she's escaped from a madhouse . . ." Joanna said slowly.

"I don't think she could have done that, Jo. In the papers Michael lodged with Lustrum was this New York address for Kelly. That's how Lustrum knew where to get in touch with her. If Michael knew where she was, her being there had to be on the up and up. And if she crossed the Atlantic, she had to have a passport. Absconders from mental institutions don't usually have those. No, no, I'd say she was released, which means that some hospital psychiatrist certified her as sane. So she probably is."

Joanna's brain was tumbling. She could at last understand Michael's determination to keep his new wife, and her family, apart from his mad daughter and the memory of her mother's suicide. But for him to have had to live with that secret, for eight years, while coping with her shenanigans and financial as well as moral crises, and never breathe a word or ask even for emotional help . . . never in her life had she felt so guilty. Or so determined to make amends

73

as best she could by doing everything she could to help this girl.

"So there we are," William said. "I'm expecting to hear from Evans again this evening. That's his time, so it will be pretty late over here."

"Thanks a million, Willie."

"What are you going to do?"

"Think."

"I think we should take legal advice as rapidly as possible," William said. "We have on our hands, at best, a recently recovered madwoman who has just become a multi-millionairess, and who holds the future of your company in the palm of her hand. We need to take every possible step to protect ourselves."

"You mean, if we can send her back to her institution, she can't inherit."

"I don't know whether she can or not. That's what we have to find out. But I also think we should find out whether, in view of her mental problem, we cannot take steps to have the Will set aside."

"And then?"

"Well . . . you are the natural next of kin. At the very least you could become her guardian, with control of her finances."

"What a devious fellow you are," Joanna said. "I'm glad you're my brother and not hers. But as you say, she must have been certified sane."

"By some psychiatrist. What do you think? You must have had a pretty good look at her over the past twenty-four hours."

"I have," Joanna said. "She doesn't act mad. She's . . . odd, and has some behavioural quirks I don't approve of, but then, so do my own children. Anyway, there's nothing we can do on a Sunday morning. Let me know the moment you hear anything more from Evans."

"As I said, it may be pretty late."

"The moment, Willie."

"And you'll let me set up a meeting with Matthews first thing tomorrow?" John Matthews was the Caribee company solicitor.

"Tomorrow's out. We've the funeral, first thing, and the reading of the Will in the afternoon. But presumably he'll be coming down for the funeral. We can have a chat afterwards."

"And the shipyard?"

"They really can't expect me to deal with their problem until after the funeral. I'm sending Raisul up there on Tuesday."

"Raisul? He's only twenty."

"The same age as me when I took over the company." Her mouth twisted. "He'll be properly instructed. And he has as much interest in this as anyone. Now, will you stay for lunch?"

"I'd like to. If only . . ."

"To meet the girl. Mind you don't fall for her."

"Me?"

"Everyone else has, virtually at first sight." She got up, frowned, hearing shouts from outside the house, followed by the roar of a motorbike engine.

"Oh, shit!" she said, and ran into the hall, William behind her. They stood on the porch and gazed at the motorbike, now nearly out of sight down the drive. Beside the Mercedes, Deardon was just picking himself up and replacing his cap. "Deardon!" Joanna ran down the steps. "Are you all right?"

"I'm all right, madam. I'm sorry, but that man just came running round the house. I told him to stop, and he charged me, headbutted me, and got on his bike and drove away."

"But you are hurt." She gazed at the blood on his tunic.

"That's not mine, madam. It was that fellow. His head was a mass of blood."

"Oh, my God!" Joanna ran round the house and into the woods, both William and Deardon accompanying her. "Kelly!" Joanna shouted. "Raisul! Where are you?"

Then they heard splashes.

"What the hell . . . ?" William asked.

"Stop right here," Joanna said. "Both of you. I'll call if I need you."

"Sis . . ."

"Just wait." She went forward cautiously, stood beside a tree overlooking the stream, watched the two people bathing. They were aesthetically beautiful, as their bodies twined together, coupling and moving apart. Her son, she thought. And . . . she didn't want to make up her mind about that. Then she saw the knife, lying on the grass. There was no blood on it. She stepped away from the trees. "I think you can come out, now," she said.

They turned, Raisul in alarm, Kelly without any great change of expression save for a bright smile. "Oh, hi," she said.

"Didn't you hear me shouting?"

"Vaguely."

"Come out and get dressed," Joanna said. "And tell me what happened."

Raisul climbed out of the water and pulled on his underpants. "It all happened so quickly . . ."

Kelly giggled. "Raisul came hustling up, just as Geoff and I were going for a dip. He looked real mad, said he was going to punch Geoff on the nose."

Raisul went on dressing, looking thoroughly embarrassed. But also, Joanna thought, considerably frightened. Kelly pulled on her jeans. "Then Geoff suddenly pulled a knife. I didn't know he had a knife."

Joanna looked from one to the other; neither was in any way hurt, or even scratched. "What did you do?"

"I hit him," Kelly said. "With that stone."

Joanna looked at the stone. It was very large, more like a small boulder, and it was definitely blood-stained. "So he dropped the knife and ran off," Kelly went on.

"Don't you think you should have done something about it?" Joanna asked. "He could be badly hurt."

"Serves him right," Kelly commented.

Joanna looked at Raisul; he was now dressed in shirt and pants, picking up his crumpled jacket and tie. "That suit will have to go to the cleaners," she remarked. "Give me your handkerchief."

Raisul pulled his handkerchief from his pocket, and Joanna picked up the knife, wrapped in the cloth. "I think we'd better be getting back."

"Jo!" William was shouting.

"Just coming," Joanna said.

Lunch was a subdued meal. Having heard the rumpus, Helen had come down, distinctly out of sorts. "You hit Geoff?" she asked incredulously. "With a stone?"

"She was protecting me," Raisul mumbled.

"Did I do the wrong thing?" Kelly asked, as innocently as ever.

"I'm sure you did the right thing," Joanna said. "I just hope that bastard doesn't go to the police."

"But we have the knife," Raisul said. "Surely we'll be able to prove it's his?"

"It'll have his prints on it. But it'll just make this drugs mess worse."

"If you're Jo's brother," Kelly said, adroitly switching subjects to a spellbound William, "then you're my uncle. Sort of."

"Sort of," he agreed.

"What a good-looking family you are."

William gulped, and looked at his sister.

"She says the sweetest things," Joanna said. "Now, I am going to take a siesta, and I think you should all do the same. We've all had a pretty traumatic morning."

"I'll be getting back up to town," William said. "Norma and I are taking the children to the zoo this afternoon. It's been a pleasure meeting you, Kelly."

Kelly kissed him on the cheek. "And for me, Uncle William. But I'll be seeing you again, I hope."

"Often," William said. "Beginning tomorrow, when we come down for the funeral."

"Oh, yes, the funeral," Kelly said.

"Kelly doesn't like funerals," Helen said, vindictively.

"Who does?" William asked, easily.

Joanna went with him to the door. "What do you think?"

"That she's a charmer."

"Like I said, she has that effect on men. Maybe on women, too. Don't forget to call me the moment you hear from Evans."

"I'll do that."

"And I am assuming that Norma and the kids will also be coming down tomorrow, for the funeral?"

He grinned. "Of course. It'll be interesting to see what Norma makes of her. Has Matilda met her yet?"

"As a matter of fact no. But it's bound to happen any moment."

"Well," he said, "have fun."

What to do, what to do, what to do? Joanna asked herself, as she showered before lying down. What she needed to do, first, was marshal her facts, place them in order of priority, and then tick off the answers or requirements, one after the other.

She lay down, on top of the sheets, flat on her back as she liked best. Fact Number One: she was again, and for the third time, a widow. What was she going to do about that? Did she want to do anything about that?

Fact Number Two: because she was a widow, her company was suddenly in financial straits. How serious depended on some of the facts still to be considered. But in the short term, she needed some kind of arrangement with the bank. Barry Andrews on Tuesday. It might be an idea to put off Raisul's trip north until Wednesday.

Fact Number Three: she had accumulated one stepdaughter, who might, or might not, have escaped from a mental institution, and who was the nearest thing to a nymphomaniac she had

78

ever encountered. But who held the key to the future financial viability of Caribee Shipping.

And who had also had a totally traumatic experience with her mother. For all her faults, Joanna desperately wanted to help her, mother her, to give her some of the happiness that seemed to have entirely passed her by. But as she had thought earlier, she didn't want Kelly's rampant sexuality to overwhelm her own children.

Equally, she had to handle the financial side of the picture with kid gloves. Kelly was, understandably, conditioned to being suspicious of everyone around her. She had also given one or two glimpses of possessing an acute mind, whether she was sub or abnormal. If she felt in the slightest way that anyone might be setting up to cheat her, or even manipulate her handling of her fortune, an explosion would almost certainly follow. Perhaps William was right, and the simplest solution would be to put her back into an institution. But it would be quite unspeakably cruel.

Knuckles brushed her door. "Come," Joanna said, hastily inserting her naked body beneath the sheets. Raisul sidled in, and closed the door behind him. He was dressed in casual clothes. "You just caught me," Joanna said. "Before drifting off. I thought you were going up to town?"

"I am. Mother, are you very angry with me?"

"Come here, you silly boy." He sat on the edge of the bed, and she gave him a hug. "No, I am not *very* angry with you. But I meant what I said. OK, so you had a bit of a traumatic experience this morning, but it must never happen again."

"It won't. Mother . . . she's not quite right. Did you know that?"

"Tell me."

"Well . . ." he bit his lip. "I went chasing after them, as you know, and that bastard drew his knife on me. I . . . I didn't know what to do. I've never faced a knife before. Frankly, I was scared stiff."

"That's understandable. So?"

"But Kelly . . . she just went berserk. She started screaming and shouting, quite incoherently, and then picked up that rock and hit him with it. I've never seen anything like it."

"And after she'd hit him?"

"He ran off, and she dropped the rock, and smiled, and this was an entirely happy, normal smile, and she said, 'I feel like a dip. Let's have a dip.'"

"And you weren't about to argue with a lady who's good with rocks."

Raisul shuddered. "It's not a joke, Mother. I *was* scared. But when I stopped to think about it, I don't know what had scared me more, that Geoff with his knife, or Kelly with her rock." He gave a shamefaced grin. "I was never so relieved as when I saw you."

"That's what mothers are for," Joanna said. "So your brief romantic fling is over."

"It never was on . . . though she's one hell of a turn-on."

"I know. But I'm so glad she's managed to turn you off. Just tell me, is everything you have said true?"

"Well, of course it is."

"I'm not accusing you of lying, silly. I just want to be sure there was no exaggeration or embroidering."

"That was what happened, I swear to God."

"Your word will do. Because you may just have to repeat all of that."

"Who to?"

"A judge. You go on up to London and see your friend. Give her my love. Will you be back tonight?"

"Would you be mad if I wasn't?"

Joanna shook her head. "It would probably be the best thing. But I'll expect you down early tomorrow, for the funeral."

"You expecting a big crowd?"

"Not really. Only family and business acquaintances."

"I'll be there." He stood up, hesitated, then stooped and kissed her on the forehead. "You've been just great. I'll repeat it to a judge, if you need me to."

As he left, Joanna smiled as she nestled into the bed. One crisis had resolved itself. In a manner of speaking. She really did need to find out who this 'friend' was in London that Raisul was so keen on. When a young man is an heir to a fortune there will always be fortune hunters knocking about. At least he hadn't made any noises about moving out, while he clearly supposed his appearance before a judge would be to do either with Helen's drug bust or Geoff's assault. For all his observations, that it might have anything to do with Kelly's mental situation had not yet crossed his mind, and Joanna hoped it would not, until it became necessary – or quite unnecessary.

Another knock. "Come," she said. "Would you believe that my sole ambition is to put in a few hours sleep? I've had an absolutely traumatic three days, I didn't sleep much last night, and I may well have a broken night tonight."

"That goes for all of us." Helen sat on the end of the bed. "Mother, I really think Kelly should go."

Joanna pushed herself up the bed, arranged the sheet across her chest, propped the pillows behind her back and head. "What's she done now?"

"Well, that display this morning . . ."

"She was protecting your baby brother."

"But going off with Geoff in the first place . . ."

"Don't tell me you still have something going for that yob?"

"Well . . ." Helen looked sulky. "He's not all bad, really. And compared with Kelly, he's an absolute innocent. Do you know she had a go at me, this morning, almost the moment you left the house?"

"She is a bit omniverous," Joanna agreed.

Helen frowned at her. "Not you, too?"

"I think she had some ideas. She has a problem."

"I can see that."

"I meant, she has the problem that for all of her adult life she has entirely lacked any love or real companionship. And any family."

81

"Her? Lacking love and companionship? She just goes out and grabs them both by the lapels whenever she feels in need."

"You can't really do that when you're locked up," Joanna pointed out.

"Eh?"

Joanna told her what William had found out.

"Holy shit!"

"This is in the strictest confidence," Joanna said.

"But if she's a maniac . . ."

"No one said she was a maniac. She had a severe nervous breakdown. Wouldn't you, if you came home one day and found me lying in my bath with my throat cut? No, I suppose you wouldn't, after all you've been through. But Kelly was only sixteen when it happened to her, and she'd had a sheltered life."

"Sure. I'm sorry for her. But you have to admit she's violent. Attacking Geoff with a bloody big rock . . ."

"He had it coming. Now, we are trying to sort the whole thing out, but until we do, I want you to be as nice as possible to her."

"You don't mind if I keep Parks in the room when we're together. And lock my door at night," Helen added.

"You're over-reacting. You could take her apart if she tried anything."

"Not if she sneaked up behind me with a rock," Helen pointed out. "Have a nice nap."

Chance would be a fine thing, Joanna thought, as she lay down again. But her sleep was this time uninterrupted. She rose at four, showered, dressed, and went downstairs, going first into the study, as was her habit to see if there were any faxes . . . and discovered Kelly sitting at her desk.

Her immediate reaction was total outrage, and then she realised the young woman was not reading any of the papers or account books taken from the drawers, but instead a volume of the *Encyclopaedia Britannica* taken from one of the bookshelves. She looked up with her invariable bright smile.

"Hi! All these books . . . we never had any books at home. Mom was no reader, and I guess Dad was too busy to read. He was always too busy. Did you find that?"

"He kept busy," Joanna agreed.

"I wanted to ask you," Kelly said. "You reckon there's going to be trouble over my hitting that jerk?"

"He may come back at you for GBH."

"What's GBH?"

"Grievous Bodily Harm. It's a serious crime."

"They wouldn't send me to prison?"

"I think we have an adequate defence. Raisul's evidence that Geoff attacked him. Backed up by the knife."

"I don't think I could stand jail," Kelly said.

"I know," Joanna said.

Kelly's eyebrows shot up, suspiciously. "You know what?"

"I know what it's like to be in prison," Joanna said.

"Sure. You were sent up for murdering my brother."

"Yes." Joanna remained standing on the other side of the desk; her muscles were tensed but her mind was curiously relaxed. "Only it wasn't murder. It was self defence."

Kelly closed the book and stood up. "That's what they all say, right?"

"I wouldn't know. I am sorry he was your brother, but he did attack me."

Kelly shrugged. "I never really knew him; he was so much older. I know Dad didn't go for him. Still, I guess a brother is a brother."

"Does that mean you're going to hold it against me?" Joanna asked.

"Now why should I do that?" Kelly asked, and left the room. Joanna sat down. She was sweating.

"Raisul?" Nicola said into the street phone. She was both astonished and angry. "What are you doing here?"

"Things are a bit fraught at home. May I come up?"

"You really should telephone a girl to let her know when you're coming," Nicola said, severely.

"I'm sorry. I thought you'd be pleased to see me."

"Of course I'm pleased to see you. But . . . oh, shit, I'm in the middle of washing my hair."

"I don't mind. I'd like to watch."

"Well, I don't want you to watch," she snapped. "Look, take a walk and come back in half an hour. OK?"

Raisul gazed at the speaker. It wasn't OK, he told himself. But he didn't want a quarrel, or a scene. "Half an hour," he said, and walked up the pavement. Her front window over-looked the street, and he reckoned she'd probably check that he had left. So he went to the corner, rounded it, and waited.

Did women usually wash their hair at seven o'clock on Sunday evenings? He couldn't recall either Mother or Helen ever doing that . . . But presumably they all had their own habits, their own routines. He was being paranoid. But he could not stop himself looking cautiously round the corner and back along the street, to watch the man hurrying in the other direction. He couldn't prove the man had come from Nicola's building. But he had certainly just materialised.

The two-timing bitch! Or was he again deluding himself, had been deluding himself from the beginning? He had been nothing but a one-night stand to her. He was the boss's son, so why not accommodate him? And he had fallen in love with her! Or he thought he had.

Dejected, he walked back to where he had parked his car.

With Raisul missing, dinner was a subdued affair. Kelly kept up her usual flow of question and answer conversation, concentrating, as earlier, on the hijack of the *Caribee Express* and the role Helen had played in regaining control of the ship, whilst Helen, under her mother's watchful eye, replied uninhibitedly. But Joanna was glad when the meal was over.

"I'm for an early night," she said. "It's been one of those

days, and tomorrow is going to be exhausting. Lots of business, Kelly." She smiled. "You'll need to keep a clear head."

"Lots of lolly," Kelly said happily. "This time tomorrow I'll be a millionairess."

"It's not all it's cracked up to be," Joanna suggested, but she also reminded herself that she had never been as rich as this girl was going to be – at least in her own right. But maybe, equally, by this time tomorrow she'd be on her way to sorting out this whole messy business.

"Your mom is feeling the strain," Kelly remarked.

"Wouldn't you be? Her husband has only been dead seventy-two hours," Helen said.

"He was my dad."

"I'm sorry. But you're not feeling the strain."

"Maybe I can keep mine under control. You didn't like him, did you?"

"What makes you say that?"

"The way you said, her husband. Did he rough you up? Try to have sex with you?"

"For God's sake, is that all you can think about?" Helen demanded. "Your father was a perfect gentleman at all times."

"But you didn't like him," Kelly persisted.

"Well . . ." Helen left the table, walked about the room. "Maybe he was too authoritarian."

"That's my dad."

"Was he ever rough on you?" Helen could not help being curious.

"Not really. We were pretty close, until Mom died. Then we kind of drifted apart."

"Because he wanted to marry my mother?"

Kelly grinned. "There were a lot of reasons. All done now."

Helen stood in front of her, across the table. "We really do feel, well, very sorry about everything that's happened," she said. "I know my mother wants to do everything possible to

85

help you . . ." She paused, because there was no response in Kelly's expression.

But she said, "Sure. I'm looking forward to that."

"Well . . . I'm for bed. Like Mother said, tomorrow is going to be a long day. You turning in?"

"Not right now," Kelly said. "I'm not tired."

"Right, well . . . see you in the morning. 'Night, Parks."

"Good night, Miss Helen," the butler said.

Kelly watched the door close. "What does one do for night life around here, old fellow?"

"On a Sunday night, Miss? Very little. There is a cinema in the village, but . . ." he looked at the clock. "The feature will have started half an hour ago."

"How about a roadhouse? There has to be one, somewhere."

"A roadhouse, Miss?"

"You know, a place where you can get a beer and maybe play a disc and meet some people."

"Ah . . . I think you mean a public house, Miss."

"I'll take your word for it."

"There is a pub in the village, Miss. It'll be open for another hour, I should think. But . . ."

"Then I'll give it a whirl."

"The village is four miles away, Miss."

"So? Miss Helen has an auto, hasn't she? I'll use hers."

"Ah . . . don't you think you should ask her first, Miss?"

"What the hell, she'd probably say no," Kelly pointed. "And don't you go telling her, or I'll have your guts for garters when I'm running this show."

"Are you intending to, ah, run this show, Miss?"

"Why not. Where would the keys be?"

"They're hanging in the front hall, Miss. But you don't have a driving licence."

"Sure I do."

"An English one?"

"What's the difference, so long as I remember which side of the road I'm on?"

86

Desperately he tried another tack. "You'll need money. I mean, English money."

"Now, there's a point. The boss keeps some in her desk drawer, right?"

"I'm afraid I wouldn't know, Miss."

"Oh, yes, you do. When I arrived yesterday, Mrs Johannsson told you to take money from her desk to pay the taxi. Right?"

"To take that money without Mrs Johannsson's permission would be stealing, Miss."

"Oh, fuck you, Parks. You're a goddamed lawyer. They all want to help me, right? So lending me a little money can't do any harm. This time tomorrow, I am going to have all the money in the world. That's what matters."

She went into the study, opened the drawer, pulled out a handful of ten-pound notes from the roll held by a rubber band. Then she went into the hall, took Helen's car keys from the hook. "Tara, Parks. Oh, say, how do I get back in? I guess you're going to bed, right?"

"You will find there is a latchkey on the ring, Miss."

"Right. I'll see you." She closed the front door behind herself.

Parks stood in the hall for several minutes. He was not a man who dealt in crises. Whilst he knew there had been sufficient of those involving this family in the old days, since he had come to work for Mrs Johannsson, following her release from jail and rehabilitation, the only crisis had been the hijacking of the freighter, involving Miss Helen, and as it had taken place on the other side of the world, it had not directly involved him, save for an inordinate number of phone calls and comings and goings. But this young woman was something else again. And she had placed him in a very difficult position. She had virtually threatened his job if he didn't do as she wished. But if he did that, his job was in danger anyway. Mrs Johannsson was a most charming woman to work for, who treated her staff with both courtesy and respect – but in return she demanded utter loyalty, at every level, and where that loyalty was not forthcoming, he knew she could be absolutely ruthless.

He sighed, and climbed the stairs, padded along the upper gallery, and knocked on Joanna's door. He had to do this several times before there was any response. Then a sleepy voice said, "Come."

Parks opened the door and went in, and Joanna switched on the bedside light, saw who it was, and drew the sheet to her throat.

"Parks? What on earth . . ." she looked at the gold clock on the bedside table. "My God, it's only ten o'clock! I was so asleep. Really Parks . . ." She sounded more disappointed than angry.

"There is something I think you should know, madam."

"What?" Joanna pushed hair from her face and hastily regained control of the sheet.

"Miss Johannsson has gone out."

"Gone out where? How?"

"She took Miss Helen's car, madam."

"Miss Helen OK'd that?"

"No, madam. Miss Helen does not know, yet."

"Oh, good lord. Why didn't you stop her?"

"It would have required physical force, madam. And well . . ."

"Oh, quite," Joanna said. "So she's gone for a drive. She'll soon be back." Or maybe she'll have an accident and break her bloody neck, she thought.

"I think she may have gone to the public house in the village, madam."

"How? She hasn't any money."

"She took some from your desk drawer, madam."

"She did, did she?" The thieving bitch, she thought. "All right, Parks, thanks for letting me know."

"Do you require me to wait up, madam?"

"No, you go to bed. I'll deal with her in the morning." Parks withdrew, closing the door, and Joanna threw herself across the bed in a fit of frustrated energy. What a handful the silly girl was proving. The phone rang. Joanna rolled back and grabbed it, uncertain who she wanted it to be. "Yes?"

"Were you asleep?" William asked.

"No, I was not asleep," Joanna said. "I had just been awakened. Have you got something for me?"

"I've just heard from Evans."

"Right."

"As I told you, he was going out to the institution where Kelly was confined, to find out what he could about her release."

"And?"

"She was released, certified sane, two years ago."

"As we supposed."

"There's more," William said. "There was some controversy over her release. It seems that Michael had to pull a good many strings and spend a lot of money to get that certification of sanity."

"Why?"

"Simply because there was a body of opinion in the institution that she was not actually sane. It seems that she was given to maniacal rages when she just went berserk. According to the people Evans spoke with, they reckoned they were lucky she didn't commit murder on more than one occasion."

"Like this afternoon," Joanna said grimly. "But they still let her out."

"Money talks. And Michael had a lot of it. But I have an idea that the institution was just happy to see the back of her."

"And after she left them?"

"She went off with her father and left the country. Didn't you know about that?"

"Nope. He took regular business trips to Canada. He never invited me to go along. So I didn't. So he set her up in New York. And now we have her. A possibly homicidal maniac, in my own home. Who is about to become a multi-millionairess."

"Evans is going to come back to me as soon as he digs up anything else."

"What else can there be to dig up?" Joanna asked.

"Well . . . it seems there's a rumour that there could have been something odd about Mrs Johannsson's death. The first Mrs Johannsson."

"I wish people would stop saying that. What was odd about it? Apart from the fact that it was a hell of an unusual and unpleasant way to commit suicide."

"That's just it."

Joanna stared at the phone. "Just what are you saying, Willie?"

"Just what Evans has gleaned. There was a rumour that something was odd about her death, and that was another reason why some of the people at the mental institution were reluctant to give Kelly the all clear. As I say, Evans will come back to us as soon as he finds out anything more."

And bang, Joanna thought, goes my night's sleep.

Part Two

The Lunatic

Wine maketh merry: but money answereth all things.
                                        Ecclesiastes

Five

Raisul had the car radio on full blast as he drove home. He'd been to several London pubs, and at one of them had had a good dinner, and he knew he was way over the limit. So he was taking a risk. What the fuck, he thought. He felt like taking risks. He could have the bitch fired. He probably would, when all this crisis died down. She deserved nothing better.

Now that he was out in the country he felt safer. All he had to do was avoid possible traps, and these were unlikely to be situated on lonely country roads. But he breathed a sigh of relief when he at last turned off the road on to the lane leading down to the Caribee House drive, and then braked hard as he saw the car slewed across the lane, its front end buried in the water-filled ditch. Helen's car!

Raisul left his engine running as he leapt out and ran to the crashed vehicle. There was someone slumped behind the wheel. Helen? What on earth would she be doing out at this hour? It was past midnight.

He pulled open the door, grabbed Kelly as she fell out. He had left his headlights on, and by their glare he saw there was blood on her face and soaking her shirt.

"My God!" he said. "Kelly!"

She gave a little groan. Even in his own alcoholic state he could smell the alcohol on her breath. But if she was badly hurt . . . it would take a repair van to get Helen's car out of the ditch. He lifted Kelly into his arms and carried her to his own car, opened the back door, and laid her on the seat. Her eyes opened.

"Raisul," she said. "My knight in shining armour."

"What happened?"

"I skidded, I guess. Boy, will Helen be mad."

"You've hurt yourself. You're bleeding."

"Oh, that . . . forget it." She grinned at him. "What are you going to do with me? Or to me. I'm your prisoner. You can do whatever you like to me."

"Don't tempt me. I think the best thing I can do is take you home and put you to bed. There's just room for my car to squeeze through."

"Raisul," Kelly said. "I don't want to go home and go to bed. Do you?"

"Well," Helen said, standing above Joanna's bed like an avenging angel. "She has got to go, Mother. She has *got* to go."

Joanna sighed; she had had a restless night, following William's call, and to be awakened by a furious Helen with tales of cars being stolen and then smashed up . . . but for the moment she knew only relief: the girl had at least come home in one piece.

"Have you looked at it? Is it a write-off?"

"Well, no, I don't suppose it is. But it'll cost a mint to put right; the front is pushed in. The insurance isn't going to pay up. She wasn't insured, she doesn't have an English driving licence, she took the car without permission, and she was almost certainly driving too fast, and under the influence."

"So I'll stand the bill," Joanna said. "We don't want to get any more mixed up with the police than we have to. How is she, by the way?"

"I haven't seen her, today. Raisul is sure she hurt herself. He says he saw blood, and there are a few specks on the upholstery in the car. But . . . she hasn't called a doctor."

"I'll have a word with her. Meanwhile, get on to the garage

94

in the village and have the car moved; we have a lot of people coming down here in a couple of hours. And tell Raisul I want to see him."

Helen went to the door. "And you're going to give her the push?"

"If Raisul is right, she may have been hurt. And today is her father's funeral," Joanna said. "And this afternoon is the reading of the Will. We just have to go softly until all that is behind us. Right?"

Helen banged the door behind herself.

Joanna chewed a piece of toast – unusually for her – and drank some coffee. Strange how she had thought Kelly might have an accident. And break her neck! That had been a terrible wish. And it had so nearly happened!

"Will you tell me exactly what happened?" she asked Raisul. "I thought you were spending the night in town?"

"My friend was out," Raisul said. He was also looking remarkably chipper.

"So you came home. After several hours."

"Well, as I was up there, I decided to have dinner . . ."

"And drank a lot. Suppose you'd been breathalysed?"

"I'd have been run-in, I suppose. But I wasn't."

"So you came home, and . . . ?"

Raisul told her about finding the car, and Kelly. "So you played the Good Samaritan and brought her home."

"Well . . . she was shaken. Naturally."

"Oh, quite. What time was this?"

"Ah . . . we must have got to the house about two."

Joanna scratched her head. "So . . . the pub shuts at eleven. Could be ten-thirty on a Sunday. And you found her about two. And it is only four miles from here to the village. Say a ten minute drive. You mean she's been lying there for maybe three hours? I'd better get Doc Buckston up here right away; she could have concussion, or internal injuries." Shades of her brother, she thought. He had died of internal injuries, after she had jumped on his stomach. And no one had realised it for at least twenty-four hours.

"Well," Raisul said. "She seemed all right."

"Helen said something about blood."

"There was some, on her face and shirt. But she didn't seem hurt."

"Well, I'll give the doctor instructions to go over her anyway. You go and get dressed."

Raisul went to the door, hesitated. "What are you going to do?"

"I am not going to curse and swear and jump up and down," Joanna assured him. "Much as I feel like it." She telephoned the doctor at the village surgery and appraised him of the situation. "It could be urgent," she said.

"I'll be right out," Buckston said. Surgery didn't start until ten, and Joanna Johannsson was one of his more important patients. Not that she was often ill. "Does she complain of any pain?"

"I haven't seen her yet. But I am about to."

"Joanna . . . have you reported this to the police?"

"No. Should I? No one was in the least bit hurt, except perhaps for Kelly herself. No damage was done to any property, save one of our cars. She lost control and skidded into a ditch. Simple as that. It's our business, nobody else's."

"You are making it mine."

"Don't tell me *you'll* have to report it?"

"If there is nothing wrong with the girl, no problem. If she is hurt, and needs hospitalisation, I will have to make a report, yes."

"Bugger it," Joanna said. "Let's hope she isn't hurt. Listen, do drive carefully; we're sort of blocked in."

Putting the phone down, Joanna got dressed and went to the Blue Room. This was in darkness. She drew the curtains, turned back to the bed. Kelly was sprawled across it, on her face and on top of the covers, naked. Joanna stood above the bed for a few minutes, contemplating her stepdaughter. She looked relatively unmarked. There were a few minor reddened patches on her shoulders and arms, but the bruises were slight. There was no blood, either on her face or on the bed; she would have washed, or probably showered, before going to bed, supposing Raisul had actually seen any blood at all and was not merely over-reacting. Joanna went to the dirty clothes basket, took out the top garments. There was more blood than she had expected on the shirt. From where? She couldn't see any cuts on the body on the bed.

Kelly had sensed there was someone in the room. She opened her eyes.

"Shit," she commented, and reached for the sheet, rolling over at the same time, and then letting the sheet go. "Oh, it's you," she said.

"Who were you expecting?" Joanna asked.

"Oh . . ." Kelly sat up, and then lay down again with a thump. "Jesus!"

"Do I gather you tied one on last night?"

"Not really. I went to this bar in the village, and had a couple of drinks, but they were shutting up, so I left to come home, and then . . . I really don't remember too much about it. I'm sorry about taking your money. I'll pay you back."

"The money isn't important. You don't remember Raisul fishing you out of the ditch?"

"I remember a man . . . was that Raisul?"

"That was Raisul. He says you were all right."

"Was I?" Kelly grinned. "I guess he was just being nice."

"You know you virtually wrote off Helen's car?"

"Gee, did I do that? Oh, I am sorry. Tell you what, I'll buy her a new one. Tomorrow. After I've become a millionairess."

"That would be very nice of you. Now, I've a doctor coming here to see you . . ."

"A doctor? Whatever for?"

"Just to make sure you're all right. It does appear you were concussed last night, and you may have an internal injury."

"I feel fine."

"You seem to have lost a lot of blood, from somewhere."

"I had a nose bleed."

"Dr Buckston will confirm that. So you get up and have a shower and clean your teeth and brush your hair and generally make yourself presentable. I wouldn't bother to dress until after he's gone as he'll need to examine you; wear a dressing-gown. Then, as soon as he says you're all right, we can get into the village and buy you some decent clothes."

"I don't like doctors," Kelly sulked.

"You'll like Dr Buckston. I'll have some breakfast sent up." She went to the door.

"When does Daddy arrive?" Kelly asked.

"Ten-thirty. The funeral is at eleven. Have you changed your mind about attending?"

"No way. I wouldn't mind seeing the old gink a last time, though."

"I don't think that would be at all a good idea," Joanna said. "He's been dead for four days."

Joanna went downstairs. This whole business was eating into her time. It was just eight o'clock, and she had to be dressed for the funeral by half-ten. Supposing Buckston arrived by half-eight, and took half an hour to look Kelly over, they'd have less than an hour to get into the village, do some shopping, and be back here. That simply wasn't on. But the girl had to have some decent clothes to wear, certainly for the meeting with the lawyers that afternoon.

She found Helen in the study, on the phone.

"Yes," she was saying. "It is an emergency. We have a whole lot of cars arriving in a couple of hours. Yes, I'd be grateful. Right." She replaced the phone, glared at her mother. "Can't be done before this afternoon," she growled. "Stupid man."

"But you talked him into coming this morning."

"I shouted him into coming this morning, if that's what you mean. How's the lady?"

98

"Remarkably fit. But I intend to make sure. Helen, I want you to do me a favour."

"Oh, yes?"

"Get dressed in your funeral gear now. Then as soon as Dr Buckston has been, providing there isn't an emergency, I want you to take Kelly into the village. Go to Charlotte's; they have some reasonable stuff there. Buy her some decent clothes. I'm thinking of a couple of smart dresses and an evening gown. Just remember, whether she likes it or not, she's in mourning."

"I don't want to go anywhere with that monster, Mother. Why can't she do her own shopping?"

"Because I shudder to think what she might buy," Joanna pointed out. "Just do it. Regard it as a job of work, and put in for danger money if you feel like it."

Matilda emerged from the door to the wing.

"Joanna!" she boomed. "What on earth is happening? I went for a walk this morning and saw Helen's car in the ditch. Is she hurt?"

"She wasn't in it," Joanna said, wearily. "It was just a skid. Nothing serious."

"Well . . ." Matilda looked disappointed, and a trifle confused. "Then who was in it?"

"Kelly. You met her yesterday, remember?"

"Briefly. She seems an odd girl. I've arranged for the children to come down today, so that they can attend the funeral."

"That's very nice of you," Joanna said. "Now you really must excuse me, Tilly. I have to go over the arrangements with Parks."

She took Parks into the study. "We've catered for twenty-four for lunch, madam. Is that about right?"

"Should be, if everyone comes. Nothing elaborate, I hope?"

"I thought lobster salad and champagne, madam."

Joanna smiled. "Nothing elaborate. Very good, Parks. I'm going to have to leave everything to you, but I know I can."

"Thank you, madam."

Dr Buckston arrived. He was a middle-aged man, who, in defiance of his profession, was both overweight and red-faced. But he had a good bedside manner.

"Did you manage to wriggle by?" Joanna asked.

"By virtually going down into the ditch. Where is the young lady?"

"In her bedroom. Would you like me to come up with you?" Joanna asked.

"How old is she?"

"Twenty-four, and somewhat febrile."

"Then it might be a good idea."

To Joanna's relief, Kelly looked spruce and clean, and was wearing one of the dressing-gowns supplied to each bedroom. She was just finishing her breakfast. "Well, hi," she said. "You come to poke and prod?"

"Hopefully not," Buckston said.

Joanna sat in the corner.

"You the chaperone, eh?" Kelly asked. "Here to make sure he doesn't try any funny stuff, or that I won't slap him with a suit."

Buckston raised his eyebrows, and began his examination. It took him only a few gentle squeezes of Kelly's stomach to ascertain that she had no internal injuries. Then he peered into her eyes with his little flashlight, and carefully parted her hair to examine her scalp.

"Tell me about this blood."

"A nose bleed," Kelly said.

Joanna showed him the shirt, and he peered into Kelly's nostrils. "I'll make out a full report and let you have it," he said. "But for the time being, Miss Johannsson, you can certainly attend your father's funeral."

"You can forget that," Kelly said.

It was Buckston's turn to look confused.

"Well, Helen is waiting to take you into the village," Joanna said. "So be a dear and get dressed." She escorted the doctor down the stairs. "Well?"

"It's puzzling," Buckston confessed. "There is no trace of any injury whatsoever. But there was too much blood on that shirt for a nose bleed. Incidentally, her nasal membranes do not indicate any recent bleeding."

"What about concussion?"

"I would say again, not a trace. And anyway, concussion does not cause blood loss, unless it is a result of a serious head injury. Which your stepdaughter does not have."

"As far as I can make out, Jeremy, she was unconscious in that car for roughly three hours. Is that possible, without some kind of visible bruise?"

"No."

"Suppose she fainted."

"Anyone who faints and stays fainted for three hours is seriously ill. Miss Johannsson is not seriously ill. She's not ill at all."

"So just what are you telling me?"

"That she did not lie unconscious in that car for three hours."

"In other words, either she, or Raisul, or both, are lying."

"I'm not going to answer that, Joanna. It is not a medical question. But it may be worth finding out exactly what did happen last night. Now I must rush. I have to fit in a surgery before the funeral."

Joanna saw him to the door herself, then returned to the study. She felt she was being engulfed by a rising tide, with no land in sight. But she had been in such a position before, and always made it to the shore. She went outside, walked down the drive to where Helen's car still waited to be removed. There were a few passers-by off the main road peering at it, who greeted her courteously. She had lived just outside the village, on and off, for more than twenty years, and if they all knew her seven-year absence in the middle of that period had been the result of her prison sentence, they still were very fond of her, and they all knew she had just lost her husband.

Police Sergeant Maltby was also there, a man of massive girth and even more massive moustache, one of the last relics of the traditional British bobby.

"You making a complaint, Mrs Johannsson? Or a report?" he asked hopefully.

"I don't intend to, Sergeant." Joanna chose her words with care. "My daughter's car skidded and went into the ditch. That's all there is to it. This is a private road, so there really is no need to involve anyone else, is there?"

"Miss Helen all right?"

"Miss Helen is perfectly all right." Joanna continued to choose her words with great care.

The sergeant scratched his chin. "Wasn't that Dr Buckston just driving out?"

"Yes, it was. He has pronounced the young lady to be absolutely unhurt."

The sergeant was clearly trying to work things out, without a great deal of success. "You'll be having the car moved, I assume. Before the funeral. Doesn't leave much space for passing where it is."

"The car will be moved within the hour, Sergeant."

"Very good, ma'am. You know where to find me."

Talk about hints, Joanna thought. She smiled at the onlookers, who smiled back, sheepishly, and moved off, aware that technically they were trespassing. Then she opened the driver's door and peered inside. There were one or two brown spots on the upholstery, as Helen had said, which might very well be blood, but it would take a forensic expert to prove it. She was more interested in the facia, which contained a clock. As she had suspected might be the case, the clock had stopped with the impact of the crash. It showed eleven forty-five. If the pub had closed at ten thirty, it had taken Kelly an hour and fifteen minutes to cover four miles, driving at such a speed that she had lost control and crashed: the skid marks were clearly visible on the road surface. That was absurd.

But then, if she had crashed at eleven forty-five, and Raisul had not found her until just before two, that left another two hours unaccounted for, two hours in which, according to Buckston, she had neither been concussed nor hurt in any way, nor, he had strongly indicated, had she even been unconscious. She had just sat there, for two hours, waiting to be rescued? She could not possibly have known that she was going to be rescued at all, as Raisul had announced his intention of spending the night in town.

She returned inside. Raisul's car was in the garage.

"Where is Mr Raisul?" she asked the housemaid, who was busily vacuuming the front hall.

"I think he went for a walk in the grounds, ma'am."

"Well, when he comes in, would you tell him I'd like a word."

At the foot of the stairs she met Helen and Kelly, descending. Helen looked very smart in a little black dress, rather too short for a funeral in Joanna's opinion, but she knew she was old-fashioned when it came to clothes, and at least the girl was wearing black tights. Kelly, as always, was in shirt and jeans and untidy.

"Which car do we use?" Helen asked.

"Deardon will drive you in the Merc, providing he can get out."

"Oh, right." Helen looked relieved.

Deardon was waiting at the foot of the steps, and the two young women sat in the back.

"Gee, what a mess," Kelly remarked as they reached the gate. The repair truck had arrived, and ropes were being attached to pull the Ford out of the ditch.

"Yes," Helen agreed grimly, as with great skill Deardon navigated round the wreck.

"Look, I really am sorry. I told your mom, I'm going to buy you a new one."

Helen glanced at her.

"Really and truly," Kelly said. "Let's be friends, huh? I do want us to be friends."

She laid her hand on Helen's arm, and Helen shifted across the seat to the far side. "We can be friends," she said. "On one condition."

"Name it."

"That you don't ever touch me."

Kelly raised her eyebrows, then turned away to look out of the window.

By ten o'clock, Helen's car having been towed away, the guests were assembling. A clutch of lawyers, Lustrum, Matthews and Sedgling, were all looking apprehensive, aware that the actual cremation might be the calm before the storm. Barry Andrews from the Bank, a somewhat cadaverous looking man, was acting suitably grave and sympathetic, but obviously itching to be brought up to date on the financial aspects of the situation. Also present were nearly the whole Caribee Shipping staff, headed by an equally grave looking Peter, who kept giving Joanna meaningful looks, the crews and officers of the two Caribee ships in port, Nicola, looking very chic in her black dress, which came discreetly below the knee, but also distinctly out of sorts, several business acquaintances of Michael's, marshalled by Reynolds, and of course the family, Matilda and her children, William and Norma and their two children, and which by this stage even included Kelly, wearing a black dress and looking most attractive.

"Well done," Joanna muttered at Helen.

The dogs barked and there was an air almost of a cocktail party until the hearse arrived, late, coming slowly down the drive. By this time Raisul had also appeared, wearing a dark suit and a black tie, but Joanna did not have the time to speak with him before it was necessary to move off, firstly to the village church, and then to the crematorium, several miles away in Windsor.

"We shouldn't be more than a couple of hours," Joanna told Kelly. "Parks will give you anything you wish."

"Do I keep this on?" Kelly asked, flapping her skirt.

"All day."

"Shit! But you like the way I look, eh? I'm even wearing knickers."

"You look like what you are," Joanna told her. "A million dollars."

"I like the sound of that," Kelly said. "Say a word for the old gink for me, right?"

"You say a word for yourself," Joanna recommended. "You can do it just as well here as in the church."

Helen sat beside Joanna in the back of the Mercedes, Raisul sat in front beside Deardon.

"How on earth did you get her into that dress?" Joanna asked.

"Oh, she's not as tough as she pretends," Helen said. "I think if she hadn't taken that stand from the beginning, she'd probably have liked to come."

"Silly girl," Joanna commented.

"You know," Raisul said. "It's odd, but this is the first funeral I have ever attended."

"It's not something you want to make a habit of," Joanna said. "They get forced on you soon enough. Do you know why Nicola was looking so blue?"

"Why should I know anything about Nicola?"

Joanna observed that his ears had turned bright red.

"Well, you were the last member of the family to have seen her," she said. "On Friday, right?"

"Haven't a clue," Raisul said.

"You didn't make a pass at her, by any chance?"

"Who, me?"

"Employers do not make passes at their employees," Joanna said.

"Or they get done for harrassment," Helen giggled.

"They get done, period," Joanna said. But she began to

105

wonder . . . she really intended to have a word with Nicola. It would be a shame to have to let the girl go; she was a very efficient secretary. While as for Raisul . . . he seemed to be laying everything in sight.

"Tell me," she said. "Last night. You're quite sure of the time you found Kelly in the ditch?"

"Yes, I'm sure," Raisul said, starting to turn his head and then changing his mind. "What is this, some kind of inquisition? Now isn't the time, Mom."

"Don't call me 'Mom'," Joanna advised.

The service took longer than Joanna had expected; nearly all the village attended the church, or waited outside. The reward of being a squire, she supposed. And everyone wanted to shake her hand when she came out. Even Sergeant Maltby was there, looking very grave.

"I know now is hardly the time, Mrs Johannsson," he said. "But do you think I could come out and have a word with you, some time? This afternoon, maybe?"

"This afternoon simply isn't on, Sergeant. We have all sorts of business matters to attend to. You could come out tomorrow morning. Early. I have to go up to town. Make it eight o'clock. I hope it's nothing to do with Helen's car."

"Only indirectly, ma'am."

Joanna hurried off to get into the Mercedes to be driven to the crematorium.

"Don't tell me the fuzz are nosing around," Helen remarked.

"The fuzz are always nosing around. When were you expecting that report from the doctor who examined you?"

"Today. Or tomorrow. Are you saying that old Maltby doesn't know who was driving the car?"

"He only knows it's your car."

"Oh, shit! So he thinks I may have been under the influence of drugs or something. We'll have to tell him."

"I'd prefer you didn't," Joanna said. "Not until after the Will has been read, and things have . . . sorted themselves out."

*   *   *

Lunch was a predictably subdued affair, but with nearly thirty
people round the table conversation soon flowed; Parks had
had no difficulty in making up the numbers as regards food.
The important subjects were carefully avoided until after the
meal, when the wake broke up.

"I will attend the reading after all. We'll use the drawing
room," Joanna told Lustrum, whom she had quite taken to;
he was a jolly little man with a red face. "And I will give
instructions that we are not to be interrupted."

"Thank you. It's a little irregular, to have the reading on the
very day of the funeral . . ."

"It's what Kelly wants. Should any other members of the
family attend?"

"Ah . . . this is very embarrassing, Mrs Johannsson. But
none of them are mentioned in the Will."

"Then none of them will attend," Joanna said. "I take it you
have no objection to me?"

"No, no. I think you should attend, Mrs Johannsson, because
while you're not mentioned, there are provisions in the Will
which may affect you. Or certainly your company."

Joanna nodded. "Then do you mind if Mr Matthews also
attends? Strictly as an observer."

"I can have no objection to that. But . . ." he peered at her.
"Are you meaning to contest the Will?"

"That depends on what happens after the reading, Mr
Lustrum. I will certainly need legal advice."

"Oh, quite. Well . . ."

"Make yourself comfortable," Joanna suggested. "I'll just
finish saying goodbye to my guests."

Barry Andrews had hung back.

"Do we still have a meeting for tomorrow morning?"
he asked.

"Of course we do, Barry. We have a lot to discuss."

"Indeed we do. But after today . . ." he hesitated.

"You were going to say?"

107

"Your financial problems will be ended, I would say."

Joanna gave him one of her bright smiles.

"Who knows, Barry? We haven't heard the Will yet." She kissed him on the cheek, then turned her attention to the hovering Sedgling.

"Things aren't going well, Mrs Johannsson."

"Tell me why not."

"Well, this accident Miss Edge has had, coming on top of the drugs bust . . ."

"Helen was not driving the car, Sedgling."

"But . . ."

"I would prefer to keep that quiet for the time being. When is the hearing?"

"On Friday."

"And will she be committed?"

"Hopefully not. If we can find the man she was out with that night, someone named Geoffrey Best. Unfortunately, I haven't been able to locate the fellow; he's not at the address given to me. Nor have I been able to have a word with Helen. Perhaps you could find out where he might be . . ."

"What is he supposed to do?"

"Give evidence on her behalf. Support her story that she thought the packet contained Ecstasy tablets. That way we might get away with a fine."

"Try the hospitals."

"Eh?"

"I happen to know that he met with an accident," Joanna explained. "But if you do find him, I wouldn't hope for too much. He and Helen are no longer friends."

"Oh, dear. Well, then . . ."

"Do the best you can. Now I really must rush; they're waiting to read the Will. Let me know if you find Best."

William was last, waiting anxiously. Norma and the children were already in his car.

"Will you let me know how things turn out?" he asked.

"The very moment I know how they turn out," Joanna promised.

"I saw Sergeant Maltby making a nuisance of himself outside the church. Did that bastard Best make a complaint?"

"Not so far as I know. Maltby is more interested in the accident. Don't worry. I can handle him. He's virtually an old family retainer." Joanna kissed him. "I'll see you in the morning, anyway."

Joanna went into the drawing room, where Lustrum, Kelly and Matthews waited. Matthews was a tall, heavily-built man with a most reassuring presence – if he was on your side.

"Just us?" Kelly asked, as Joanna carefully closed the double doors.

"I'm afraid so. Mr Lustrum doesn't have very much to say. Do you, Mr Lustrum?"

"No, indeed." The solicitor had opened his briefcase and laid his papers on the table beside his chair. "Shall I begin?"

"Please."

"Well, as you say, Mrs Johannsson, this is a relatively brief document. It is the Last Will and Testament of Michael Avery Johannsson. The Will was originally made in Vancouver in 1976, but was copied exactly, and re-registered in London, on 8 May 1978, Mr Johannsson at that time having moved his domicile to Great Britain. There are a few minor bequests to persons living in Canada, and I have informed these beneficiaries. None of them amounts to more than a thousand pounds. As for the bulk of the estate, Mr Johannsson states very simply that: I leave all my worldly goods, including my properties and such shares as I hold in various companies, as well as the cash in my bank accounts, whether on deposit or current, to my wife Eleanor, and should she predecease me, to my daughter Kelly." He looked over the tops of his glasses. "That's it."

Matthews looked at Joanna, who looked back, eyebrows arched.

"There is no mention of the current Mrs Johannsson at all?" Matthews asked.

"No, there isn't," Lustrum said. "As far as I am aware, when the Will was first executed, Mr Johannsson did not know that Mrs Orton, as she then was, existed."

"He knew who I was in 1978, Mr Lustrum," Joanna said. "I had been sent to prison for murdering his son, and he was trying to contact me. He was writing me letters."

"Ah. Yes. But had he yet indicated his wish to marry you?"

Joanna shrugged. "I burned most of the letters, unread." She forced a smile. "I suppose I wasn't in the mood."

"Quite. Well . . ."

"The point is," Matthews interrupted, "within a year of the Will being registered in London, Mr Johannsson and the then Mrs Orton were married, although she was still in prison. Yet he did not alter the Will?"

"I'm afraid he did not," Lustrum said.

"Say, what is this?" Kelly asked. Hitherto she had kept quiet, looking from face to face. "You guys trying to take away my inheritance?"

"Of course we are not," Joanna said.

"However, it is very unusual for a man not to make provision for his wife, certainly over a seven-year marriage," Matthews said. "In fact, it is illegal for him not to do so."

"Then you intend to contest the Will?" Lustrum asked.

"That decision must by my client's," Matthews said.

"Could someone be a sweetie and tell me just what is involved?" Kelly asked, smiling at Lustrum.

"Ah . . ." he lifted another sheet of paper. "Much of these figures are necessarily estimates, as share holdings fluctuate. However, let me see . . . the house in Vancouver. I have been in touch with the agents over there and they consider it to be worth about three million dollars."

"Fuck the house," Kelly said. "I don't ever want to see it again. It goes on the market, now."

"I will of course require your instructions in writing, Miss Johannsson. Then there are several other properties, mainly of

110

the holiday variety, but also the flat in London. Together with various cars, and a yacht moored in Vancouver Harbour, we are talking of perhaps another three million – pounds in this case."

"What about this house?" Kelly asked.

Once again Joanna and Matthews exchanged glances.

"Ah, no," Lustrum said. "This house belongs to Mrs Johannsson. The present Mrs Johannsson." Even though she had known what his reply would be, Joanna gave a little sigh of relief.

"And the Mercedes?" Kelly asked. She really was as sharp as a button, Joanna thought.

"The Mercedes also belongs to Mrs Johannsson. There is a Rolls garaged in London that belonged to Mr Johannsson. That is now yours. Now, cash. There is, in various current accounts here and in Canada, seventy-five thousand odd pounds. There are also, in various deposit accounts, here and in Canada, two hundred thousand odd pounds."

"That doesn't sound very much," Kelly remarked.

"Cash is unproductive, Miss Johannsson. Even in a deposit account. Your father liked to make his money work. Now, shares. Sixty per cent of the shares in the Johannsson mining corporation. That is six million shares. The present price per share is just over eleven dollars."

"Sixty-six million dollars," Kelly said.

"Approximately. Various other share holdings in Canada and the United States, currently valued at a total of twenty-seven million dollars. And forty per cent of the share holding in Caribee Shipping." He glanced at Joanna. "That is four hundred thousand shares, currently valued at seven pounds per share. Two million eight hundred thousand pounds. The total worth of the estate you have inherited therefore amounts to just over one hundred million dollars. This is currently producing an income of approximately six million dollars, say four million pounds, a year. Now there will be substantial death duties to be paid, and there are also some small outstanding liabilities . . ."

111

"What liabilities?" Kelly demanded.

Lustrum produced a third sheet of paper. "There is an outstanding tax bill of eighty-four thousand pounds, but this is in the hands of Mr Johannsson's accountants, and will be settled out of the estate. There is also an endorsed loan of just over ten million pounds . . ."

"Daddy lent someone ten million pounds? But that can't be a liability. Or is the gink refusing to pay it back?"

"Your father didn't actually lend the money," Lustrum explained. "He backed a borrowing for, well . . ." He looked at Joanna.

"Michael endorsed a loan for me at my bank," Joanna said.

"For ten million pounds?"

"Twelve originally. To finance the building of two new ships."

"So where are these ships?"

"One is at sea. The other is on the stocks in a Glasgow yard. It is only a third completed."

"And how is this money to be repaid?"

Joanna kept her patience, and her smile. "The loan is being repaid out of operating profits. Once the new ship is operating, it will be repaid even quicker."

"How long do you reckon this will take?"

"Oh, several years, I'm afraid. But the bank is perfectly happy as long as they have that endorsement."

"And they're getting the interest. What about the interest on the endorsement?"

"That does not enter the equation," Lustrum said. "Your father did not actually pay out the money. He merely assured the bank that he would repay the loan if anything happened to prevent Mrs Johannsson from doing so."

"But that money has to be kept aside, right?"

"Usually it would have to be. But in view of Mr Johannsson's extreme wealth, the bank was happy with just his signature."

"You reckon?" Kelly demanded. "You say I've just inherited a hundred million dollars, right? How much is that in pounds?"

"Ah . . . sixty million, odd."

"Of which I am going to have to give forty per cent to the government, and now you tell me another sixteen per cent has to be tied up in this loan thing."

Lustrum permitted himself a quiet smile.

"I don't think, in any event, Miss Johannsson, that you are ever going to starve. You will have the full use of at least thirty million pounds."

"Fuck me," Kelly said. "Half." She looked at Joanna. "You and me need to talk, Stepmother."

Six

"I think we do," Joanna agreed. "Mr Lustrum, thank you very much for all your trouble."

Lustrum merely looked relieved to have got the reading behind him without the two women having come to blows.

"Then I take it you have no objection to my applying for probate?"

"I think you should wait for a day or two, Lustrum, until my client and I have discussed the matter," Matthews said.

"What the fuck," Kelly said. "Don't I get my money?"

"You will get your money, Miss Johannsson," Lustrum said. "These are, I am sure, mere formalities. Ladies. Matthews." He hurried from the room.

"Am I going to see you again?" Kelly asked Matthews.

"That depends on Mrs Johannsson, Miss Johannsson."

"I'll be in touch," Joanna said.

"I hope so." He hesitated, looking as if he wished to stay, perhaps to protect her, Joanna thought. "Goodbye." He followed Lustrum.

This time it was Kelly who closed the doors, then turned to lean against them.

"Looks like I have a few strings that need pulling," she remarked.

"Do you?" Joanna sat down and crossed her knees. "Tell me about them."

Kelly looked at her watch. "Four o'clock. What do you drink around here, mid-afternoon?"

"Tea."

"Fuck that. I thought champagne was your usual tipple."

"It is, at the usual time."

"I think right now would be a good time. I have a lot of celebrating to do."

Joanna got up and rang the bell. Parks appeared immediately; she suspected that he, and all the staff, had been eagerly awaiting the outcome of the lawyers' meeting.

"Bollinger, Parks," Joanna said, and sat down again. She didn't doubt she could drink her stepdaughter under the table, if she had to.

Kelly sat opposite.

"The first thing is, I reckon I now have a controlling interest in your company."

"Say again?"

"Well, I have forty per cent of the shares, not that they're worth a lot, apparently. And I also have a ten million pound stake in your new ship. At the share price quoted by Lustrum, that's the equivalent of more than another hundred and forty thousand shares, which would put me over the half million mark. That's control."

"The ten million is not a stake," Joanna said quietly, even as the adrenalin started to flow. "It's an endorsement. Thank you, Parks."

"So what's the drill if I decide to cancel it?"

"That would be between myself and my bank manager," Joanna said. "Cheers."

Kelly swallowed some champagne.

"Who owns the other shares in your company?"

"I own fifty per cent. Peter Young, that's my Controller and general Company Secretary, owns five per cent. Raisul and Helen have two and a half per cent each. Your father set that up, so that I could never be replaced as chairman."

"Chairperson," Kelly said thoughtfully.

"If that's how you like to think of it."

"I don't want to fight with you, Stepmother."

"I'm so glad."

"But you realise that I could make life pretty difficult."

"I'm sure you can."

"So let's talk turkey. I'm willing to help you, all I can. Like I'll continue that endorsement for you . . ." Waves of relief started to seep through Joanna's mind. "But I think I'm entitled to a quid pro quo, right? I mean to say, Dad let you have the money because you were letting him have your body. Right?"

"It's one way of putting it."

"But you aren't going to let *me* have your body, are you?"

"I'm afraid not," Joanna said.

"So I have to look elsewhere, right?"

"Not in this house."

Kelly grinned. "What about the house?"

"Say again?"

"This house. It's just grand, with the grounds and everything. And that stream. That's out of this world. That pile in Vancouver is nothing like this So how about it? I reckon it's probably worth a couple of million. I'll buy it with the Caribee shares. Now there's a real deal for you." She certainly had the gall of a rampant rhinoceros, Joanna thought. "And like I said," Kelly went on, "I'll continue the endorsement. Doesn't that sound grand? You won't just have fifty per cent of the company, you'll have ninety. And you'll have your new ship."

"I'm sorry," Joanna said. "This house is not for sale."

"Every house is for sale, if the price is right."

"Not this one. I began my adult life here. I feel I've lived in it all my life. I inherited it from my first husband, who was maybe the only man I ever loved . . . I'm sorry, but that was it. Your father and I had a sexual relationship, and a business one, to be sure. But nothing more. I lost the house when I was sent to prison, and your father bought it back for me, as a wedding present. I intend to die here, for the memory of both him and Howard."

"Isn't that something," Kelly remarked. "Falling in love with a house. It sure takes all sorts." She put down her champagne glass. "I should warn you that I can be real mean when things don't work out."

"I'm sure you can be," Joanna said.

"So, if you won't sell me this house, I'm gonna pull the rug from under your precious new ship."

"Do that, and I will be forced to contest the Will."

The two women glared at each other.

"You think that'll work?" Kelly sneered. "What, the poor injured woman left penniless? You've just admitted you never loved my father. You've just confessed that he married you to get his hands on those tits and that ass. You're a jailbird, Stepmama. If Dad hadn't come along you'd still be looking out through those bars. When all that is dragged through the courts you won't have a leg to stand on."

Joanna fought back the temptation to slap her face. But she knew how to hurt as well.

"I will contest the Will, and I will win, because in view of your time in a mental institution, my lawyers will prove that you are unfit to handle large sums of money."

She had never really intended to say that, but she had quite lost her temper. Now she watched the attractive face in front of her dissolve into a mask of hatred and anger.

"You fucking whore!" Kelly screamed. "Murdering bitch!" She scooped the champagne bottle from its bucket, fingers wrapped round its neck, and swung it, regardless of the liquid which came bubbling out.

Joanna leapt to her feet and jumped backwards, tripping as she did so, to land on the carpet with a jolt that seemed to drive her backbone out through the top of her head. Kelly bore down on her, again swinging the now empty champagne bottle, although her dress was soaked. Desperately Joanna rolled to one side, kicking her legs as she did so. Even hampered by her skirt she gained some momentum, and her high-heeled shoe struck Kelly on the ankle; the girl in turn fell to the carpet with a thud, losing her grip on the bottle, so that it rolled across the floor.

Joanna picked it up as she regained her feet, panting. She ran for the bell rope and pulled it, then turned back to face Kelly, who was getting up, kicking off her shoes as she did so, her face still a crumpled mask of rage.

"You come near me and I'll brain you," Joanna said.

Kelly was panting in turn, as she glared at her, and the door opened to admit Parks.

"Madam?"

"Miss Johannsson is leaving," Joanna said. "Tell Mrs Beckett to pack her things and bring them down. Then tell Deardon to have the car ready."

"You think you can just throw me out?" Kelly snarled.

"Yes," Joanna said, and couldn't resist a sudden giggle.

"You think it's a joke?"

"Fifteen years ago," Joanna said, "Your brother and I had a set-to in this very room."

"And you killed him."

"Yes," Joanna said. "But don't worry, I'm not going to kill you." Kelly took another step forward. "But I will knock you down if you attack me again," Joanna said. "Now, I'm sure you'd like to go and change that wet dress. By the time you've done that, and packed up, Deardon will be waiting."

"To take me where?"

"Anywhere you choose to go," Joanna told her. "Before you leave, you may telephone Lustrum and have him arrange some instant credit for you, and somewhere to stay. But you are not spending another night in this house."

"I am going to bury you in shit."

"I am sure you are going to try," Joanna said, and waited for her to leave the room.

It seemed the entire household had gathered in the hall to listen to the fracas in the drawing room. Kelly stalked past them all without looking at them, went up the stairs.

"Mother?" Helen asked. "Is everything all right?"

"No," Joanna said. "Nothing is all right."

118

She desperately wanted to go upstairs and lie down; she felt utterly exhausted, and her dress was also wringing wet – with sweat. But she didn't want to encounter Kelly again. She sat on the settee, and Helen sat beside her. Raisul also came in.

"What *happened*?" he asked.

"Very simply," Joanna said, "Kelly started to throw her financial weight around. She offered to continue the backing provided by her father, if I would sell her Caribee House."

"The house?" Helen was aghast. "Whatever for?"

"Seems she's been taken with it. When I refused, she became abusive, and . . ." Joanna sighed. "I suppose I became abusive back. So she attacked me with the champagne bottle."

Helen looked at the soaked carpet and wet floor. "Oh. Mother."

"So you're throwing her out?" Raisul commented. "Isn't that a bit drastic?"

"She's a bit drastic," Joanna said. "I wanted to help her. I really did. But . . ."

"You've done entirely the right thing," Helen said.

"I'd better go and . . ." Raisul started for the door.

"You are not going anywhere until she has left this house," Joanna told him.

"Now, Mother . . ."

"I don't think she's quite sane," Joanna said. "You saw how she behaved at the stream, yesterday morning. You told me about it."

"Well . . . she was protecting me from that nutter."

"That doesn't alter the fact that she behaved like a maniac. I do not wish you to see her again. I do not wish you to do anything that might compromise our position."

"You mean you're going to fight the Will?" Helen asked.

"I have no choice, now."

"Yippee," Helen said. "You'll win, and put that runt right where she belongs."

"She's coming down," Raisul whispered.

Joanna stood up and faced the open doors. Kelly was

accompanied by both Parks, carrying her kitbag, and Mrs Beckett, looking like a jailer; she had changed back into shirt and jeans. She stopped at the foot of the stairs, and looked into the drawing room. All the anger had faded from her face, and she looked serene.

"My family," she remarked, contemptuously. "I'll be in touch, Stepmama."

"Do you wish to use the phone before you go?" Joanna asked.

"Fuck you," Kelly said, and went out the front door.

"Whew!" Helen said. "Do you think we could all have a drink?"

Deardon kept one eye on the woman in the back seat of the Mercedes, adjusting his rear view mirror. He didn't know exactly what had happened at the house, but he did know there had been an almighty row. Hard to believe, really, looking at the slim, attractive figure behind him, with the gently composed features. Who appeared deep in thought. They had been driving for nearly an hour when she apparently noticed that they were in a built-up area. Kelly sat up. "Where are you taking me?"

"I'm driving into London, Miss. But I am to take you wherever you wish to go."

"Right. Take me . . . to Caribee Shipping." It would never occur to Joanna that she might go there. And she thought she might be able to do herself some good, as no one there would be aware of the row, or that she had left Caribee House for good.

Deardon obediently turned at the right corner.

"It's past five," Kelly remarked. "What time do they shut up shop?"

"Usually about six, madam. Except on a Friday, then it's about four. Today, though, what with the funeral . . . but there's always someone there. A night watchman."

"Just get me there before six."

"I think we'll manage that, Miss."

But the traffic was heavy, and the minutes ticked away.

"How long have you worked for Mrs Johannsson, Deardon?" Kelly asked.

"Three years, Miss."

"That's not very long. Hires and fires, does she?"

"Oh, no, Miss. Mrs Johannsson isn't like that. My predecessor drove her for nearly twenty years."

"Is that a fact. But she got rid of him in the end, eh?"

"No, miss. He died in service. He was killed combatting Indonesian pirates, defending Mrs Johannsson."

"Now, that is something. I guess you wouldn't care to be killed by Indonesian pirates, Deardon."

"Frankly, no, Miss."

"So, how'd you like to work for me? I'll double your pay and eliminate your risks. Pretty good, eh?"

"Work for you, madam?"

"Sure. Here's the deal. You keep on working for Mrs J, collect your pay, and I'll double it. All you have to do is keep me informed of what she does, where she goes, who she sees."

"You mean you would like me to spy for you, Miss."

"Why not? It means money, man, money."

"I'm afraid spying is not my scene, Miss. Mrs Johannsson has been good to me. I intend to be good to her." He pulled into the kerb. "Caribee Shipping." He got out to open her door, took her kitbag from the boot.

"Deardon," Kelly said, "to me, people are divided into two classes, my friends and my enemies. I can be pretty mean to my enemies."

"I will bear that in mind, Miss."

Kelly got out and he closed the door, then got back into the driver's seat, engaged Drive.

"Just where do you think you're going?" Kelly inquired.

"Mrs Johannsson said I was to deliver you to wherever it was you wished to go, miss. She said nothing about waiting. Good night."

The Mercedes drove away. Kelly stared after it for a few seconds. There's a motherfucker needs dealing with, she thought.

She picked up her bag and went to the door of the Caribee Building. This was unlocked, but inside, seated behind a large desk and three computers was a small, military looking man.

"May I help you, Miss?"

"Who're you?" Kelly asked.

"My name is Harris, Miss."

"And you're the security guard, right? My name is Kelly Johannsson. You savvy?"

Harris goggled at her. He had not attended the funeral, but he had heard about Kelly Johannsson from those who had.

"Of course, Miss. What can I do for you?"

"Nothing," Kelly said. "I just thought I'd introduce myself. I'm going to leave this bag in your care for a while." She placed the kitbag beside his desk and went to the elevator.

Harris watched her go, uncertainly. He didn't know what authority this woman had, but he did know she was heavily involved in the firm. The lift doors closed, and he picked up his phone, punched a number.

"Nikky? Mr Young still here?"

"He left over an hour ago," Nicola said. "Didn't you see him?"

"I only came on duty half an hour ago," Harris said. "Listen, Miss Johannsson is on her way up."

"Miss Johannsson? Kelly Johannsson?" Nicola's voice contained a frown. "What does she want?"

"She didn't tell me. Just thought you'd like to know."

"Shit!" Nicola commented. "There's the lift." She put down the phone and went into the lobby.

"That thing needs replacing," Kelly remarked. "I thought it wasn't going to make it." She looked Nicola up and down; Nicola was still wearing her black dress and tights. "You were at the funeral."

"That's right, Miss Johannsson. I'm Nicola Outridge. I'm Mrs Johannsson's secretary."

"Great. Look, Joanna said I could have the use of her office for an hour or so. Okay?"

"Well . . ." Nicola was quite sure Joanna would never allow *anyone* the use of her office. "I really should check with Mrs Johannsson."

She went back into her own office, and Kelly followed her to stand in the doorway. "I'd prefer it if you didn't." Nicola, already reaching for the phone, checked. "I'm not going to steal anything or break anything," Kelly said. "Although I'd like to borrow some company notepaper, if I may."

"I have some here." Nicola opened one of her drawers and took out several sheets of headed paper.

"Great." Kelly put the sheets into her windcheater pocket. "Now I need to use the phone. Right?"

"Oh," Nicola said. "Well . . . you can use this phone. The fact is, Mrs Johannsson is very particular about who uses her office."

"And she's the boss. Can't I even have a peek? At the seat of power?"

"Well . . . a peek," Nicola conceded, following her into Joanna's office and biting her lip as Kelly sat in the chair behind the huge walnut desk, and swung herself to and fro.

"Sure gives a feeling of power," Kelly remarked. "You know, I could be sitting here permanently, in a little while."

"Could you?" Nicola asked, uncertainly.

"Didn't you know I've inherited the whole shitting she-bang?"

"You've inherited Caribee Shipping?" Nicola was aghast.

"I've inherited enough to give me a controlling interest," Kelly said.

Nicola sat down in the chair before the desk. "Does Mrs Johannsson know this?"

"She just found out."

"Good lord! What did she say?"

"She's not a happy bunny. So she threw me out."

"She . . ." Nicola swallowed. "You said she'd given you permission to come here."

"I lied. So, it's war," Kelly said. "But it's a war your boss is sure to lose. I have too many big guns, too much ammunition. She's up the creek with not a paddle in sight. Now tell me, how long have you been working for her?"

Nicola licked her lips. "Two years."

"What happened to your predecessor? Don't tell me she got killed too?"

"Killed?" Nicola's voice rose an octave. "Too?"

"Didn't Mrs Johannsson's last chauffeur get killed?"

"Ah . . . I heard something about it. But I hadn't joined yet. Maybe it had something to do with the last secretary quitting. She said it was too stressful."

"Do you find it stressful?"

"I haven't, up to now."

"Well, I can tell you it's going to become real stressful over the next few weeks. You don't want to get involved."

"But . . ."

"You are involved. Right. How'd you like to guarantee your future?"

Nicola stared at her as a rabbit might have stared at a snake. "I'm not asking you to give up your job, or anything like that," Kelly said. "All I want you to do is be my friend. Would you like to be my friend? I treat my friends real good."

"I'll happily be your friend," Nicola said, not quite sure whether or not she was dreaming.

"Right. In fact, I'd like to take you on as my secretary too. Whatever Mrs Johannsson is paying you, I'll double it. How does that grab you?"

"She pays me very well," Nicola muttered.

"So you'll be rich. In return, I just want you to keep me informed of everything she does, everyone she sees, and especially any financial transactions she has."

"I couldn't do that," Nicola protested.

"Why not?"

"Well . . . it would be betrayal of trust. Dishonest."

"Fuck that. You'd be getting rich, and you'd be making me happy." Kelly got up, walked round the desk, and leaned against

124

it, next to Nicola. "I've an idea you'd be a dab hand at making me happy." Nicola blinked at her, and Kelly stretched out her hand, and ran it over Nicola's collar, then slipped it down the bodice of her dress. "I know I could make you happy," she said. "And not just with money."

"Ah . . ." Nicola desperately sought time to think. Right this minute she was quite off the Johannssons, after the way Raisul had walked away from her. But this was something else again. "May I think about it?"

"Sure. I'll give you five minutes. Now, do you have the number for this guy Lustrum? Daddy's lawyer?"

"He'll have gone home by now."

"Okay, so give me his home number."

"It'll be in the book." Nicola looked it up.

Kelly punched the numbers. "Hi! Mr Lustrum about? . . . Kelly Johannsson . . . Hi, Mr Lustrum. I'm sorry to bother you out of hours, but I have a problem. Things turned kind of nasty after you left. I'm not going to bother you with all the gory details, but in the end Mrs Johannsson threw me out . . . That's right . . . Oh, sure, we need to have a meeting about it . . . Tomorrow? Why not? . . . Ten o'clock? Right. My problem is tonight. I don't have any money, and I don't have any place to stay . . . From . . ." she glanced at Nicola. "A friend's apartment . . . Yeah, I guess so. But you'll have some money waiting for me in the morning, right? . . . Oh, a couple of thousand will do for starters, and some line of credit . . . Oh, sure, a card would be great. Okay, Mr Lustrum. See you at ten." She replaced the phone, gazed at Nicola. "I guess the five minutes are up."

"Well . . . I suppose I could help you."

"Listen. Are you working for me, or not?"

Nicola drew a deep breath. "Yes. I'll work for you, Miss Johannsson."

"Then you can call me Kelly. And you can give me a bed for the night."

"What?"

"You heard what I said to Lustrum. Right this minute I don't have any money and I don't have any place to go. But this time tomorrow I'll have all the money in the world. So your salary will start then. Tonight you can give me a bed, on account."

"I . . . I only have the one bed."

"So we'll share." Kelly put her arm round Nicola's shoulders, and gave her a squeeze. "Let's have a fun night. I'm feeling randy as shit."

Joanna lay in bed and stared at the ceiling, only half aware that it was daylight. She had broken the rule of a lifetime and taken a sleeping pill. It had made her sleep all right, but it certainly hadn't done anything for her tranquillity. Of all the God-awful messes. She had lost her temper. That was unforgiveable. She had honestly wanted to help the girl, had understood that most of Kelly's problems arose from her background . . . and she had let the downside of the girl's character get to her. Did her character have an upside? But that was cruel.

She sat up, pushed hair from her eyes, and gazed at Helen, seated as usual at the foot of the bed. Helen was fully dressed, but in shirt and jeans rather than city clothes.

"You were sleeping like the dead," she remarked.

"I needed to be."

"What's the programme?"

"I have so much to do I hardly know where to begin. Look, I may need you at the office. Go and dress yourself and you can come in with me."

"Right. Am I really going to have to go to court on Friday?"

"I'm afraid it looks like it. Sedgling is one of the people I, we, have to have a word with. Raisul up?"

"And dressed."

"Good. We'll go in together." She picked up her house phone. "I'll breakfast now, Parks."

"Yes, madam. Shall I ask Sergeant Maltby to wait?"

"Sergeant Maltby? Here?"

"He said you had an appointment, madam."

126

"For eight o'clock . . ." she looked at her watch. "Jesus!" It was a quarter past. "Why didn't you wake me?" she asked Helen.

"I didn't think I should. As you said, you needed a solid night's sleep. What do you think old Maltby wants?"

"Something to do with the accident."

"You going to pull the rug on Kelly?"

"Damn! I don't know. Are you still there, Parks?"

"Yes, madam."

"Give me ten minutes, and then bring the sergeant up with breakfast."

"In your bedroom, madam?" Parks was shocked.

"I'm sure he knows how to behave himself, Parks." She got out of bed, ran to the bathroom, cleaned her teeth and brushed her hair, put on a nightgown but decided against adding any make-up. Let him see her as she really was. Not that she had ever needed much make-up, anyway.

"You sure you know what you are doing?" Helen asked.

Joanna grinned. "Putting on the beautiful distressed woman act. And knowing he'll be scared out of his wits to be standing there with me in bed wearing only a nightie." She got back into bed. "When you hold the high ground, darling, you don't ever give it up except for the victory charge. Off you go. We leave the house at a quarter to nine sharp. Tell Raisul."

Helen left, and a moment later there was a tap on the door. "Come," Joanna said. Parks entered, wheeling the breakfast trolley. Joanna could see Maltby hovering in the background, shifting from foot to foot. "Oh, come in, Sergeant," she said. "I hope you brought an extra cup, Parks."

"I will fetch one, madam." Parks left the room, and Sergeant Maltby sidled in. He had left his helmet downstairs and didn't seem to know what to do with his hands.

Joanna was sitting up, the covers folded across her groin; the nightie did not leave a great deal to the imagination. "Good morning, Sergeant. I'm so sorry I kept you waiting. I overslept. The fact is, I took a pill. Yesterday was pretty harrowing."

"I can imagine, madam. If it's not convenient, I can come back later."

"I think it has to be now, Sergeant. I'm going up to London in half an hour, and heaven knows when I'll be back. Is it about the car?"

"Only in a manner of speaking. Coincidentally, you might say."

Parks returned with a spare cup and saucer. "You'll take a cup of coffee, Sergeant?" Joanna poured. "Do sit down. Do you mind if I eat?"

"Please do, madam." Maltby sat down, cautiously, on the stuffed chair by the bed, took his cup while Joanna buttered toast, again breaking the habit of a lifetime.

"You were saying?"

"Ah . . ." Maltby sipped, made a face, and put down his cup. "I'm afraid I must ask you straight out, Mrs Johannsson: was it Miss Helen driving her car on Sunday night?"

"And I must tell you no, it wasn't."

"Ah. I was pretty sure, mind. The people in the pub would have recognised Miss Helen. Then it must have been Miss Johannsson. The woman was described as tall, slim, attractive, with reddish-brown hair. Wearing a shirt and jeans."

"That's a fair description."

"This young lady is American, I believe."

"Canadian."

"Ah. Just arrived in the country."

"Yes." Joanna munched.

"Would she have had an appropriate driving licence and insurance cover?"

"She did not," Joanna said. She really owed Kelly nothing, now. "I have to tell you that she took the car without permission. And then crashed it. I was not going to proceed with the matter, as no one was hurt, but if you intend to act . . ."

"No, no, Mrs Johannsson. As you say, no one was hurt, and the accident took place on private property. Of course Miss Johannsson was breaking the law, driving while unlicensed

128

and uninsured, but we won't pursue that providing she obtains
a licence and insurance cover in the immediate future. However
. . . I would like a word with the young lady."

"You won't have it here. She left last night and went up to
London."

"Ah. Would you have an address?" Maltby took his notebook
and pencil from his breast pocket.

"I'm afraid I don't. But I have no doubt I shall be in touch
with either her or her solicitor this morning. I'll get an address
from one of them and let you know. But . . ." she frowned as she
finished her toast. "If you are not intending to proceed about the
car, why do you need to interview her?"

"It's just that we are hoping the young lady may be able to
help us in some inquiries we are making concerning a missing
person."

"A missing person?" Joanna was mystified.

"Yes. You see, ma'am . . ." he flipped some pages in his
book. "Miss Johannsson was seen, in the pub, with a young
man named Adam Benham. He's not a local man, but he uses
that pub quite often. He and Miss Johannsson were seen in
conversation, and when the pub closed, they left together. But
Mr Benham never went home. His parents were concerned
when he was not in the following morning, and they contacted
the police who naturally contacted me."

"Which is why you mentioned it to me at the funeral. I'm
terribly sorry, Sergeant; if I'd known what it was about I'd
have fitted you in earlier. I assume the young man has been
located?"

"No, ma'am, he hasn't."

"He's been missing for two nights?"

"Yes, ma'am. And his car is still in the pub car park. Now,
he lives a dozen miles from the village, so I don't imagine he
decided to walk home, even if he had had a few. Anyway, we
have thoroughly searched the route he usually used. So, we're
left with Miss Johannsson being the last person to have seen
him. Obviously it would be a great help if she could tell us

where he was going when they parted, what sort of a mood he was in, if . . . well, you know what young people are."

"Yes," Joanna said, thoughtfully. "Well, as soon as I get hold of Miss Johannsson, I will ask her to get in touch with you, Sergeant."

"We'd be most grateful, ma'am." He stood up, gave the undrunk cup of coffee another glance, and went to the door. "Thank you for your time."

"My pleasure." Joanna watched the door close. At least she now knew what Kelly had been doing between leaving the pub and winding up in the ditch. She really was a bitch on heat. Or more likely, she had absolutely no sense of moral values. But that went for all the young, nowadays. She found herself smiling. Had she been any different, in the swinging sixties? Or even the sober seventies, come to think of it.

But what had happened after sex? The blood on her shirt! Obviously the young man had been in the car when she had pranged it, and probably cut himself. He had then got out and walked away, leaving her unconscious? But Dr Buckston had said she couldn't have been unconscious for more than a few seconds.

Well, Joanna thought, whatever had happened was no longer her business, thank God!

She showered and dressed and found Raisul and Helen waiting.

"Sorted out the fuzz?" Raisul asked.

"I think so." She led them down the steps to the waiting Mercedes.

"Good morning, madam." Deardon opened the car door for her, and she suddenly remembered that the chauffeur might hold the answer to Kelly's whereabouts.

"Good morning, Deardon." She sat down, and Helen and Raisul got into the other side. "Tell me, where did you drop Miss Johannsson last night?"

"I took her to Caribee Shipping, madam."

"Why on earth did you do that?"

"You told me to take here wherever she wished to go, madam."

Joanna looked at Helen, who shrugged.

"Was anyone there?" Raisul asked.

"The night watchman, sir. And there were still lights on in the building. It wasn't quite six, you see, when we got there."

"And she went in?" Joanna asked.

"I believe so, madam. I didn't wait."

"Curious," Joanna commented.

"What are you going to do about her?" Helen asked.

"Nothing, personally. She's an adult, she's very rich, and the world is her oyster. Let her get on with it."

"But the endorsement . . ."

Joanna nodded. "We will have to contest the Will. I'd hoped to avoid that, but if that's the way she wants it . . ."

"What about Glasgow?" Raisul asked.

"I'm having a meeting with Barry Andrews this morning. I'll let you know after that. But act on the assumption that you will be going up there tomorrow."

Harris had gone off duty, but the receptionist had his night diary, and he had, as required, entered the visitor, Miss Kelly Johannsson, at five minutes to six, and leaving again, in the company of Miss Outridge, at six thirty-five.

Joanna swept into her office, accompanied by Helen; Raisul went off to where he had left his pile of company reading and computer records.

"Good morning, Mrs Johannsson." Nicola had shadows under her eyes, although she was immaculately dressed, as always.

"You look as if you tied one on, last night."

"Well . . . I felt sort of desolate."

"And you had company."

"Miss Johannsson came here, yes. She wanted to telephone her solicitor."

"And did she?"

131

"Yes. She arranged to meet him this morning, to obtain funds."

"I hope you charged her for the call. Where did she spend the night?"

"I have no idea," Nicola said, meeting her gaze. "I didn't hear what she said to her solicitor. I assume he arranged some place for her to stay."

"I see," Joanna said. "But you took her with you when you left."

"Well, there was no one else in the building, save for Harris downstairs. I didn't want to leave her here on her own."

You, Joanna thought, are lying. She really was a most deceitful girl. But getting rid of her would have to wait. She sat behind her desk.

"We have a lot to do. I want to speak with Mr Lustrum just as soon as he gets to his office."

"Yes, ma'am." Nicola made a note.

"I also need to speak with Mr Sedgling, and Mr Matthews, as soon as they get to their offices."

"Yes, ma'am."

"And I am expecting Mr Andrews at ten."

"Yes, ma'am."

"That will be all for the moment."

"Yes, ma'am." Nicola gave a nervous smile and left.

"Close the door," Joanna said.

Helen did so.

"Weren't you a bit short? I thought she was a treasure."

"So did I. Now, Helen, we have got to get hold of your friend Geoff. He must testify on your behalf if we are going to keep you out of jail."

Helen sat down. "I gave Sedgling his address."

"And he wasn't there when Sedgling tried to contact him. So tell me where he might be."

"Hm. Sedgling did try the hospitals, I suppose?"

"I believe so. Let us assume Best is not in one."

132

"Well . . . he has a friend he might have gone to. I know he's been there before when he's been in trouble."

"M or F?"

"Oh, M. He's a bit of a push-me-pull-you."

"And you let him get between the sheets with you?"

"Actually, he's a bit of a dream between the sheets," Helen said.

"And you are nearly as randy a bitch as Kelly," Joanna pointed out. "Give me the address of this friend."

"I'll go down there and see if I can dig him out."

Joanna pointed. "You are going nowhere near that bastard again. I don't suppose this friend has a telephone?"

"I don't think so. He lives kind of wild."

"Birds of a feather. Okay, give me the address and I'll sort it out."

"You, Mother? These characters play rough."

"I've observed that. I shall take Deardon. Just write down the address." She looked up as the door opened to admit welcome. "Welcome to happy hall."

William did not look at all happy. "Where's Kelly?"

"I have not the faintest idea."

"I thought you might bring her in this morning."

"Kelly has departed, lock, stock and barrel. At my request. I'm afraid she went right over the top after the reading of the Will, and we both lost our tempers."

"Oh." He glanced at his niece. "Do you think we could have a word, alone?"

Helen had been writing down the address. Now she stood up. "I know when I'm not wanted. Morning, Uncle Willie." She kissed him on the cheek, closed the door behind herself.

William sat in the chair Helen had just vacated. "I've had Evans on the phone."

"Your tireless watchdog. What has he to say now that we don't already know?"

"That Kelly may be guilty of murder."

Seven

"I'm not very bright this morning," Joanna said. "And I know I need to be. Would you mind saying that again?"

"It's all a matter of how you regard these things," William said.

"Tell me."

"Well, as you know, the official line is that Kelly came home from school, and found her mother dead in the bath, her throat cut."

"Don't tell me she did it?"

"I'm afraid she did. At least, that is what the police thought. Still do."

"And she wasn't arrested?"

"It was a tricky one. Kelly's fingerprints were on the handle of the razor. But she said she had taken it from her mother's hand in horror at what had happened. Forensic evidence disputed this. There were various other prints on the bath that indicated that Kelly had held the side while presumably wielding the razor, and then there was the angle and direction of the cut. But by the time they worked this out she had flipped, completely. And Michael stepped in to say that it was at the very worst a mercy killing, in that she could no longer bear to see her mother in pain. As she was going to be certified in any event, the murder charge was never aired."

"Well, I suppose that's fairly consistent with what we know of her," Joanna said.

"Save for something else. According to quite a few people,

134

friends as well as servants, Mrs Johannsson, the first Mrs Johannsson . . ."

"The next person who says that to me is going to get a black eye," Joanna threatened.

William grinned. "They say that Mrs Johannsson was not actually in a lot of pain, was quite resigned to the fact that she was in the last year of her life, was determined to get every moment of enjoyment she could in that year, and had never at any time given the slightest indication that she was considering suicide."

"So Kelly just picked up a razor and cut her mother's throat? There must have been a motive."

"The consensus is that she and her mother quarrelled. Seems Kelly had planned to go away for the summer with a friend, a male friend, and Mrs Johannsson had refused to let her. She was only sixteen, remember. And Kelly reacted violently."

"We've seen her do that," Joanna agreed.

"So you'll see why there was some difference of opinion over whether or not she was ready to be released from the institution. But again, Michael's millions told."

"And then?"

"She appears to have left Canada, and therefore she swam out of Evans' ken, as it were. Obviously she went to the States. Canadian citizens don't need visas to get across the border, so no one would have been interested in her background. What she's been doing the last couple of years is anyone's guess, but it would seem that Michael has been paying her an allowance . . ."

"Just as he did with Sean," Joanna said thoughtfully. "Thanks a million, Willie. You have, as always, been marvellous. Now, for the moment we keep this strictly between you and me. It's ammunition, which we will only use as and when we need to."

"You going to contest the Will?"

"I have no choice, the way things have turned out. But it's going to be very nasty if it comes to court. Just consider: I was convicted of murdering this girl's brother. I then married her father; we were married for seven years, but he never altered his

Will in my favour. All of that is going to suggest, in the hands of a skilful advocate, that he did not altogether trust me, or worse, that during our marriage he discovered reason to doubt that I *was* innocent of Sean's murder. And now they have me trying to steal the crust from Sean's sister's mouth. I shall be lambasted from here to Vancouver and back. That's why we keep this latest piece of information under our hats. We have to get a settlement out of court, and when I talk with Lustrum I have to have so much ammunition he will be forced to agree. I'm not asking for anything more than a continuation of that endorsement with no chance of a renege on her part. Let us have that and she can take off and murder who she likes."

William swallowed, but he knew his sister's single-mindedness. "You're the boss. But I have asked Evans to obtain documentary proof of what he told me and sent it over."

"Good thinking, Now . . ." Joanna's intercom buzzed. "Yes?"

"Mr Andrews is downstairs, ma'am," Nicola said. "And I have Mr Lustrum on the phone."

"Put Mr Lustrum through, and apologise to Mr Andrews. Tell him I'll be with him in a few minutes. Go keep him happy," she told William, and picked up the outside phone. "Good morning, Mr Lustrum."

"Good morning, Mrs Johannsson." His tone was cold.

"Ah," Joanna said. "Kelly has been in touch."

"We spoke on the phone last night," Lustrum said, "and I am expecting her here any moment."

"Right. Well, when she comes in, will you ask her to contact the Berkshire police."

"Why should she do that?"

"Because they wish to have a word with her," Joanna said. "It is quite important. And after that, you and I need to have a chat."

"My dear Mrs Johannsson, you are not my client; Miss Johannsson is. I can only speak with you if she is present, or with her permission."

"Lustrum," Joanna said. "Let me tell you something: if you

do not agree to meet me, with or without Kelly's permission or
her presence, I am going to blow a very big hole in her hopes
for the future. I'll expect you tomorrow morning at eleven."
She hung up, picked up the piece of paper on which Helen had
written Geoffrey Best's friend's address, and regarded it for a
few seconds. Then she pressed her intercom. "Ask Mr Young
to come in."

Peter was immediate. "You all right?"

"Don't I look all right?"

"There are all manner of rumours . . ."

"Aren't there always? Yes, Kelly and I have had a difference,
and she has departed."

"My God! Does that mean . . . ?"

"In the short term, certainly."

"You know Andrews is here?"

Joanna nodded, and tapped her intercom. "Ask Mr Andrews
to come in, Nicola. And Mr Grain as well."

"What are you going to tell him?" Peter asked.

"As much as he needs to know. Barry!" She stood up, her voice
like velvet, and Peter Young reflected, not for the first time, that
she could charm the fire-breathing tongue out of any dragon.

"Joanna!" Andrews kissed her on each cheek. "My, you're
looking well. Yesterday must have been exhausting."

"I slept well. Do sit down, all of you."

William arranged chairs, and the three men sat in front of
the desk.

"So, how does it feel to have a few dozen millions at your
disposal?" Andrews asked.

"I imagine it feels great. If you're talking about cash or
disposables, I have never been in that position."

A faint frown appeared between Andrews' eyes. "I thought
the Will was being read yesterday afternoon?"

"It was. The entire estate was willed to my stepdaughter, Kelly
Johannsson."

"You mean that pretty little red-haired girl?"

"That is one way of describing her," Joanna agreed.

137

"I see. Does that include Mr Johannsson's forty per cent of Caribee stock?"

"It does."

"Good lord! But in that case, perhaps she should be in on this meeting."

"I don't see why. Michael never sat in on any of our meetings."

"No, of course he didn't. So you think this young woman will be similarly disinterested in the operation of the firm?"

"No, I don't. I think she is going to be as disruptive as she possibly can. She has told me so."

"Oh, dear," Andrews said.

"However, I do not regard that as a serious problem," Joanna said. "Her forty per cent does not give her the power to change company arrangements, providing she cannot obtain any more."

"Yes, but she does have the power to cancel her father's endorsement."

"And she will do that," Joanna said. "I imagine you will be hearing from Lustrum later on today."

"Oh, dear," Andrews said again.

"I don't suppose you'd feel up to continuing the loan, unsecured? Presently it stands at . . ." She looked at Peter.

"Ten point one million," he confirmed.

"Ah . . . I would love to say yes, Joanna," Andrews said. "But in the present climate . . ."

"I have got to have that ship, Barry."

"Oh, quite. Well . . . how about selling one of the older vessels? Or even two."

"And leave myself with four ships to cover six routes? Once I give up one of those routes, much less two, Caribee Shipping will be on a slippery downwards slope. Once it is even rumoured that I am selling ships we'll take a beating on the market. How long would you be prepared to carry us, unsecured?"

"You mean while you see if you can arrange alternative financing? Well, of course, for an old and valued customer like you, Joanna, we'll bend over backwards to help. I think I could go for six months. But . . ."

"Six months will be more than adequate. I hope it won't take anything like that long."

"I hope so too. But I was going to say, it will have to be on terms that at the end of six months the loan must either be covered or liquidated, or we shall have to call." He looked truly distressed. "I really am sorry about this, Joanna."

"Don't be. You are doing your job and being very generous. Six months. I assume I'll get the usual letter?"

"Tomorrow. That is, assuming I receive a negative from Lustrum. If your step-daughter could be persuaded to carry on the endorsement . . ."

"She won't."

"I suppose one has to be realistic. Ah . . . purely personally, do you already have an alternative source of financing in mind?"

Joanna smiled. "I'll think of something. However, in the very short term, I need a draw of a quarter of a million for the yard. I assume that will be in order?"

"Of course. Well . . ." He shook hands with William and Peter, kissed Joanna again. "As always, it's been a pleasure. I just wish I could have been more helpful."

"Six months, Barry," Joanna said. "That's all I need."

"I wish someone would tell me what is going on," Peter complained. "If that young woman really does mean to pull the plug, well . . . I don't see where we are going to raise ten million in six months, without selling something fairly substantial."

"We have nothing to sell," Joanna said. "Nothing that I am prepared to sell, at any rate. What I am going to do is contest the Will."

"But . . . that can't possibly come to court in under six months."

"We are going to obtain an out-of-court settlement," Joanna said. "William has some very useful information which I propose to put to Lustrum at our meeting tomorrow."

139

Peter scratched his head. "Cloak and dagger."

"More dagger than cloak. Now, Peter, will you call the yard and tell them that their requested draw is coming up to them tomorrow, and will be delivered personally by my son Raisul. And Willie, I'd like you to hold the fort here for the rest of today; I have to go out."

He frowned at her. "Kelly business? You're not going to do anything rash?"

"It is not Kelly business. I have no intention of even thinking of her until this time tomorrow." She pressed her intercom. "Nicola, ask Mr Edge to come in, will you, and ask Deardon to bring the car to the door."

Raisul appeared a few minutes later.

"Your journey north tomorrow is on," Joanna told him. "You'll be taking a draft for two hundred and fifty thousand pounds, which should keep the yard happy for a week or so. Hoever, my original instructions stand: inspect and be critical."

"Right. How do I get up there?"

"Train or plane. It's up to you. Nicola will make the arrangements. OK, everybody, I'll see you tomorrow."

Raisul followed Nicola into her office and closed the door.

"Train or plane?" she asked, sitting behind her desk.

"Oh, plane. Then I can be back tomorrow night."

"Makes sense." She checked her list of numbers.

He sat on the desk. "Still mad at me?"

"It's not the business of an employee to be mad at her boss," she remarked, found the number she wanted and picked up the phone. "Anyway, I gained the impression you were mad at me."

Raisul waited while she booked his flight.

"You can pick up the ticket at the desk," she said.

"Thanks. I was mad at you. Then I realised I can't run your life. Not out of the office, anyway. You did say you didn't have a partner, right this minute." He waited.

140

"So it was an old friend who arrived inexpectedly. I put you off because I felt you might get the wrong idea. Which you got anyway."

"So let's forget it. Can I come round tonight?"

"I'm afraid not."

"Another old friend?"

"You *are* going to make me mad at you. Yes, I have a guest staying with me. A female guest. So . . ."

"Good God!" He pointed. "My stepsister!"

Nicola flushed. "Well . . . she had nowhere to go. No money. No nothing. I felt sorry for her."

"Does my mother know this?"

"No, she does not. And I don't want her to. She'd think I was being disloyal. All I was trying to do was help a stray."

"Some stray. And you reckon she'll still be there tonight? After her get together with Lustrum? She'll be on her way to the Savoy."

"I think she'll come back for her things. And in all the circumstances, I don't think it would be a good idea for you to meet."

"I have no quarrel with Kelly. In fact, well . . ." His turn to flush. "We've been rather close, from time to time."

"You only met her last Saturday."

"She's a fast worker." He grinned. "So am I. I've had her."

"You what?"

"More than once," Raisul said. "Well, she wanted it. The first time was practically rape. In reverse, if you follow me." Nicola leaned back in her chair; it was difficult to determine her expression. "So I thought," Raisul went on, "if I came round tonight, not only could I perhaps patch things up, but we could have a bit of fun."

"I'm not sure my bed is big enough for three," Nicola pointed out.

"But we'd be on top of each other," he grinned. "Two of us, anyway."

Nicola's tongue came out and slowly circled her lips. "I've never done that."

"Neither have I. But one should try everything once, don't you think?"

"But Kelly . . ."

"Tell you what," Raisul said. "I'll bet she's tried it before."

"The person we are going to see is your old friend with the knife," Joanna told Deardon, as the Mercedes drove out of London, heading south.

"In the New Forest, madam?"

"I believe he could be hiding out with a friend. If he is not there, we shall have to persuade the friend to tell us where he can be found."

"There is just the one friend, madam?"

"I don't know that. So we need to be prepared for any eventuality."

"Yes, madam." Deardon did not seem bothered by the prospect. "You just wish to speak with this man?"

"A little more than that. I wish him to accompany us back to London and make a sworn statement before a solicitor."

Deardon considered this. "And if he does not wish to come, or make such a statement?"

"We shall have to talk him into it," Joanna said.

"Yes, madam. How much force am I allowed to use? If it becomes necessary?"

"How much force have you got?"

Deardon smiled. "Thank you, madam. And if there is a charge?"

"I bail you out and take full responsibility."

"Of course, madam."

Joanna leaned back as the villages and trees and overhead cables raced by, as well as the usual stream of other traffic. She was actually rather hoping that Geoffrey Best would refuse to co-operate; she was in the mood for a punch-up – it might relieve some of the steadily building tension in her brain. Of course Peter and William, not to mention Matthews, would throw their hands into the air in despair if they knew what she was doing. But she had always gone straight for the jugular in times of crisis. She was determined on only one thing: Helen was not going to jail, not even for a single night.

Deardon pulled to a gentle stop, and unfolded his map.

"Are we lost?" Joanna asked. They were certainly within the official boundaries of the New Forest, although for the moment there was more open ground than trees.

"No, madam. Just checking. I think we take the next turning on the left."

He released the brake and the car slipped forward. Joanna deliberately allowed the tension, the adrenalin, to flow into her arms and legs and stomach. Now they were within a deeply wooded area, with trees rising thickly to either side. Deardon turned off the road and down a track, which twisted for some way, before he braked and they looked down a slope at a clearing in which there was a parked caravan, disconnected from a very ancient car. Both were surrounded by a considerable amount of rubbish. Between them there was an open fire, from which a thin plume of smoke rose into the still air, giving off a pungent odour of overcooked food left to burn.

"Not very edifying, madam," Deardon remarked. "Shall I go in?"

"I'll go in," Joanna said, and pointed at the motorbike parked beside the car. "We know he's here. You're the back-up."

"This is the young man with the knife we are talking about, madam?"

"I'm afraid so."

"Then, if I may recommend . . ."

"I am the one going in, Deardon," Joanna said.

"Very good, madam. Just shout if you need me."

She got out of the car, took a couple of steps down the slope towards the caravan, and checked to look over her shoulder, watching the chauffeur remove both his cap and his tunic and tie, and on his head place what looked a motorcyclist's crash helmet, which he had apparently carried on the floor of the front seat. She smiled. He was a most reassuring sight.

She continued on her way, and reached the fire, nose wrinkling. Then the caravan door opened, and a young man came out. His hair was as yellow as her own, worn even longer than hers, and whereas hers was in a bun, his was loose, clouding past his shoulders. For the rest of him, he was fairly tall, but underweight, had not shaved in about a week, she estimated, and wore jeans and a dirty shirt. A male equivalent of Kelly, she thought, without the water fixation.

"You're trespassing," he announced.

"How much of this land do you own?" she riposted. "Squatters' rights?"

He pointed. "You come here looking for trouble?"

"Actually, I'm interested in whether you have an MOT certificate for that pile of junk."

"Lady . . ."

"When you've told me that, you can tell Geoff Best to come out."

"He a friend of yours?"

Geoff appeared behind him, in the caravan doorway.

"She's the bitch who's Helen's mother," he said. His head was bandaged.

"I'm the bitch who's going to cause you a lot of trouble if you don't do as I say," Joanna said.

"You and who else?"

His friend was looking up the slope, and not liking what he saw. "Jesus!"

Geoff also looked up the slope, at the huge figure of the chauffeur. "Bugger him," he muttered, and came down the steps. "Just what do you want, lady?"

"I want a signed and witnessed statement by you to the effect that that packet originally belonged to you, or certainly not to Helen, that you gave it to Helen telling her it was Ecstasy, and that you knew, or at least suspected, that the friend you had just accumulated in that bar was an undercover policewoman. I'm afraid you will have to make the statement in the presence of my solicitor, so you'll have to come up to town with me. I'll have you delivered back here, afterwards."

"So I go to jail instead of your precious daughter."

"That will have to be up to the court."

"Yeah?" He looked up the slope again; Deardon had not moved, still waiting to be summoned.

"Inside," Geoff suddenly snapped, at the same time seizing Joanna by the shoulder and jerking her forward.

She was taken completely by surprise, and cannoned into him. His arms went round her and lifted her from the ground. Her own arms were pinned against his body, but she kicked him as hard as she could, only her shoes had come off and she thought she hurt herself more than him.

"Deardon!" she shouted.

"Inside!" Geoff shouted again. "Help me!"

The blond woke up and picked up Joanna's legs. She tried to kick again, but he was too strong for her. Between them they carried her up the steps and into the caravan, closing and locking the door just before Deardon reached them.

"God Almighty!" the blond gasped. "What are we going to do?"

"Wait for him to go away," Geoff said. "He can't get at us in here. Meanwhile . . ." They dumped Joanna on the bed, and when she tried to sit up, pushed her flat again, Geoff squeezing her breasts as he did so. "Shit! There's a lot more here than your daughter has."

Joanna was regaining her breath.

"You are definitely going to jail," she said. "For a very long time." There was a thump on the door. "Come and get me, Deardon," she called. "If you have to take this thing apart."

"Yes, madam," Deardon said.

"Shit," the blond muttered.

"Threats," Geoff sneered. Joanna reckoned they were both high. "Let's have a bit of fun, anyway. Christ, this is a lot of woman. Hold her arms, Sammy."

Sammy obeyed, grasped Joanna's wrists and dragged them above her head. She kicked at Geoff, but was hampered by her skirt, until he seized her thighs and pushed the skirt right up to her waist, seizing the tights to drag them and the knickers down together. She panted and again tried to kick him, but as he was beside her and Sammy still held her wrists, pinning them to the bed, she was just flailing air, while Geoff, slowly and with great glee, pulled the knickers right off to leave her naked from the waist down. "Some thing," he said, seizing her pubes and squeezing it, bringing an exclamation of pain.

But she refused to scream, even if, having again run out of breath, she was temporarily incapable of movement. Geoff kicked off his underpants, grasped her legs to part them, and knelt between.

"I'm going to enjoy this, lady," he said. "Maybe you will too."

He was certainly big enough to do her a serious injury, she thought, as she listened to the sound of splintering wood, while the whole caravan trembled.

"Shit!" Sammy cried, and released Joanna's wrists.

Immediately Joanna sat up and slashed her nails to and fro across Geoff's face. He gave a shout of pain and fell backwards, still between her legs. She got them both up, placed her feet on his chest, and pushed as hard as she could. Geoff gave another shout and fell off the end of the bed. Joanna rolled sideways and scrambled to her feet, to be caught from behind by Sammy. At the same time Deardon launched another assault on the door of the caravan, and this time it gave way. The big chauffeur tumbled into the interior.

Joanna jabbed behind herself with her elbow, and Sammy gasped and let her go again. Geoff was just getting up, and ran straight into Deardon's swinging boot. He cannoned across the limited space and hit the wall opposite. Joanna turned to face Sammy, who had retreated up the far end of the caravan.

"Don't hurt me," he begged.

Joanna didn't know whether he was referring to herself or Deardon. "Tie him up," she told the chauffeur.

Deardon advanced, and Sammy surrendered without opposition. Deardon took off the young man's belt and secured his wrists behind his back, then took Geoff's belt to secure his ankles. Geoff was slowly recovering, shaking his head.

"Now," Joanna said, kneeling beside him, their situations reversed, for he was now naked from the waist down, whilst her skirt had dropped back below her knees. "Are you going to co-operate?"

"Fuck off," he said. "I am going to have the law on you. Breaking in here, assaulting my friend and me, causing me grievous bodily harm . . ."

"And having myself raped?" Joanna suggested.

"You can try that one," he sneered. "It'll be your word against mine. That lug don't count: he's in your pay. You can't prove I ever laid a finger on you."

"Good point," Joanna agreed. "Then we'll just have to prove you did, won't we? Tie him up, Deardon. Use the sheets off the bed."

Deardon tore the sheet into strips, bound Geoff's wrists behind him. Like Sammy, Geoff had more sense than to try to resist.

"Just what the hell do you think you're doing?" he asked.

"You wanted to have sex with me," Joanna said. "Well, your wish is going to be granted. My way. Hold his shoulders, Deardon."

Deardon obeyed, face crimson as he realised what his mistress intended.

"Now," Joanna said, picking up her discarded knickers and sitting astride Geoff's legs. "Unlike what you were going to do to me, you may well enjoy this as much as I am going to."

Joanna went outside to wash her hands from the tap.

"You can untie him now, Deardon," she said. "And have him dress himself. But keep an eye on him."

"Yes, madam," Deardon said, his voice subdued.

Joanna wondered if he was dreaming of being similarly at her mercy, one day. She was in fact still breathing hard, both from her exertions and from what she had done. She regarded it as a surgical exercise; she was not going to let a bastard like Geoff get away with any counter-charges. But she couldn't help but be left feeling as randy as hell.

Geoff emerged, Deardon close behind. Both looked at her in a mixture of awe and terror.

"What about the other one, madam?" Deardon asked.

"Untie him, and tell him to stay inside until we have driven away." Deardon went back to the shattered caravan.

Joanna put on her tights, folded up the stained knickers.

"Now," she told Geoff, who was sitting on the step, still looking dazed. "I am going to offer you two alternatives. Which you choose is up to you. You are coming into London with me, and we are going to the office of my solicitor. There you are going to make the statement that I require, that Helen had no idea it was heroin you had given her, that you told her it was Ecstasy, and that you also knew, or suspected, that the woman you told her to offer it to was an undercover cop. Do you understand that?"

Geoff snorted.

"If you do that," Joanna said, "I will not charge you with rape. If you do not co-operate, we will take you to a police station, and formally bring charges against you. You may suppose that it will be the word of Deardon and myself against that of yourself and your friend Sammy, but your discharge into my knickers, which can be related by DNA to you, will I think carry the point."

"And when I tell them it was you who jerked me off?"

"You'd have to prove it, Geoff." She was gathering hair as best she could into a reasonably neat pile on the back of her head. "Do I look the sort of woman who would go around jerking off a lout like you?"

He stared at her. "One day . . ."

"One day never comes," she said. "All set, Deardon?"

"Extraordinary," John Matthews said, as he finished reading the statement on his desk. He looked over his pince nez at Geoff, seated beside Joanna in front of his desk. "You do realise that this, ah, confession, puts you in a serious position, young man?"

"That stuff was given me by someone," Geoff said.

"But here you admit to knowing what it was."

"Well . . ." Geoff glanced at Joanna. "I suppose I did. We thought it was a laugh."

"A laugh which may have very serious consequences," Matthews said severely. "I will pass this on to Mrs Moore's solicitor, and he will no doubt give it to the police and produce it in evidence. You will be called upon to appear."

"Big deal," Geoff said. "Can I go now?"

Matthews looked at Joanna. "Yes, you may go," she said. She opened her handbag and took out two twenties and a ten. "Take a taxi home."

"Bitch," he muttered, and left the office.

Matthews leaned back in his chair. "Just how did you manage that?"

"I have my little ways," Joanna said.

"And you always get what you want. However . . . did you know you look a bit, well . . . stressed?"

"It's been a fraught afternoon," Joanna agreed. "But I had Deardon. My chauffeur. He's very useful to have around."

"And there is no risk that young thug will bring a charge of GBH against you? That cut on his face?"

"None at all," Joanna said. "I scratched him in self-defence, and he accepts that." The stained knickers were in her handbag.

"Well, then, dare I say that all's well that ends well?"

"It's not ended until Helen is free of any charge," Joanna said. "Now I am going home to a bath and an early night."

"And this Will business? Am I to draw up the papers for a contest?"

"I'll let you know. I'm having a meeting with Lustrum tomorrow morning, and possibly Kelly will be there as well. At that time we shall discuss the whole issue, and hopefully bring it to a satisfactory conclusion. All I am seeking is a guaranteed continuation of the endorsement."

"And you think you will get it?"

"Yes, I do."

"Well, judging by the success of this little foray, who am I to doubt it?"

"I don't think I'll go back to the office, Deardon," Joanna said. "Just take me home, and then I'd like you to go back for Miss Helen and Mr Raisul."

"Yes, madam."

Joanna picked up the car phone, punched the numbers.

"Oh, hello, Nikky. All well?"

"I think so, ma'am." Her voice was curiously breathless, as it had been that morning.

"Well, I won't be coming in again today. Tell Miss Helen and Mr Raisul that the car will be coming for them at six."

"Miss Helen has just come into the office, ma'am. I think she wants a word."

"Mum? How'd it go? I've been so worried."

"There is nothing more to worry about."

"You found Geoff?"

"I did. He was staying with that friend you suggested."

"And what happened?"

"We had a quiet chat, and I persuaded him that it was best to tell the whole truth."

"And he agreed?" Helen was incredulous.

"Oh, yes. He really is a very sensible fellow. So he made a statement in front of Matthews, which is being forwarded to Sedgling, who will take it from there. I would say the worst you will get is a fine and maybe some community service."

"Oh, Mum! You are a treasure!"

"Thank you. I'll see you for dinner."

She replaced the phone, watched Deardon's ears glowing.

"I think you re a treasure, too, madam," Deardon said.

Eight

"Isn't it marvellous?" Helen asked Raisul. "Mum has fixed the whole thing up. My drugs bust, I mean."

"That's what Mum's are for," Raisul agreed, studying his computer, with its lists of ships and cargoes.

"She's sending Deardon to collect us," Helen said. "I reckon we're going to have a celebration."

"Ah . . . I'm staying in town tonight," Raisul said.

"Whatever for?"

"Because I want to. I'm going up to Scotland first thing in the morning, and I feel like a night out."

"If you are going up to Scotland first thing in the morning," Helen pointed out, "then you need to pack something."

"It's only for the day."

"Well, at least you need a good night's sleep."

"Look, Sis, be a sweetheart and bugger off? I'm a big boy, now."

"You are going to spend the night with your girlfriend," Helen accused.

"What if I am?"

"Oh . . ." she stalked away, and Raisul's buzzer went.

"Would you stop in to my office for a moment before you go, Raisul?" Peter Young asked.

"I'll come right up."

Peter gave him an envelope.

"That contains a bank draft for a quarter of a million pounds, payable to the yard," he said. "That's to keep them happy for the next few weeks. Just don't lose it."

151

"I'll carry it next to my heart." He went along the floor to Nicola's office. "OK?"

She stopped typing.

"Do you know, I'm quite excited."

"So am I. I hope she turns up."

"She has to, some time. All her things are there."

"Did you give her a key?"

Nicola nodded.

"Then she may have come and gone."

"I think she'll be there," Nicola said. "We're very fond of each other."

"On one night's acquaintance?"

"Well, as you said, she works very fast." Nicola flushed. "Turns you on, does it?"

"Well . . . is there anything in it for me?"

"I don't see why not. You claim to have had us both. You weren't all that bad . . ."

"Thanks a bunch."

"Well, you must admit you were new to the job."

"And Kelly is not," Raisul said thoughtfully. "You afraid of her?"

"Why should I be afraid of her?" But Raisul knew she was lying.

"She's so intense, and she gets these moods . . . do you know she was in a nuthouse for a while, after her mother died?"

Now Nicola did look frightened.

"I didn't know that. How do you know?"

"Mum had her investigated."

"The bitch. I'm sorry. It just slipped out. It's just that I found Kelly so vulnerable . . ."

"I've seen her attacking a man with a stone," Raisul said. "Mind you, he had it coming. He was attacking me with a knife."

"What an exciting life you lead," Nicola said, clearly not believing a word of it. "So, have I put you off coming home with me tonight?"

"I wouldn't miss it for the world."

The little flat was so filled with boxes that Nicola and Raisul could hardly get in the door. The parcels came from all over London: Fortnum and Masons, Harrods, Debenhams, Selfridges . . . some of them had been opened, and expensive lingerie was scattered around the place, together with a couple of furs and a selection of shoes.

"She's bought half of London," Nicola said in wonderment.

"What do you reckon this lot cost?" Raisul asked in equal astonishment.

"Somewhere a little over ten grand, I would say." Nicola closed the door. "Anyone home?"

"In here," Kelly said as she emerged. As usual, she had been showering; her hair was wet and she was naked and towelling vigorously.

"Sorry," Nicola said. "We have company."

"Him?" Kelly asked.

"Nice to see you," Raisul said.

Kelly turned round to allow him to look at her back. "All of it." Then she stared at Nicola. "You didn't tell me you and he were an item?"

"We're not," Nicola protested. "We're just good friends."

"That's what they all say. Hey, boy, can you open a bottle of champagne?"

"I think so."

"There are a couple of bottles in the fridge. Pour."

Raisul glanced at Nicola, who shrugged. He opened the first bottle of Bollinger. Nicola didn't have any flutes, so he used ordinary wine glasses.

Kelly wrapped herself in the towel, from the waist down, and sat on the settee. Nicola was still staring at the new clothes.

"Old Lustrum got me a credit card," Kelly said. "One of those gold things. And a packet of cash." She gestured at the little desk, on which were several rubber-banded bundles of twenty pound notes. She took the glass from Raisul and raised it. "Here's to being rich. Now tell me, what's the old bitch at?"

Raisul sat beside her.

"I suppose you are referring to my mother?"

"Who else. She gonna contest the Will?"

"I don't think she's made up her mind yet."

"Siilly cow. She doesn't have a hope. I'll bring her business down about her ears."

"It's my business too," Raisul said mildly, unable to keep his eyes off her breasts.

"Maybe I'll take it over," Kelly said. "And employ you as office boy, eh?"

"Must you be so unpleasant all the time?" Raisul asked. "I came here tonight to try to be friends."

"Your mom send you?"

"Mother doesn't know I'm here. She'd go spare if she did."

"Then what you really came for is to fuck Nikky."

"Well . . ." Raisul flushed. "It's just that, I'm off to Scotland in the morning, to see about the new ship."

"The one I'm guaranteeing?"

"Well, at the moment. Or have you already cancelled that?"

"Not yet. I gather your mom wants a meeting tomorrow morning."

"She did say something about it. She's looking for a decision, I suppose."

"Let her look. So you're off to Scotland. Where in Scotland?"

"The yard is on the Clyde. Just outside Glasgow."

"Right. I'll come with you. I've never been to Scotland. How do we go?"

"Well . . ." Raisul glanced at Nicola, who was not looking pleased.

"He's flying. Early," Nicola said.

"Okay, Nikky. You're the secretary bird. Get me on the same flight."

Nicola opened her mouth and then closed it again. "They'll need some kind of payment."

"The card's in my new handbag. Would you believe I've never had a handbag before? Give them the number."

Nicola swallowed, found the card, and called the airline.

"How long are we going for?" Kelly asked.

"Up in the morning, back in the afternoon. I'm to look at the ship, give them a payment, and come back."

"Fuck that. Let's live a little. We'll go to the Highlands. I've read about the Highlands."

"Well . . ." Again Raisul looked at Nicola. "Just how long were you thinking of?"

"Maybe a week."

"Mother will . . ."

"Go spare. Whatever that means. You an adult, or what? Say, you got any shares in the Company?"

"Some."

"Then you're a shareholder, like me. Your mom can't interfere with you. Don't tell me you're chicken? Chicken, chicken, chicken."

"Of course I'll stay with you," Raisul said hotly.

Nicola hung up. "You're booked," she said. "I made it open so you can come back whenever you like. Did you say you were going to stay a few days? What about me?"

"You're going to hold the fort," Kelly told her.

"But what do I tell Mrs Johannsson?"

"Don't tell her anything, unless she asks."

"And when she asks? She'll fire me."

"For what? You don't know where I've gone, or what I'm doing. You don't know anything about Raisul, save that he's gone up to Glasgow. You don't know anything about anything. Play the dumb brunette."

Nicola sat down, clearly wishing she had not brought Raisul near her flat. "And what about all this stuff?"

"Keep it for me. I'll be back." She giggled. "You can wear some of it, if you like."

Nicola stared at Raisul, who stared back. And then gulped. "But . . . if we're going to stay a few days, I don't have any clothes, or shaving kit, or a toothbrush."

"What were you going to use tomorrow morning?"

"Well . . ." he flushed as he looked at Nicola.

"He uses my stuff when he spends the night," Nicola said. "But I don't have any of his clothes."

"So what?" Kelly demanded. "Listen, I'll buy you whatever you need when we get to Glasgow."

"You mean, a new suit, and . . ."

"Everything else that goes with it. So you'll be a kept man. I've always wanted a kept man."

Once again Nicola and Raisul gazed at each other, both overwhelmed by her personality and the extreme wealth with which they were suddenly surrounded.

"Listen," Kelly said, "give me a good time and I might let you talk me into continuing that endorsement. Then your mom will be proud of you, right?"

"Well," Raisul said. "If you'd do that . . ."

"I said if you give me a good time. Starting now. Come to bed. Nikky, see if you can rustle us up some grub."

"So you reckon he's really hooked," Joanna said at dinner.

"I'd say so," Helen said.

"But you have no idea who she is. Or what. Or how old."

"Afraid not. Do you want me to put in some leg work?"

"Well, I'm interested. I'd not really like him to come home with a female equivalent of Geoffrey Best."

"Touché," Helen said. "But I had that one coming." She leaned across the table to squeeze her mother's hand. "I can't tell you how grateful I am. But you took such a risk . . ."

"I told you, I had Deardon with me."

Helen watched her mother climb the stairs. She had a distinct feeling that there was a great deal going on of which she knew absolutely nothing. But things that involved Deardon! And Mummy? That was impossible, especially after Mum's lecture at dinner. What would she say . . .

But at the moment she had nothing to say. It was an idea, roaming about both of their minds. She didn't know if she wanted it to happen. But she knew she did. If she dared.

Joanna went up to her room, undressed, switched off the lights, and lay on her back to gaze at the invisible ceiling. There was no use pretending that what had happened that afternoon had not had a powerful effect on her senses. All her senses. She supposed in some ways that she was still on a high. But she was a woman who needed the stimulus of sex, regularly. Michael had not been in her bed for several weeks before his death. She frowned. Did that mean his heart had been playing up that long ago, and he'd refused to admit it, even to himself? That certainly made sense; people didn't just drop dead of heart attacks without some warning signs, even if they chose to ignore them.

Poor old Michael. Maybe thinking of him would stop her doing something stupid. Like . . . this afternoon had been quite traumatic, in an obscenely delicious way.

She got out of bed, went to the French windows. Her room also had a balcony. But unlike Kelly she had never stood there naked. She thought that amusing. She was a woman regarded as utterly amoral and utterly liberated, who had spent her life doing what she felt like whenever she felt like doing it. And she had never stood naked on a balcony!

She opened the doors and stepped out into the cool night air, felt her nipples tighten. Caribee House was shaped like a U. She and her family occupied the centre, looking down the drive. To her right was the wing occupied by Tilly. To the left was the servants' wing. There were only four of them who lived in: Cook, Mrs Beckett, Parks . . . and Deardon. The housemaids came in every day. As she employed no one without a personal interview and a personal overseeing of their settling in, she knew that Deardon's was the end apartment on the first floor of the wing, and there was a light on.

She found she was breathing quite hard. Deardon! She didn't even know his first name. Of course she did; it was on his file in the study. But she had forgotten it because she had never used it. Another oddity. She and Charlie Hatch had been virtually on first name terms; certainly she had always used his first name. That was because she had inherited him from Howard, and he had known all about her various peccadilloes before she had become his boss. He had cosseted her, looked after her, defended her, gone to prison for her . . . and the thought of having sex with him had never crossed her mind. Yet he had been everything she liked in a man: big, powerful and bold. The same description went for Deardon. Additionally, he was much better looking than Charlie, and, she thought, better educated. And they spent so much of their time alone together, driving to and from London, or wherever else she wanted to go.

Like this morning. He had been there, watching. And he had seen her virtually naked, even if briefly. The thought gave her goosepimples. Or was it the chill?

She went back inside, closed the windows, switched on the light. She picked up her dressing gown, put it on, went to the door . . . then turned back and sat on the bed. She had to be stark, raving bonkers! Here she was, having just sorted out Geoff Best, having told Helen she didn't want Raisul bringing home any female yobboes . . . and she was contemplating having sex with her own chauffeur? Of course Deardon was not a yobbo. He was a highly trained driver and bodyguard. And a gentleman. But still . . .

She took off her dressing gown again, threw it across a chair, switched off the light and got back into bed. But not immediately to sleep.

"Good morning, good morning, good morning." Joanna swept into the office with her usual exuberance. "Good morning,

Nikky." She peered at her secretary. For the second morning
running Nicola was looking distinctly peaky. "I do think you're
overdoing it," she remarked. "You'll be telling me next you
have a boy friend."

"I do not have a boy friend, ma'am." Nicola placed the mail
on Joanna's desk.

"Then perhaps you need one." Joanna flicked through the
correspondence. "Mr Edge in yet?"

"No, ma'am. I don't think he intends to come in this
morning. He's on an early flight, and he told me he would
go straight to the airport. But you know that."

Joanna leaned back in her chair.

"I did not know that, Nikky. Mr Edge decided not to come
home last night. Do you have any idea where he might
have slept?"

"Me, ma'am?"

"Well, I hope his clothes are wearable and that he makes
a good impression on the yard." Joanna pressed her buzzer.
"Good morning, Peter."

"Morning, Jo. I'll be right in."

Nicola departed. "Did you give Raisul that draft?" Joanna
asked.

"Last night before he left. Didn't he tell you?"

Joanna sighed. "Peter, Raisul is twenty years old, and
believes in doing his own thing. No, he did not tell me,
because he didn't come in last night."

Peter sat down. "This doesn't concern you?"

"Of course it concerns me. But what am I supposed to do
about it? I believe he has accumulated a mistress."

"Anyone we know?"

"I have no idea."

"Hm. Bit bothering, him going off to spend the night with
some dolly bird with a cheque for a quarter of a million pounds
in his pocket."

"It was a bank draft, wasn't it? Made out to the yard?
Whatever his faults, Raisul has the welfare of the Company at

159

heart. Now, I am expecting Lustrum and Kelly in this morning
at ten. I think it might be a good idea for you to sit in."

"Certainly. Anyone else?"

"Matthews doesn't want to be involved at this stage, because
we may be able to wrap the whole thing up right away. He'll
come in if we need to go to court."

"I was thinking of William."

"No, just you and me, Peter. William has enough on
his plate."

"Mr Lustrum is downstairs, ma'am," Nicola said into the
intercom.

"Ask them to come up, please. And ask Mr Young to
come in."

"Yes, ma'am. But . . . you said them. Mr Lustrum is
alone."

"Is that a fact? All right, ask him to come up."

Joanna leaned back in her chair. So Kelly had ducked out.
Was that good news or bad? She felt a little cheated; she
had spent the past half-hour getting the adrenalin flowing in
anticipation of a fight. She stood up as the door opened.

"Good morning, Mr Lustrum. As you're alone, I thought we
would have this meeting in here rather than in the boardroom.
I hope that suits you?"

"No problem," Lustrum said, shaking hands and putting
down his briefcase.

"You know Mr Young, of course."

"We met at the funeral," Lustrum said.

"I do not wish to be interrupted during this meeting, Nicola,"
Joanna said.

"Yes, ma'am." Nicola closed the door.

"Now," Joanna said. "I had expected Kelly to come with
you. I hope she's all right?"

"As far as I know, Mrs Johannsson."

"Which hotel is she staying at?"

"I have no idea. As the Americans would say, Mrs Johannsson,

Miss Johannsson is free, white and over twenty-one. She is also a millionairess. I am merely her solicitor, acting on instructions from her. Thus I have supplied her with both cash and a credit card to keep her going until the estate of her father can be wound up. What she does with her money or herself is her business, unless she instructs me to make it my business."

"Simmer down," Joanna recommended. "I was only being polite. Right. Instructions. Has she given you any instructions regarding the endorsement?"

"Yes, Mrs Johannsson. Her instructions are that it is to be terminated. I have written to the bank to that effect."

"You realise this leaves me with no alternative other than to contest the Will?"

"You are at liberty to do so, if you choose, Mrs Johannsson. However, I do feel that it would be unwise. Perhaps your own solicitor should be present."

Joanna smiled, icily. "My solicitor will interfere when I instruct him to do so, Mr Lustrum. Perhaps you would be good enough to tell me why it would be unwise? It is quite unheard of for a man to die and leave his widow nothing."

"Mr Johannsson left you a great deal, Mrs Johannsson, in the form of the settlements he made on your behalf before his death. He bought back your company for you, he bought back your house, he re-established you in the financial world . . . I have accountants working out the precise figures now, but they already estimate that they are going to come up with a sum in excess of twenty million pounds for what your late husband spent on you. This analysis will be produced in court, if necessary. That you chose to plunge for another twelve million was your decision, and that he elected to back you again was his. It does not have to be a decision agreed to by the beneficiary. In addition . . ." He gave a gentle cough.

"You will also introduce the evidence of my having been convicted of the murder of Mr Johannsson's son, and the seven years I spent in prison."

"If that becomes necessary to protect my client, I am afraid

I will have to do so, Mrs Johannsson. Would it not be a great shame, after eight years, eight very successful years for you, in which time all of that, shall we say, murky past has been largely forgotten, to have it once again splashed all over the tabloids and the media? You would surely be the loser. All the world would be against you, a highly successful businesswoman who has surmounted insuperable odds challenging the inheritance of an unfortunate young woman, haunted by the suicide of her mother and the sudden death of her father, the sister of the man you murdered . . ."

Joanna held up her finger.

"I apologise," Lustrum said. "I meant, sister of the man of whose murder you were convicted . . ."

"Etc, etc," Joanna said. "Obviously, Mr Lustrum, if you intend to fight with knuckles quite so bare, I should be obliged to do the same."

"My dear Mrs Johannsson, the facts are there, and are indisputable."

"Indeed they are. But one needs to be in possession of all the facts. I don't think Miss Johannsson has been entirely honest with you."

"If you mean her confinement in a mental institution for a few years, she has told me all about that. It was entirely predictable that she should have a breakdown, in the circumstances, and perhaps entirely in character that her father should choose just to shut her away rather than himself attempt to give her the tender loving care she so obviously needed. I may say that episode is likely to increase rather than diminish public sympathy for her. In any event, she was discharged from that institution as being fully recovered."

"Then you are not aware that Kelly was sent to that institution, not for having found her mother dead, but for actually killing her mother while she sat in the bath?"

Lustrum's brows seemed to draw together. "Do you expect me to believe that?"

"I have proof," Joanna said. "Kelly cut her mother's throat.

162

She claimed it was to prevent further pain for a woman who was already dying. But there is evidence that Mrs Johannsson . . ." – and here she smiled – ". . . the *first* Mrs Johannsson, was not in pain and was perfectly content with her lot, and that the murder, because it *was* murder, Mr Lustrum, was the result of a quarrel."

Lustrum took off his glasses and polished them.

"So you see," Joanna went on, "my late husband was in the position of either having his daughter stand trial for murder, in which case she would have been certified insane and sent to an institution for a very long time, or of hushing up the facts and having her sent to an institution for a short period as suffering a nervous breakdown. With his money and influence he was able to do this, and he was able to secure her release after six years. But the decision to release her was not unanimous. I can, and I will, if necessary, bring staff from that institution across to give evidence in support of what I have just said."

Lustrum replaced his glasses. "I will, of course, have to discuss this development with my client, Mrs Johannsson . . . just what would you be attempting to prove?"

"That Miss Johannsson is not a sufficiently fit person, mentally, to have control of a very large sum of money. No one is trying to take her inheritance away from her, but it needs to be properly administered by a trustee."

"And you see yourself as the trustee."

"Well," Joanna said. "She does not appear to have any blood relatives left. And I am her stepmother. I would have thought that was quite reasonable."

"And you would, of course, immediately reinstate the endorsement."

"How I would administer my stepdaughter's estate is entirely my business, Mr Lustrum."

Lustrum was red in the face. "You'll never get away with it."

"We'll have to wait and see, won't we? However, I do not have all the time in the world. I suggest you get hold of Kelly immediately, put the facts to her, and receive her instructions."

"And if, as I expect her to, she flatly denies any involvement in her mother's death, apart from finding the body?"

"I have said, Mr Lustrum, that I can prove my allegations. You need to bear in mind that there is no statute of limitations on murder, even if the murder might be represented as a mercy killing. If this were to come to court, Miss Johannsson might well face a request for extradition from the Canadian government, to face charges."

Lustrum polished his glasses a last time, stood up, and closed his briefcase. "We shall have to wait and see."

"I require an early answer," Joanna said.

"I don't know that will be possible."

"OK, so perhaps you can't get hold of her until tonight. You can come back to me tomorrow morning."

"I cannot speak with Miss Johannsson tonight, Mrs Johannsson, because I do not know where she is, or what she is doing. I can only wait for her to contact me. I'm sorry, but that is how it is. Good day to you. Young." He left the office.

"Whew!" Peter said. "Now what?"

"We wait. I think we made our point."

"Yes, but suppose the young lady doesn't get in touch? He said he's fixed her up with money and a credit card. She might not need him again for weeks."

"Then we will just have to find her." She pressed her intercom. "Ask Mr William to come in, will you, Nikky."

William appeared in five minutes.

"How did it go?" he asked, and Joanna outlined the conversation. "Great," he said. "Are you going to hand the whole thing over to Matthews?"

"We need to find Kelly first. And see which way she jumps when we put the facts squarely to her."

"Suppose she simply jumps up and down and starts throwing rocks?"

"That would be ideal," Joanna said. "I mean to have both

Lustrum and Matthews present when we meet, and if they catch a glimpse of the real Kelly, then that's to our advantage. Can you find her, Willie?"

"I should think so."

"Then will you drop everything else and do so? I really would like to get this mess cleaned up."

"Carte blanche?"

"Absolutely."

William went into Nicola's office and closed the door. She watched him with some alarm. He grinned.

"I'm not going to bite you, Nikky. Just ask you some questions. I'm told that when she left Caribee House on Monday night, Miss Johannsson came here."

"That's right," Nicola said, watchfully.

"With what in mind?"

"As I told Mrs Johannsson," Nicola said, "she wanted to telephone Mr Lustrum and arrange for some funds."

"But this was after six o'clock at night. She didn't have a bank account. What was he supposed to do, get some of his own money and give it to her?"

"Ah . . . she was prepared to wait until yesterday morning, Mr William."

"OK. So we have her sitting on a fortune, but for the moment penniless and homeless. Makes you weep. Where did she say she was going to spend the night?"

"Ah . . ." Nicola gave a nervous glance at the door.

"This is confidential," William said. "All my sister wants to know is where she is now. Would you happen to know that?"

Nicola licked her lips. "She's in Scotland. With Mr Edge."

"Come again?"

"Mr Edge went up to the shipyard this morning. Kelly . . . Miss Johannsson, went with him."

"How do you know?"

"I . . . I booked the passage for her."

William scratched his head. "When was this?"

"Last night."

"You were with Kelly last night? Good lord! She's been staying with you!"

"I was only trying to be helpful," Nicola protested. "Like you said, Mr William, she was homeless and penniless . . ."

"That was on Monday night. By last night she had her money."

"Well . . ." Nicola shrugged. "We had become friends."

"And how," he remarked. "Why didn't you tell Mrs Johannsson this?"

"I didn't know how she'd react. I really didn't know what was going on."

"Well, get the yard for me, will you. I think I'd better speak to Raisul. Hold on a moment, though. Just how did Raisul get in on the act? I mean, how did Kelly discover Raisul was going up to Scotland and get him to agree to her going as well?"

"Well . . ." Nicola flushed.

"As you say, well, well, well," William commented. "I think you and I need to have a serious chat, Nikky. But right now, get me Raisul."

William returned to Joanna's office. "Kelly is in Scotland. With Raisul."

"Say again?"

William repeated the gist of his conversation with Nicola.

"I'm afraid I don't understand," Joanna said. "OK, maybe I can understand Nikky giving her a bed for the night. One night. You think they have something going?"

"Well . . ." William's turn to flush.

"Wouldn't surprise me," Joanna said. "She's omniverous. But Nikky? And how the hell did Raisul get into the act?"

"I think maybe it's a threesome."

Joanna leaned back in her chair. "I told him not to go near that girl again."

"Libido is a powerful driving force."

"And he appears to have his father's libido," Joanna said. "I am going to have a serious word with him when he gets back."

166

"As long as he brings Kelly back with him . . ." The intercom buzzed.

"Excuse me, Mrs Johannsson, I have the yard on the line."

"Tell them to put Raisul on," Joanna said.

"That's just it, ma'am. He's not there."

"I'm not with you," Joanna said. "Where is he?"

"He was there, Mrs Johannsson. He landed at nine, went straight to the yard, handed over the draft, looked at the ship, briefly, and then left again."

"Left to go where?"

"The yard manager doesn't know, ma'am. Mr Raisul didn't say."

"Did he have Miss Johannsson with him?" William asked.

"The yard manager says he had a female companion, yes, sir."

William and Joanna looked at each other.

"He must be on his way back," William suggested.

"Nikky," Joanna said. "What flight was Mr Raisul catching this afternoon?"

"He's booked on the five o'clock, ma'am."

"And presumably Miss Johannsson was also booked on that flight?"

"I wouldn't know, ma'am. She took an open ticket."

"Well, get on to the airline and find out if Mr Raisul has changed his flight to an earlier time, and also if Miss Johannsson is on the same flight." Joanna clicked off the intercom. "I wish I knew just what that little nutcase is playing at."

"She certainly seems to have Raisul wrapped round her little finger," William said.

"That was obvious from the moment he saw her standing starkers on the balcony," Joanna growled. "Anyway, thanks a million, Willie."

He got up.

"About Nicola. I promised her immunity if she came clean."

"You did, did you?"

"So I'd be grateful if you'd let it drop, Jo."

"Oh, very well. She's a good secretary. But she and Raisul have got to stop. It just isn't on for the future boss to be having it off with my secretary."

"I'm afraid there is no record of Mr Edge changing to an earlier flight, ma'am," Nicola said, hovering nervously in the doorway. "The airline computer still has him down for five o'clock. And Miss Johannsson's name isn't on their passenger list at all."

"So they've swanned off somewhere together," Joanna said. "This is really very bad of you, Nicola."

"I'm sorry." Nicola licked her lips. "Does that mean . . ."

"I am not going to fire you, or anything like that. But this strenuous love life you seem to be enjoying, and now letting Mr Edge and Miss Johannsson go off together without telling me . . ." she sighed. "I suppose the only good thing about it is that when Raisul comes back he'll bring her with him."

Joanna waited at the office until six, but there was no word from Raisul. Nicola checked.

"He wasn't on the five o'clock," she confirmed.

"Shit," Joanna said. "How many more are there?"

"Two. Would you like me to wait here?"

"Of course I would not like you to wait here," Joanna snapped. "Go home. But call me the moment you hear from him or see him." She went home herself, curled up in the back of the Mercedes.

"Bad day, madam?" Deardon asked.

"Mostly."

"Anything I can do?"

His head never wavered, and she saw only the back of his neck. Once again, extreme temptation. So who was she to criticise Kelly?

"What's your first name, Deardon?" she asked. "Forgive me, I ought to know it."

"Colin, madam."

"Thank you. Colin. I like that. I really just need to think, Colin."

"Of course, madam."

They finished the drive in silence. Think, Joanna thought. But her brain kept going round in circles. Raisul had obviously fallen far more heavily for Kelly than she had suspected. Now they were off together in Scotland, presumably on her money. Did that mean he was in the opposite camp? Or that Kelly might be weaned back into theirs? Look on the bright side, she told herself. Or did it mean that she was bent on destroying the family?

The car pulled into the drive, and braked. There were two other cars parked in the drive. One was Raisul's, as he had gone into town with her that morning. The other was a police car! Joanna leapt out of the Mercedes before Deardon could open the door for her. Obsessed with the fear that something had happened to Raisul, she ran into the house, past an astonished Parks.

"What is it?" she demanded.

"Sergeant Maltby, madam. He would like a word. I put him in the drawing room."

Joanna hurried into the drawing room, and Maltby stood virtually to attention. "What is it, Sergeant? Something about my son?"

"Your son?" Maltby's eyebrows went up and down. "Has something happened to Mr Edge?"

Relief flooded Joanna's mind.

"No. Not if you haven't come to tell me. Sit down, Sergeant." Maltby cautiously lowered himself on to the edge of a chair. Parks appeared with a tray and a bottle of Bollinger. "Or are you on duty?" Joanna asked.

"I'm afraid I am, Mrs Johannsson."

"Well, I hope you won't mind if I do. It's been a long day. Tell me."

"You were going to ask Miss Johannsson to get in touch with us."

Joanna nodded. "I've been trying all day to get Miss Johannsson to get in touch with *me*, Sergeant. But she's gone off."

"Gone where, madam?"

"I think she's in Scotland," Joanna said. "She'll be back soon enough. I won't forget to tell her to contact you."

"I'm not sure how long we can wait," Maltby said.

"You've decided to press charges after all?"

"About the car? No, madam. But the situation has become grave. We have located Adam Benham."

"And where has he spent the last couple of days?"

"In a ditch, madam. Dead."

Part Three

The Fugitive

I kiss'd thee ere I kill'd thee.
William Shakespeare

Nine

J oanna spilt her champagne.

"Dead? You mean . . ."

"I'm afraid the young man was murdered, madam. He was stabbed. The knife was left in the wound, a rather nasty, long-bladed affair."

"And you think . . . oh, my God!"

"Well, madam, Miss Johannsson certainly seems to have been the last person to see Mr Benham alive. We need to interview her very urgently."

Joanna got up and went into the study, opened the desk drawer. She hadn't thought to look before. But when Kelly had taken the money she had also taken Geoff's knife. Maltby stood in the doorway.

"Madam?"

"Come in and sit down."

The sergeant obeyed, and Joanna told him about the assault made by Geoff on Raisul.

"You didn't report this, madam?"

"Frankly, it seemed better not to, at the time. I didn't know as much about Kelly then as I do now. Is it possible she was acting in self-defence? When she stabbed Mr Benham?"

"If she was, madam, she over-reacted. Mr Benham was stabbed several times. It was what one might call a frenzied attack. And why did she take the knife in the first place? She couldn't have known she was going to have to stab somebody."

173

A frenzied attack, Joanna thought. A maniacal attack. And now she is somewhere in Scotland . . . with my son!

"So, as I was saying," the sergeant went on, "if there is the slightest possibility of your discovering where the young lady is . . ."

"Can't you put out a bulletin on her?"

"Well, you see, madam, we are not at this time accusing her of anything. We would like her to help us with our inquiries. But the murder could have been committed by somebody else."

"You have the knife. Won't it have her fingerprints on it?"

"It has fingerprints on it, yes, madam. If they are hers, then it will place her in a very serious position. But until we can obtain a sample of her prints . . ."

"I'm sure I can do that," Joanna said. "She spent last weekend here. You have my permission to dust her room, or whatever it is you do."

Maltby was looking puzzled. "You really think this young lady, your step-daughter, could have carried out such a vicious crime?"

"I don't think, Sergeant," Joanna said. "I know. Let me fill you in on her background."

Maltby listened gravely. "Quite a story," he said when she finished. "Did you say you can substantiate it?"

"I can prove it."

"Then it could be that we have a very dangerous maniac on our hands."

"She is currently shacked up, somewhere in Scotland, with my son."

"Good heavens. We'll need to move right away." He looked at his watch. "May I bring our fingerprint people down here tonight?"

"You bring them just as fast as you can."

"There is the point that the prints in the room Miss Johannsson was using won't all be hers."

"You bring your people down, and you may take the prints

174

of everyone in this house. Raisul's prints will be in his room. Those that are left will be Kelly's."

"Right," he said. "I'll hope to be back in an hour."

"Meanwhile, do you object if I put out some sort of message on television to the effect that my son should contact me immediately?"

Maltby pulled his ear. "It'll cost a bit. I mean, you can't go accusing Miss Johannsson of anything as yet. They'll have to run it as a regular ad."

"I'm not bothered about the cost," Joanna said. "I want my son back."

The sergeant left as Helen arrived.

"Flap?" she asked, and Joanna told her. "Shit!" Helen commented. "Why, do you think? She seems to enjoy sex from any angle, so it can hardly have been defence against rape."

"Something touched her off. Something he said, maybe an allusion to her mother . . ." Joanna frowned. "When we first met, I referred to her mother, and she gave me a look that quite froze my blood."

"What are you going to do? Putting out a private APB on the telly won't do much good. I doubt they'll be watching."

"Someone must have seen them."

"Don't let's panic about this, Mother. Think. If Kelly does happen to find herself in front of a television set and discovers she's wanted by the police, that's as likely as anything to touch her off. Right now she's enjoying Raisul. She seemed fond of him. Let them get on with it while we track her down."

"How do you suggest we do that?"

"I'll go up to Glasgow tomorrow morning. We know they were at the yard this morning. We know that when they left the yard they didn't catch a flight back down. So we must assume they are still in Scotland. But someone at the yard must have seen them go, and how they went. Once we know that, I can trace them."

"Good thinking. I'll come with you."

"No," Helen said. "We need you here, acting as a back-up. They may come back down before I can catch up with them."

"That's good thinking too," Joanna said. "OK. You to Scotland, me holding the fort here. But you will be careful. If she *is* in the habit of knifing people who get on her nerves . . ."

"I'll be careful. The important thing is to get Raisul out of her clutches, right?"

"Right. Now tell me, how did your meeting with Sedgling go?"

"He's getting quite optimistic. He's issued a subpoena for Geoff to appear on Friday."

"Do you think he will?"

"If he doesn't, that's a strike against him for a start. And we have his signed statement." She wrinkled her nose. "You *are* going to tell me how you got him to do that?"

"I exerted all my womanly powers," Joanna said.

"Stop the car," Kelly commanded.

Raisul obligingly braked to a halt at the side of the lonely road. "Problem?"

"I just want to admire the view. Isn't it something?" She got out of the car. The road was halfway up a hillside, and below them the lake was dark and still; there was no wind. Beyond the lake the ground rose steeply again, reaching up towards the mountains. "Some thing," she said again. "They call those things lochs, right?"

"Right." Raisul got out to stand beside her. It was dusk, and the valley was filled with a somewhat eerie half-light.

"It looks deep," Kelly remarked.

"It is deep. Some lochs are more than a thousand feet deep."

"Is that the one with the monster?"

"No. That's further north. This is just a little fellow. We should be looking for some place to have something to eat, and a bed for the night."

"Yeah," she said, and leaned against him. "It's been a fun day. I've never seen a ship being built before."

"It's our business," Raisul said proudly.

"Yeah," she said again, and got back into the hired car.

It had come with a map, and Raisul studied this, bending low in the half light. "There's a village a few miles away. It'll have a pub. We'll probably get a room there."

"You're the boss," she said.

Which he didn't believe at all. She had quite taken over his life. He didn't resent that. He had fallen for her from the moment he had seen her on the balcony, without in any way supposing they could ever get together. Of course she frightened him when she got into one of her violent moods, but the only time she had actually done that in his presence had been to defend him. He thought the idea of having a woman like Kelly always at his shoulder was out of this world; it would make him physically invulnerable. And financially!

Equally of course there was her background. Mom hated her, but Mom hated anyone who tried to interfere with her business, much less wreck it. She was going to be absolutely furious when she found out what he was doing. But he felt he could play an important part in solving the current problem. If Kelly was as fond of him as she seemed to be, surely he could persuade her to continue the endorsement. While her love-making was like nothing he had ever supposed possible. She made Nicola appear like a schoolgirl.

"Brown study," Kelly remarked. "Don't you think we should have lights on?"

Raisul obligingly turned the switch. "Sorry. I've a lot on my mind."

"Tell me about it."

"When we're sorted out. There's the village."

The pub was easy enough to find; it dominated the single street. Raisul pulled into parking, and led Kelly into the lounge bar.

"What'll it be?" asked the landlord.

"We'd like a bed for the night," Raisul explained.

The landlord looked him up and down, and then did the same for Kelly. "Ye're from the south," he observed.

"Yes. We're on a driving tour."

"And ye've nae booked?"

"Well, it's early in the year . . ."

"Always book," the landlord recommended.

"You mean you're full."

"I mean, we don't have rooms, here."

"So, sh . . . shoot," Raisul said. "Do you think there'd be an hotel anywhere near?"

"Aye, well a few miles, to be sure. But I'll no guarantee they'll take ye in."

"What's the matter with us?" Kelly inquired.

"I'm not saying there's anything the matter wi' ye," the landlord said. "The place may be full. Listen. The widow Maclain does bed and breakfast. I don't think she's got anyone there tonight. She's just along the road. There's a sign."

"Splendid," Raisul said.

"I could gi'e her a ring and make sure," the landlord offered.

"Would you? That'd be great."

"Ye'll want a drink while ye're waiting."

"Oh, yes, of course. I'll have a pint of lager."

"And the lass?"

"The same," Kelly said.

He stared at her for several seconds. "Two pints of lager," he said, half to himself. He went through to the public bar, returned a moment later with the two tankards. "My wife's making that call for ye." He returned to the other room.

"Dig that accent," Kelly said. "Tremendous. I feel like we're really adventuring."

"We have to go back sometime."

"Sometime. Quit worrying."

"Mum will be going bonkers."

"Like I said, you have to remember some time that you're an adult," Kelly said. "Why don't you call her?"

"Could I?"

"What's to stop you? But listen, don't tell her where we are. Just say you're with me and we're having a bit of fun."

"And if she says, come straight home?"

"Stand up for yourself. Tell her you'll be home when you're ready."

Raisul swallowed, felt in his pocket, located the necessary coins, and went into the corridor to use the public phone. Kelly followed him.

"Raisul?" Joanna asked. "Raisul! Oh, thank God! Where are you?"

"I'm in Scotland, Mum."

"Is that . . . is Kelly with you?"

"She's right beside me."

"Hi, Stepmother," Kelly said into the phone.

There was a brief silence. Then Joanna said, "Hi. Let me speak with Raisul, please."

Raisul took the phone back. "I'm sorry, Mum. We just wanted to have a couple of days alone together. Listen, Mum, I think I may be able to persuade her to continue the endorsement. She was very impressed with the new ship. She . . ."

"Raisul," Joanna said. "I want you to come home, tonight."

"Now, Mum . . ."

"I can't explain over the phone, but it is most important that you do this," Joanna said. "Both of you."

"We'll be back in a couple of days," Raisul said.

"Raisul!" Joanna shouted. "At least tell me where you are."

"Scotland," Raisul said. "See you soon." He hung up.

Jonna dialled the operator.

"Is is possible to trace a call from Scotland?" she asked.

"Is the other person still on the line, madam?"

"Well, no, he isn't."

179

"Then I'm afraid we can't help you," the operator said.

Joanna slammed down the phone. "Helen!" she shouted. "Helen! Come in here, please."

Sergeant Maltby arrived a few minutes later, together with his fingerprint people. Joanna told him of the phone call.

"Well, Mrs Johannsson," he said, "I know how worrying this is for you. Now here's what we're going to do. We're lifting prints from upstairs now. You said we could take the prints of everyone in the house. Including yours?"

Joanna nodded wearily, and then smiled. "You have mine already."

"It'll be quicker to take them again, here, than try to look up the file. Then we'll go back to the station, and see if we can match any of them to the knife. If, as seems likely, the unidentified prints are on both, then we have reasonable grounds for obtaining a warrant for the arrest of Miss Johannsson on a charge of murder. If that is the case . . ." He looked at his watch; it was just coming up to eight o'clock. "We should be able to make the ten o'clock news, and of course the bulletin will be repeated tomorrow morning. That should turn something up. You wouldn't happen to have a photograph of the young lady?"

"I'm afraid not. But we do have one of Raisul."

"That would be a help."

"So long as it is made perfectly clear that he is not involved in the murder inquiry, and knows absolutely nothing about it."

"Absolutely," Maltby promised.

"She sounded a bit cheesed off," Kelly remarked.

"Well, I knew she would be. She . . . well . . ."

"She doesn't approve of me," Kelly said. "Sure. And what was that about me continuing the endorsement? I've already cancelled it."

"I had to say something like that, to stop her losing her rag.

Anyway . . ." he began before kissing her. "I'm still hoping to change your mind."

"Chance would be a fine thing."

She led him back to the lounge bar, where the landlord's wife was waiting.

"I've spoken with Mrs Maclain, and she'll gi'e ye a bed for the night." She peered at them. "Married, are ye?"

"Oh, yes," Kelly said.

The landlady looked at Kelly's left hand. She was wearing two quite expensive rings, bought the previous day – but neither was on the third finger. "Ye need to be married," she said. "Mrs Maclain is a wee bit old-fashioned."

"We are married," Kelly said, positively. "Now say, does this lady serve dinner?"

"No, no," the landlady said. "It's B&B only. But there's a café just down the road. Ye can eat there."

"This country may be lovely to look at," Kelly remarked, peering into her soup. "But the people sure are stiff."

"Good thing you brought along that bag," Raisul said. "Or she probably wouldn't let us in at all. What are we going to do about the ring?"

"No problem." Kelly took the ring off her forefinger and placed it on her third, turning it over so that only the band was exposed. "All I need to do is not let her see the stone. Now listen, don't sign your real name."

"You mean . . . Smith?"

"I shouldn't think she'll go for that, either. Make it . . . Dorminton."

"Why Dorminton?"

"Just came into my head. Nobody fakes a name like Dorminton. What *is* this?"

"I'm not sure."

Kelly pushed the plate away. "Hey," she shouted at the waitress.

"Is something wrong, madam?"

181

"You got any real food in here?"

"The main course is steak and kidney pie."

Kelly looked at Raisul.

"That should be good," he said.

"Then bring on the pie," Kelly said. "Talk about slumming."

"I suppose, once you've got all your money, you're only going to eat at the best places."

"You bet. You going to work for me?"

"Eh?"

"I'm offering you a job, asshole."

"What as?"

"Live-in lover, general factotum . . ."

"I'd like to marry you."

Kelly regarded him for several seconds, then regarded the plate that had just been placed in front of her. "You sure this ain't dogfood?"

"Madam, you are welcome to leave."

Raisul placed his hand on Kelly's arm as she seemed about to rise; he didn't think she meant to leave. "It'll taste good, believe me."

"It'd better," Kelly growled, and tried some. "Say, that ain't half bad. Marry you? What do you think your mom would say to that?"

"Well, like you said, she can't really stop us."

"Marry you," Kelly said again, and giggled. "It'd be a hoot. Any chance of you inheriting that Arab throne?"

"None whatsoever, I'm afraid."

"What about if I bought it for you?"

"Kelly, the annual income of the Emir of Qadir is about ten times your inheritance."

"But still, you're a prince, right?"

"I suppose so."

"Then you should start using the title. Then if I married you, I'd be Princess Kelly of Qadir. Now there *is* a hoot. Sounds good, though."

"I don't have any right to use the title," Raisul pointed out. "My father specifically renounced it, for him and his heirs."

"But they still bumped him off. Seems to me they cancelled the renunciation by doing that, if you follow me."

"It's a point. But if I started using the title, they might just come after me."

"That scare you?"

"Well . . . it would be a difficult situation to live with."

"Don't worry about it. I'll protect you."

"I'm going to break every bone in that boy's body," Joanna said, as she and Helen finished dinner. The house was still filled with policemen.

"He's young, he's in love . . ."

"And he's wandering around the country with a murderess."

"Do you still want me to go up there tomorrow?"

"Yes. I'm sure you'll do as good a job as the police in tracking them. Just keep your distance, and let me know what you find out. Now, I'm going to bed." She said goodnight to Sergeant Maltby, toyed with the idea of taking a sleeping pill, decided against it. It was not a habit she wanted to get into, and there was always the chance Raisul might ring again. If the police did get the message out on the ten o'clock news . . .

She switched on the set and sat up in bed. After the usual scandals and international crises, the presenter said, "Berkshire police are anxious to interview a Miss Kelly Johannsson, whom they think may be able to help them in their inquiries as to the suspicious death of a young man last Sunday night. Miss Johannsson is in her early twenties, tall and of strong build, with red hair. She is at present thought to be in Scotland, and is travelling with a male companion, a Mr Raisul Edge." The photograph of Raisul appeared on the screen. "It should be emphasised," the presenter said, "that Mr Edge has nothing to do with the police inquiries, but he is urged to get in touch with them as to the whereabouts of his companion as quickly as possible."

Joanna switched off the set. That should accomplish something, she supposed. The phone rang, and she snatched at it.

"Jo! Have you seen the news?"

"Yes."

"Did you know about it?"

"Yes, Willie. I knew about it."

"But . . . are they saying that Kelly had a hand in that man's death?"

"Kelly killed him."

"God Almighty! And Raisul . . ."

"Is blissfully unaware of this, or anything else in her past life, and is swanning around Scotland with her, apparently having the time of his life."

"Jesus! What are you going to do?"

"What can I do? We now have the police looking for them, and presumably they will find them. We can only pray Raisul is still in one piece. Helen is going up tomorrow to see what she can do."

"Do you wish me to go too?"

"No," Joanna said. "You and I are going to hold the fort here. I'll see you in the morning."

She hung up as her door was thrown open.

"Jo!" Matilda boomed.

"Yes, Tilly, I have seen the news."

"But . . . what are you doing about it?"

"I'm not in the snap my fingers and let's have a miracle class," Joanna said, "Everything that can be done is being done. Now, Tilly, I really would like to get some sleep."

"I just wanted you to know that we're all behind you. I'd like to break that girl's neck."

"I'm sure you'd make a good job of it, Tilly." They'll find them tomorrow, she thought, as she switched off the light.

*　　*　　*

"Ye'll be Mr Dorminton," Mrs Maclain said, blinking at Raisul through heavy glasses. "Mrs Forsythe telephoned from the public house." She was a short, thin, middle-aged woman with a sharp nose.

"That's me," Raisul said. "And this is my wife, Kelly."

Mrs Maclain regarded Kelly with disfavour. "I expected ye some time ago."

"We stopped to have something to eat," Raisul explained.

"Aye, well, that was wise, nae doubt. I'll show ye the room."

She led the way up the stairs. In the front room the television was on; it was just coming up to the ten o'clock news. "Here ye are." She opened the door. "That's my room opposite. Ye'll nae be making a noise?"

"Wouldn't dream of it," Raisul assured her.

Kelly entered the room. "Where's the bathroom?"

"Just along the corridor."

"You mean there isn't one in the room?" Raisul squeezed her hand.

"I'm nae an hotel," Mrs Maclain pointed out. "Breakfast is at eight sharp. Sharp, mind. And ye'll be out of the room by nine. That'll be five pounds."

"Oh, ah . . ." Raisul took out his wallet.

"I have it." Kelly produced a roll of twenty pound notes. Mrs Maclain blinked at the money in astonishment. "Don't you like cash?" Kelly asked.

"I'll have to get change." She took the note. "Ye can have it in the morning. Eight o'clock sharp." She went back down the stairs.

"What a hoot." Kelly kicked off her shoes.

Raisul tested the bed. "Backache tomorrow."

"Frontache tonight. I'm as randy as hell."

He took her in his arms, kissed her. "Where are we going tomorrow, anyway?"

"Who cares? Just let's drive a bit. North. I'm real keen on seeing this monster."

"You may have to hang about awhile. He doesn't show very often."

"He'll show for me," she said confidently.

Remarkably, they both slept heavily, despite the sagging mattress. But it had been a long day. Raisul awoke to see daylight streaming through the window.

"Jesus!" he exclaimed. He looked at his watch. "Half-past seven. We'd better rush, or we'll miss breakfast."

"Ugh!" Kelly tumbled out of bed, went to the door.

"You can't go out like that," he protested. "Suppose the dragon's about?"

Kelly inhaled the smells coming up the stairs. "I'd say she's cooking breakfast. Anyway, it'll give her a thrill." She picked up her washbag and hurried to the bathroom. Raisul joined her to shave, and they stood at the basin shoulder to shoulder. "Just like if we *were* married," Kelly giggled.

They dragged on their clothes and hurried downstairs, into the kitchen.

"Ye're just about late," Mrs Maclain remarked. But she seemed in a better mood than the previous night as she placed three five-pound notes beside Kelly's plate. "Did ye sleep well?"

"Very," Raisul said.

"I heard the bed creaking," Mrs Maclain said, perhaps wistfully. "Honeymooning, are ye?"

"Right," Kelly said.

"Aye. It makes the world go round." She placed before each of them a plate of bacon, eggs, tomatoes, mushrooms and friend bread. "That'll start ye off."

"No juice?" Kelly asked. "I gotta have some juice."

"Nae juice," Mrs Maclain told her. "Drink some tea." She poured.

"Tea? I only drink coffee."

"Nae coffee," Mrs Maclain said. "Take it or leave it." She looked at the clock. "Time for the news. I missed it last night, showing ye to your room." She went into the front room.

"Silly old bag," Kelly muttered. "Tea?"

Raisul poured. "Britain's most popular beverage, so they say."

"Which cost them an empire." Kelly peered into her cup.

"Eat up," Raisul said. "It's pretty good."

"Brrr . . ." she took a mouthful, and stopped chewing.

"Repeat of last night's police bulletin," the voice in the next room was saying. "Police are seeking the whereabouts of Miss Kelly Johannsson, in connection with the death of a young man in Berkshire. Miss Johannsson is reported to have fled for Scotland, with a male companion. She is described as being twenty-four years old, about five foot eight inches tall, strongly built, attractive in appearance, with auburn hair. She may be wearing jeans and a windcheater. Her companion is a Mr Raisul Edge, who may also be using the name of Johannsson. Mr Edge, shown in this photograph, is twenty years old, and is described as being five feet ten inches tall, slight build, with dark hair and a swarthy complexion. It should be emphasised that he is not involved in the police inquiries, but he is urged to contact the nearest police station as soon as possible."

The set went dead, while Kelly and Raisul stared at each other.

"Shit," Kelly said. "Shit, shit, shit! That's your fucking mother."

"It was a police message," Raisul said. "What are we going to do?"

"Finish breakfast and get out of here," Kelly said. "These yobboes won't . . ." she paused, again in mid-chew, staring at the doorway, and Mrs Maclain.

"I thought there was something . . ." Mrs Maclain started, checked herself and turned away.

"Get the phone!" Kelly commanded.

Raisul knocked over his chair as he leapt to his feet and ran into the hall He and Mrs Maclain reached the phone at the same time, and he tore it from her grasp and threw it on the floor. Mrs Maclain gasped, and turned for the front door, but Kelly had now joined them, and she held the older woman's shoulder and jerked her back with such force that she spun round and fell to her knees. Her glasses came off and Kelly stepped on them as she again ran at her.

Mrs Maclain reacted violently, kicked behind herself, and caught Kelly on the knee. Kelly went down with a thud, and Mrs Maclain, after another glance at the front door, in front of which Raisul was still standing, reached her feet and ran for the back.

"Stop her!" Kelly shouted. Blindly obeying her, as he could think of nothing else to do, Raisul ran across the kitchen and caught Mrs Maclain as she was unlocking the back door. He grasped her shoulder and she turned and threw him off, revealing a strength he had not suspected her to possess. He stumbled into the table, scattering plates and food and cups of tea, and she leapt away from him again.

But now Kelly had caught them up, and she threw the woman against the wall. Mrs Maclain collapsed, panting, and now weeping as well.

"We'll have to tie her up," Raisul panted.

"Tie her up, shit," Kelly said. "You hold her."

Raisul held Mrs Maclain's shoulder, and pulled her to her feet. "Listen," he said. "We don't mean you any harm."

"Murderers," Mrs Maclain snapped at him.

Raisul blinked. In the excitement of stopping her getting away, he had quite forgotten the earlier part of the bulletin. He looked at Kelly. "You didn't."

"He was a bastard," Kelly growled. "They're all bastards. Hold her," she shouted, as Mrs Maclain made another abortive effort to get free.

Raisul tightened his grip, but Mrs Maclain was exerting all her strength, and she turned him away from Kelly to face the wall.

"Please," he panted. "We just want to leave. Please."

Something raced past his head and crashed into the back of Mrs Maclain's skull. He gazed in horror at the matted hair and blood and bone, and instinctively released her to step away. Mrs Maclain slid down the wall to her knees.

"Out of the way!" Kelly ordered.

Raisul sank to his knees, realising that Kelly was wielding the large frying pan that only a few minutes earlier had been cooking their breakfast.

"My God!" he shouted. "You'll kill her!"

"Yeah," Kelly said. Mrs Maclain was trying to crawl to the door, moaning, blood dribbling down her cheeks. "No, you don't," Kelly said, and swung the frying pan again. This blow landed on Mrs Maclain's shoulders, and she went down with a shriek. "Fuck it!" Kelly stepped forward, the frying pan raised, and Raisul hurled himself at her, reaching for her arm. She turned, violently, pushing him backwards so that he fell on to a chair, and stood above him, frying pan raised. Never had he seen such maniacal fury in anyone's eyes. "I ought to smash your face in," she said. And turned back to find Mrs Maclain.

The police car drew up outside the public house. Forsythe was standing on the steps.

"Now, what's all this, Jamie?" asked PC Weir. "Ye say ye had these people in your house, last night? And didna report it?"

"I didn't know it was them, then," Forsythe said. "We were busy, and I wasn't looking at the box. Anyway, they were only here for a few minutes. Young couple, looking for a place to stay the night. It was only when I saw the news this morning that it occurred to me they fitted the descriptions of the people ye're looking for. I'm not saying it *was* them, mind. Only that it could have been."

PC Weir sighed. But he could understand the unwillingness of people to become involved in something that might cost them valuable time giving evidence in court.

"All right," he said. "They were here for a few minutes. Then they left. D'ye have any idea where they might have gone?"

"God Almighty!" Forsythe said. "Like I said, they wanted a room for the night. I recommended the widow Maclain. My wife telephoned for them and booked it."

Weir looked at his watch. "Then we have them. It's only half-past eight. I'll be going along there."

"I'll come wi' ye." Forsythe got in beside him.

They drove along the still half-asleep village street, and came to the house on the outskirts of the village.

"No car," Weir observed. "Damn and blast, they must've left already. Did ye get a look at it?"

"Never saw it."

"Well, they can't be too far. Let's have a word with the widow; she must've seen it. I can't put out a call if I don't know what they're driving." He went up the steps, rang the bell. "Come on, woman." He pressed the bell again.

Forsythe was peering through the stained glass as best he could.

"I think we should break down the door."

"We can't just break into someone's house without a warrant," Weir protested.

"We can if it's a matter of saving life." Forsythe drove his elbow at the glass, shattering it.

"I hope ye know what ye're doing," Weir grumbled.

"Take a look."

The policeman peered through the broken panel, at the feet just visible on the kitchen floor.

"Holy Jesus Christ!" he shouted, and thrust his hand through the aperture, twisting the latch. The door swung in, and the men half fell into the house. Weir ran along the hall to the kitchen door, looked at the scattered blood and the head battered almost out of recognition.

"Holy Jesus Christ!" he said again.

Ten

"I'm going to be sick," Raisul moaned.

"Well, get on with it," Kelly said. He pulled the car to the side of the road, opened the door, and vomited. "You have the guts of a field mouse," Kelly told him.

"Did you have to hit her, again and again. Kill her?"

"When I start, I can't stop," Kelly said. "Come on. Let's *go*."

"Where?"

"Some place we can ditch the car. Find a loch." She opened the glove compartment, took out a map. "Just over there."

"They have our descriptions," Raisul said, driving as fast as he could. "We may as well give ourselves up."

"Fuck that," Kelly said. "How many people pay attention to descriptions? Save where they leave a photograph lying about. There." They topped a rise, and the water gleamed on their left. "Drive down to it."

"Did you really kill that man?" Raisul asked.

"He had it coming."

"Oh, God, oh, God, oh God! Do you realise we're going to be locked up for the rest of our lives?"

"They don't lock up people worth sixty million pounds."

"I wouldn't count on that," Raisul said.

"Listen," she said. "You're in this as much as me, now. So you just stay close and do exactly what I tell you. Right? And the first thing is to dump the car."

"And then what?"

"Get another, stupid. The people who rented us this one have my name and card number."

"So will the people who rent us the next."

Kelly grinned. "Who said anything about renting?"

Raisul braked. "Now what?"

There was no fence, and the water was only a few feet away. Kelly got out. "You sure it's deep?"

"They usually are."

"Right." She took out her bag, folded the map and put it into her pocket. "Turn it off the road." Raisul cautiously turned the car so that it faced the bank of the lake. "Put it in neutral and take off the brake," Kelly commanded. Raisul obeyed and hastily got out as the car slid a few feet. "This will be easy," Kelly said. "Push." They put their shoulders to the back of the little car, and pushed. It went forward, and over the edge, hung there by the exhaust and rear wheels.

"And again," Kelly said. One more heave and the car went into the water. It floated for a couple of seconds, but the windows were open, and it soon filled and went down. "Now we can start again," Kelly said.

"Someone's coming," Raisul said.

"Take cover."

They crawled down the embankment themselves, and lay against it, feet almost touching the water, while the car came round the corner behind them, at considerable speed.

"Oh, shit," Raisul said. "That's a police car. That means they've found Mrs Maclain's body."

"And they're chasing us. Let them go." The police car raced by above them.

"They'll come back," Raisul said.

"So? We won't be here." She watched the police car out of sight. "Let's go find some wheels."

"What did you say?" Joanna asked into the phone.

"I'm afraid it's true, Mrs Johannsson," Sergeant Maltby said. "The old lady was battered to death by a frying pan."

"Are you suggesting Raisul had anything to do with that?"

"I can't say, Mrs Johannsson. But it appears he was there.

192

That is to say, he spent the night at the house, with Miss Johannsson, and they have both disappeared. I mean, disappeared. The Scottish police got the make and number of the car they hired in Glasgow – a Renault Clio – and this has been circulated throughout the area. But no one has seen it, or the young couple. Of course it's still early. Maybe a sighting will come in by lunch. But the fact is that they are both now wanted, on a murder charge."

Joanna stared at the phone in total consternation. She simply could not believe that Raisul could ever kill anyone. On the other hand, she knew Kelly was capable of killing, and she also knew that Raisul was absolutely besotted with the woman. How in the name of God had so much misfortune come to this family?

"Mrs Johannsson?" Maltby was anxious.

"I'm all right, Sergeant. It's just been a bit of a shock, that's all. Will you keep me informed?"

"Of course, madam. At the house?"

"No," she said. "I'll be at the office." Life had to go on. Besides, to stay at home, alone, would be to go stark raving mad. Helen! Joanna leapt out of bed, ran along the corridor, threw open the door.

Helen was fully dressed and putting some things into an overnight bag.

"Hi. Just leaving," she said.

"Well, you can stay."

"Eh?"

Joanna sat on the bed, told her what the sergeant had just reported. Helen sat beside her.

"My God! Raisul . . ."

"I know he's innocent," Joanna said. "I just know it."

"But he was there. If he doesn't turn her in, he's an accessory."

"I know. Anyway, with all the police in Scotland looking for them, I don't think there is anything you can do. I'm going in to the office. You'd better come along."

Helen held her hand. "I'm so sorry, Mummy."

Joanna forced a smile. "Who'd be a mother, eh?"

They drove in silence, Deardon looking rigidly ahead. And he didn't even know the worst, yet. William and Peter were waiting in her office, together with a hovering Nicola.

"We saw the news," William said.

"That news is old hat," Joanna said, and repeated Maltby's conversation.

"Shit," William said. "So now we just wait for the police to bring them in."

"As they appear to have got rid of the car," Peter Young said, "it could take a while. Isn't she well-heeled?"

They looked at Nicola.

"She had something like two thousand pounds on her," Nicola said.

"Hell, they could even get out of the country on that," William said.

"Raisul doesn't have his passport," Joanna said. "And sitting here like a lot of cackling hens isn't going to help matters. Peter, William, business as usual. Just to make sure, William, would you check with the yard that work is proceeding on the ship. Reassure them that my family problems are going to have no bearing on the firm's viability. Peter, I'd like you to do the same with the captains of all our ships, wherever they are."

"Will do." Peter and William left the office.

"Anything I can do?" Helen asked.

"Business as usual," Joanna said again. "Tell you what, though: chase up Sedgling and find out if he's heard from Best. Your hearing is the day after tomorrow."

Helen nodded and followed the men.

"I can't tell you how sorry I am," Nicola said.

"So don't try. Now, I wish to speak with Mr Matthews and Mr Lustrum."

"Mr Lustrum has actually been on the phone just a few minutes before you came in."

194

"Get him first, then." Joanna watched Nicola go to the door, then asked, "Did you have something going with Kelly?"

"I . . ." Nicola licked her lips. "I was just trying to help."

"Yes," Joanna said. "Well, here's another one: did you have something going with Raisul? And don't tell me you were just trying to help."

"He wanted it, so very badly, Mrs Johannsson."

"And you don't mind in what shape, size, or sex it comes in."

"It's well . . . doing what comes naturally, Mrs Johannsson."

"It wasn't on your CV."

"Are you going to fire me?"

"No, Nikky. Not right now. But you simply have to start proving that you're one of us. Get Lustrum."

She waited, fingers drumming on the desk.

"Mrs Johannsson!"

"Good morning, Mr Lustrum."

"I assume you have seen the news?"

"Yes, Mr Lustrum. I have also been in touch with the police."

"What a mess, eh?"

"Oh, indeed, but some messes are bigger than others."

There was a moment's silence while Lustrum deduced exactly what she meant. Then he said, "I assume you mean to put things on hold until the, ah, criminal aspects of this situation have been sorted out?"

"That could take some time, Mr Lustrum. No, I am today instructing my solicitor to prepare a brief for the contesting of my late husband's Will."

"It will be nasty."

"These things always are. However, I am sure there is no judge or panel of judges in Great Britain who will determine that a young lady who is a convicted murderess and also has a record of criminal insanity is capable of managing an estate of sixty million pounds."

"May I remind you that your son is also involved?"

195

"Won't work, won't trade, Mr Lustrum. As you say, Raisul is now, unfortunately, involved. But that is a personal tragedy for me and my family. It does not affect the Company, and it cannot affect Kelly's right, or otherwise, to that money."

Lustrum digested this. "I sometimes wonder if you have blood or iced water in those veins of yours."

"It has been suggested from time to time."

"You understand I have no right to act on my own. It must be in consultation with my client."

"I entirely understand. However, I assume the police will tell you where Miss Johannsson is being confined, when they pick her up. In the meantime, I am instructing Mr Matthews to proceed."

"Ah . . . what kind of a settlement did you have in mind? I need to know this to put it to my client."

"You know what I want, Mr Lustrum. Businesswise, I require that endorsement to be renewed, with a guarantee of its being maintained. Personally, I really do not think Kelly should be allowed the management of that money, except under the most careful supervision. I will recommend to the court that it be placed in trust."

"And you would wish to be one of the trustees. Perhaps the only one."

"I think that would be quite appropriate."

"Suppose I were to repeat this conversation in court?"

"I'm sure it would amuse many people, Mr Lustrum."

Another short silence. Then he asked, "When do you expect Miss Johannsson to be arrested?"

"I would have thought, some time around now, Mr Lustrum. I look forward to hearing from you."

"A sticky business," John Matthews commented. "I shall of course prepare your case, Joanna. What are you planning to do about Raisul?"

"That depends on what he is finally charged with. I would hope you will take that on as well?"

"Of course."

"There's no way the two can be involved, is there?"

"I don't think so, legally. Whatever Raisul may have done when in the company of Miss Johannsson, as far as we know that has nothing to do with her inheritance. But of course, the two things will be connected in the public perception."

"Don't remind me. I'm still hoping Lustrum will persuade Kelly to settle, now that the odds are so heavily stacked against her. That will leave us with just Raisul to worry about. I'll be in touch." She hung up and leaned back; she was bathed in sweat.

Helen came in.

"Sedgling wants me to go round there again. He's a bag of nerves, and he hasn't heard from Geoff yet. Do you mind if I use Deardon? I'm really not in the mood for public transport, or even a taxi, at the moment."

"Of course take Deardon," Joanna said. "I'll be lunching in." She pressed her intercom. "Perhaps you'd get me a sandwich and a cup of coffee, Nikky."

"Right away, Mrs Johannsson."

Peter came in.

"Mind if I join you?" he asked.

"I'd love you to. Nikky, make that a double. All well at sea?"

"They're in a fairly agitated state. Understandably."

"But you reassured them."

"I hope I did. How are you doing?"

Joanna sighed. "I wish I knew. I think I can straighten out the firm's finances, by playing the wicked stepmother. But Raisul . . . he's going to prison, Peter."

"There's a chance, certainly. But if it can be proved he was only an accessory after the fact, and that he was forced or coerced into helping her . . ."

"How are we going to prove that? Do you really suppose she'll admit it? She's as vicious as they come. If she goes down, she'll want to take him with her. So it'll be his word against hers . . . what a mess."

Peter peered at her. "You need a break."

"How do I do that? Life is rushing by, carrying me with it."

"You can sidestep it for an hour or two."

"Doing what?"

Nicola arrived with the cardboard boxes containing the sandwiches and coffee.

"We'll take these with us," Peter said. "Mrs Johannsson and I are going out this afternoon, Nicola. Probably we won't be back."

Nicola looked at Joanna for confirmation.

"If that's what the man says," Joanna said. Nicola fled in confusion. "The masterful male," Joanna said. "Where are you taking me?"

"Somewhere far away from all this. Just for a couple of hours. We can eat on the way. But you can't help matters by staying here, brooding."

"And when the police call to say they've arrested Raisul?"

"Good thinking." He pressed the intercom. "Nicola, we'll be using my car. You can reach us on that phone. But only with news of Mr Raisul. Understood?"

"God," Raisul said. "I am exhausted. And thirsty. And I could eat a horse."

They had spent several hours tramping through the heather and up and down hills, staying off the roads, going to ground whenever they saw a car in the distance. At least the police hadn't as yet mounted a helicopter search, because they supposed the fugitives were still using the car and would eventually be picked up, or the car found abandoned to give a clue as to their whereabouts.

"No horses," Kelly said, lying on her stomach to survey the next valley. "There's another loch, though. We can have a drink."

"It won't be very sanitary. We could catch something."

"For Christ's sake, what does it matter, if they're going to hang us anyway?"

"They don't hang people in England nowadays," Raisul said. "They send you to prison. For twenty-five years, if it's murder. But if you behave yourself you're normally out after ten."

"What a soggy system. Prison." She shivered. "I've been there. But say, ten years! I'll be thirty-four. And I'll still have my sixty million. What a hoot."

"So, now you intend to give yourself up. And me?"

"No way. Let's have a bit of fun. If all they're gonna do at the end of it is lock us up for ten years. What we need to do is get south."

"And then what?"

"Listen. That guy, Geoff, who drew a knife on you. Before you came he was trying to get me to go off with him. Seems he has this pal of his living in some forest you all have on the south coast . . ."

"The New Forest," Raisul said.

"That's it. Seems this friend lives rough, and whenever he's in trouble, Geoff stays with him until the pressure's off. Nobody ever goes there. He gave me the directions to find it. He thought it might be a good idea for us to shack up for a while. Well, maybe it is a good idea, after all."

"Kelly," Raisul said. "That was before you hit him with a rock."

"He'll have got over that." She grinned. "I'll make him get over it. It's our best bet. That's cute, eh? Our *best* bet. All we need is transport. And a drink. Let's go down." They went through the trees towards the gleaming water, but had not reached it when Kelly checked. "Holy shit! Do you see what I see?"

"People. We'll have to forget it."

"Forget hell. That's an automobile, right?"

"Of course it's a car. It belongs to those people."

"Four people," Kelly said. "A momma and a poppa and two small kids."

"Kelly, if we go down there, they'll report having seen us, then the police will know where we are, exactly."

Kelly was still staring down the slope. "What number plate is that?"

"Ah . . ." Raisul shaded his eyes, "Ends in EL. I think that's Hampshire."

"And this is Scotland, right? So that car began life in Hampshire, and now its resting by the banks of a Scottish loch while the owner and family picnic. Right?"

Raisul sighed. "Right."

"That means they're on holiday, right? Therefore nobody back at their home is going to be interested in them for probably the next week at least. And even if they're booked into a hotel for tonight, the hotelier isn't going to go wild if they don't show up. He'll just write them off as uncouth sassenachs, not to be trusted. Right?" She giggled. "The great thing is, Hampshire is right where we want to go, *right*?"

Raisul was beginning to get the message. "You mean to steal their car?"

"You got it."

"Kelly," he said, as patiently as he could. "We are not more than a few miles from the nearest village. You take that car, and those people are going to walk into that village and report it. Then the police will not only know where we are, or at least started from, but they will know what we are driving. We wouldn't get twenty miles."

"Supposing they didn't report it?" Kelly asked. "Then nobody would know where we are, or what we're driving, or where we're headed."

Raisul frowned. "I'm not with you. Of course they'll report it."

"Like I said, nobody is going to start looking for that lot for at least a week. In that time we'll have got down south, ditched the car, and gone to ground. Right?"

Raisul stared at her, then down the hill at the picnickers, then looked up at her again. "You must be out of your mind." He gulped. She *was* out of her mind.

"Don't give me any of that crap," she said. "Once you've

done it once, it's easy." She opened the bag and took out a twelve-inch long kitchen knife, with both a point and a sharp blade.

"Holy shit!" Raisul exclaimed. "Where'd you get that?"

"Took it from that woman's kitchen. Seemed like it might come in handy."

He caught her arm. "You can't! You can't just kill people, children, because you want their car."

"How else are we going to get it without their spilling the beans?"

"Kelly . . ." he licked his lips. "For God's sake, this can't go on. Listen, we'll walk into the next village, and we'll give ourselves up, and we'll call it a day."

"Fuck that. You coming?"

"No," he said. "I won't let you."

She considered him for a moment. Surprisingly, her face was quite relaxed. Then she said, "You sure are a pain in the ass, little boy," and drove the knife forward. Raisul gasped and twisted away, and fell on his face. The pain was immediate, seeming to cut his body in two. The morning, the earth, the trees, the sky, seemed to be going round and round. He expected another blow, but there wasn't one. He tried to turn again, and look up, and found he couldn't move, His head flopped forward, and hit the ground.

"Hi," Kelly said, as she came through the trees. She had cleaned the knife on Raisul's pants, and now it was stuck through the belt at the back of her jeans, nestling between her buttocks, invisible beneath her windcheater. She had also wiped as much blood as she could from her hand with Raisul's handkerchief. Then she had gazed at him for several seconds, lying there on his face, motionless, while the blood gathered in a pool. Silly little boy, she had thought. We could have had something going. But he belonged to yesterday.

"Well, hello." The man stood up. He was in his middle

thirties, with a pleasant face and thinning sandy hair. He obviously liked what he was looking at.

"You guys on holiday?" Kelly asked.

"Yes. You?"

"Some. My car broke down, just across the top."

"Heck, that's bad luck."

"You know anything about cars?" Kelly asked, ruffling the hair of the little girl.

"A little."

"You wouldn't care to give me a hand?"

"Well . . ." he glanced anxiously at his wife.

"How far is your car?" the woman asked.

"Like I said, just the other side of that hill. Boy, was I glad to see you guys. This is no place to get stuck without transport."

"Absolutely," the man agreed. "I'll be right back, darling." His wife made a face, but didn't argue.

"Can I come too?" the boy asked.

"Sure," Kelly said, "why not?" The wife looked relieved. Kelly sat in the front beside the man. "My name's Jennie."

"And you're from the States."

"That's right. And you are . . . ?"

"Clive."

"Great. I like Clive."

"And I'm Robert," the little boy said.

Kelly smiled at him over her shoulder. But she also looked through the rear window; they were out of sight of the lake.

"Would you pull over a moment?" she asked.

"Ah . . . of course." Clive pulled in to the side of the road. "Something wrong?"

"I just need to pee."

"To . . . ah. Right. But not in front of the boy, if you don't mind. You can go behind that bush."

"Oh, don't be a stuffed shirt," Kelly said. "You come too."

He gazed at her, and licked his lips. He looked left and right, but the road was deserted. He got out, came round the car.

"Jennie and I won't be a minute," he told his son. "You just stay put, eh?" He followed Kelly into the bushes. "You're quite a girl."

"Not really Jennie. Kelly." They were out of sight of the car. She stepped against him, drove the knife into his chest, and then again, jumping back to avoid being soaked in the blood that spurted from his shirt. But her right hand was again covered in it. Clive lay on the ground, already dead. Just to be sure, she cut his throat, and saw that almost no blood came out. Then she returned to the car.

"Where's Dad?" Robert asked.

"Somewhere nice, I'm sure," Kelly said. "Let's see if you can catch him up."

"Shit," Helen said as she got back into the car. "Shit, shit, shit."

"Problem, Miss?" Deardon asked.

"Not a word from Mr Bloody Best," Helen growled. "And the useless Sedgling is bothered about how we'll stand if he doesn't appear."

"Won't he be breaking the law if he doesn't respond to the subpoena?"

"Not half so much as if he does."

Deardon waited, his hands on the wheel.

"I bet he's shacked up at that place in the New Forest," Helen said. "You know where that is, don't you, Deardon? You took my mother there yesterday."

"Yes, Miss," Deardon said, ears glowing.

"Just what happened, anyway, that had him crawling behind her like an obedient dog?"

"Your mother has a way with her, Miss."

"I've noticed. Well, let's see if I have a way with me. Take me down there."

"You, Miss?"

"Who else have you got?"

"Now, Miss?"

"Yes, now. Mother said I could have you for as long as I need you."

Deardon made no comment, engaged gear, and began threading his way through the London traffic. Helen looked at her watch.

"Tell you what. We'll stop and have a pub lunch on the way."

"That would be very nice, Miss." He drove out of town, and they stopped in a village in Surrey. "Where would you like to eat, Miss?"

"You're embarrassed about being in uniform?"

"I was afraid you might not think it proper, to be seen eating with me, in uniform."

"I hadn't thought about it. Okay, we'll eat in the garden." She opened her bag. "Here's twenty pounds. Lunch, and a bottle of wine."

"I'm driving, Miss."

"You can have a glass," Helen said. "I'll drink the rest."

She waited, at an Olde Worlde table in the beer garden, while he brought the tray and set it down.

"I'll be mum." She served. "Good choice. Boy, was I hungry." He apparently was too. Helen poured the wine. "What do you think of it all, Colin? That's your name, right?"

"That is right, Miss. Think of what all?"

"Working for this crazy family."

"It is exciting, Miss."

He was such a good-looking man. And his presence was curiously reassuring.

"It's been more exciting in the past," she said. "You know about me?"

"Only what I've read in the papers, Miss."

"And that was quite a lot. You ever been married?"

"Yes, Miss. It didn't work out."

"Neither did mine. So, who's the lucky girlfriend?"

"There isn't one, right this minute. Working for your mother doesn't really give one much time off."

"And now I'm taking up your afternoons as well."

"I can't think of anything I'd rather be doing, Miss."

"Than driving me around England?"

"Than being in your company."

She looked into his eyes. "You know I have, from time to time, been a very bad girl?"

He smiled. "Maybe I'm counting on that."

"You got it." She finished the wine. "Let's go."

He followed her back to the car. "Where to, Miss?"

She got into the front beside him. "I don't really care. Someplace private."

Deardon drove out of the pub yard, and soon found a quiet country lane, still driving south. It was early afternoon, but there was still a lot of traffic.

"Privacy is hard to come by in this country." Helen said, and slid her hand up and down his tunic, releasing the buttons. "I'm getting to the bursting stage. We're supposed to be going to the New Forest."

"To Best's hideout?"

"We can stop somewhere first. Or I won't be able to concentrate."

Deardon was already finding it difficult to concentrate, as her hand was sliding over the front of his breeches. His brain was in a whirl. He had accepted that she wanted to flirt with him. He hadn't really expected it to be taken so much further so very quickly. She had the hots. But she was the boss's daughter. She also, as she had admitted, had had a very chequered life; there were even those who doubted her emotional stability. Shades of Miss Kelly! The boss's daughter!

They were amongst trees, and there was a lane leading off.

"There," Helen said.

Deardon obeyed, brought the car to halt as soon as they were out of sight of the main road. Helen switched off the ignition and put her arms round his neck "I want a man who's going to be my man. Who's not going to betray me or trick me or hurt me. Are you such a man, Colin Deardon?"

Deardon kissed her mouth, while his hands slid under her jacket to caress her breasts. "I want a woman who will give me her all, who will not take drugs, and who will be a mother for me."

"Then call me Helen," she suggested.

"What's this?" Joanna asked, opening her eyes. It had been so relaxing, sitting beside Peter as he drove, she had no idea where. Or even for how long. But now the car was slowing, and turning into a drive.

They were on the outskirts of a country village; she had no idea which county they were in. There were no houses nearby, apart from the cottage immediately in front of her, but she could see a church steeple on the far side of the field.

"It's a little place I retreat to, from time to time," Peter said, then got out and opened the door for her.

"With your lady friends?"

"I only have one lady friend," he said. "And she's never been here."

Joanna glanced at him, and waited while he opened the door, then entered the small lounge.

"Cute," she murmured.

"Just right for two." Peter closed the door, watched Joanna wander into the kitchenette. "There's just the one bedroom."

Joanna looked at the stairs. "If I go up there, will I be raped?"

"Only if you want to be."

Again she glanced at him. "But I suppose now is not the time," he said.

"I don't know. It may take my mind off things."

Joanna climbed the stairs.

"I have loved you," Peter Young said, "from the moment I first laid eyes on you." And I love you more than ever now, he thought, as he gazed at her flushed and still excited body. That the Joanna he had wanted for so many years could be so abandoned, could have thrown herself about the bed with the enthusiastic sexuality of a young girl, he would never have supposed possible. For those tumultuous moments she had been his, and he could only imagine what splendid moments Howard Edge and Prince Hasim, and perhaps even Michael Johannsson, must have enjoyed. Now he could never let her go.

"That is a terrible lie," Joanna said. "The first time you saw me, you hated me. You felt I was going to disrupt all of Howard's plans."

"No, no," he argued. "The first time I saw you was the night Howard bailed you out of jail following that drugs bust. I thought then, gosh, if that's his latest, he's a lucky man."

"The drugs bust," she mused. More than twenty years ago. She had been sixteen, a total innocent who had had no idea what sort of a party Dick Orton was taking her to. At that, they had only been smoking grass. How times change.

"I'll admit I became alarmed when he told me he was going to marry you," Peter said, lying on his back and stretching. "But even then I was envious. Since then . . . I think I have fallen more in love with you every day."

She rolled on her side to look at him. He had retained more of a figure than she had had any right to expect, for a man of over sixty. She hoped he felt the same about her, for a woman of over forty. And as rapes went, that had been the best. He had been so gentle, so thoughtful . . . that he had also been slow had suited her perfectly.

"And you never said anything about it," she said.

"Who was I to compete with Prince Hasim? Or even with Orton. I know that didn't work out, but he was your oldest friend. And then Michael . . . he was such a huge man, in every way."

"All gone."

He turned his head. "Would you marry me, Jo?"

"Do you realise what you'd be taking on?" she smiled.

"Quite apart from the fact that my husbands have a tendency to to die suddenly."

"Having had you in my arms, I'd die tomorrow, happily. But I think I can struggle on for a year or so yet."

She sat up, went to the bathroom. "Ask me again when we've sorted out this Kelly mess, Peter. Then . . . I've a notion the answer will be yes. Now we'd better be getting back. God knows what has been happening while we were having it off."

He watched her dress, with quick, precise movements. Without warning she had changed from being the most sexually exciting woman he had ever known to the mistress of industry, and a mother with her brood to protect. He dressed himself, followed her downstairs.

"I think this cottage is a treat," she said. "Will you bring me here again?"

"Just name the day."

She kissed him, got into the car, called the office.

"Mrs Johannsson!" Nicola cried. "Oh, Mrs Johannsson! Thank God you called. I've been trying to reach you."

"They've been found?" Joanna asked.

"Only Raisul. Mrs Johannsson . . . they think he's going to die."

Eleven

Peter Young drove as fast as he dared. Neither of them spoke. Joanna was hunched in her seat, her fists clenched. All the staff of Caribee Shipping were assembled in the lobby to greet her. None of them had known Michael Johannsson all that well, as he had seldom come to the office. But Mr Raisul was known to them all.

"Will you take over, please, Peter?" Joanna asked.

"Of course. But wouldn't you like me to come with you?" She shook her head. "I wish you to hold the fort, here."

William was upstairs. "My God, Jo . . ."

"Where is he?"

"In a hospital in Glasgow."

"With what?"

"A stab wound in the abdomen. That in itself wouldn't have been life threatening, but he wasn't found for two hours. All that time he was bleeding . . ."

Joanna looked at Nicola, whose eyes were red with weeping.

"I've booked you on the four o'clock," she sobbed. "You can still make it."

"Where's Deardon?"

"I don't know, Mrs Johannsson. He went off with Miss Helen. I've been trying to raise them, but the car phone seems to be switched off."

"Keep trying." She looked at William.

"I'll drive you," he agreed.

"We'll have to hurry."

William concentrated on the road, but in mid-afternoon the traffic was light.

"What about Kelly?" Joanna asked. "Have they got her?"

"No. She's done another of her vanishing acts. They're hoping Raisul may able to help them with her plans, if . . . when he regains consciousness."

"When," Joanna said fiercely.

William made no reply for several minutes. Then he asked, "Did you have any idea something like this could happen?"

"No," Joanna said. "Would you believe that after what you told me I actually felt sorry for the girl, wanted to help her? Anyway, she and Raisul seemed to have something going. I can't imagine what happened."

"I would say he tried to stop her doing something else criminal."

Joanna relapsed into silence herself. If Raisul were to die, coming on top of Michael . . . and it had happened while she was having her first real sex in six months. She wondered if she would ever be able to have sex again?

The airline knew who she was, and seemed to have some idea of what had happened; they were cloyingly solicitous. But Joanna made it plain that she wanted to be left alone, and have no one beside her either. As it happened, she was the only passenger in first-class, and she was able to remain wrapped in her own thoughts.

Once again, no tears. She was too angry, with Raisul, for becoming involved with that witch, with herself, for allowing it to happen, and most of all with Kelly, merely for existing. Why, oh why, had they ever abolished hanging? She thought that if she was the first to get to her, she would willingly throttle her there and then.

A police car was waiting for her at Glasgow Airport, together with an inspector.

"A mighty sorry business, Mrs Johannsson," he remarked.

"What are my son's chances?"

"They're pumping him full of blood. He lay there for two hours, ye see. It was a passing motorist saw him and called the police."

"Two hours," Joanna muttered. "And Miss Johannsson? Did they have a car?"

"It seems not. There were no tracks near the body . . . near where Mr Edge was found."

"Then surely Miss Johannsson can't have got very far, on foot."

"Ye're making an assumption, Mrs Johannsson, that it was Miss Johannsson stabbed Mr Edge."

"Well, really, Inspector, who else could it have been?"

"We'll have to wait for Mr Edge to tell us, madam. As for the lady, I agree that she should still be in the neighbourhood, but there's been no sighting of her."

"Then she's stolen a car."

"Well, there's been no report of any car being stolen, either . . . we're working on it."

"I'm sure you are," Joanna said. "Are you intending to charge my son?"

"Well, madam, he does seem to have been involved in a murder. That of Mrs Maclain in the village of Dumrooie. She was beaten to death with a saucepan, ye ken."

"And you think my son did that?"

"Somebody did, Mrs Johannsson. And your son left in a hurry, with Miss Johannsson."

"Who was already wanted in connection with the murder of Adam Benham in Berkshire," Joanna snapped. "And I have evidence that she committed murder in Canada as well."

"Quite a little serial killer," the inspector remarked. "I'd give all of that evidence to your solicitor."

"I already have."

"Well, then . . . but ye'll understand that we must proceed on the facts as they are known to us. We'll just have to wait on the lad, to be sure."

* * *

The hospital was as solicitous as the airline. But there was a uniformed constable sitting outside the door of Raisul's room. Joanna stood by the bed and looked at her son. His face was invisible beneath the oxygen mask, but his skin was abnormally pale, and he was motionless. A nurse sat beside him monitoring the flow of blood and various intravenous drugs.

"It really is a miracle he's alive at all," the doctor said. "He must have a very strong constitution."

"Is he going to make it?" Joanna asked.

"I think he is. But . . ."

"But what?"

"There may be collateral damage. The blood loss was so great that certain parts of the body were virtually without any for some time."

"You mean he may lose the use of one of his limbs?"

"I was thinking more of the effect on the brain, Mrs Johannsson." He caught her arm as she swayed, and assisted her to a chair. "It's not inevitable. We won't know until he regains consciousness. But it's best to be prepared for these eventualities."

"When will he regain consciousness?"

"Hard to tell. Maybe today, maybe not until tomorrow. Will you stay?"

"Yes," Joanna said.

He nodded. "I'll arrange a bed for you."

"Oh," Helen said. "Oooh!" She had never had sex in the back seat of a car before, and presumably a big Mercedes was as good a place to start as anywhere. But then, she had never had sex like this before, anywhere. Deardon kissed her, again and again. She kissed him back.

"How long did you say you wanted to get between my legs?" she asked.

"From the moment I first saw you. But . . . it wasn't a matter of getting between your legs. I wanted to . . ."

"Kiss me all over."

He held her shoulders and gave her a gentle shake. "Do you think of nothing but sex?"

"There's not a lot else, is there?"

"There's a whole lot else," he said fiercely. "There's being with someone, sharing things, doing things together that you both want to do, smiling at each other, knowing that you can rely on each other . . ."

"You felt all of those things about me?" Helen was amazed. But pleased.

"I want to, and more. Because when you've achieved all of those things, together, you come up to marriage, and children."

Helen pushed herself up, instinctively felt on the floor for her knickers. "Are you asking me to marry you, Colin?"

He sighed. "You reckon you're a bit out of my class, do you?"

"Do I? My mother married money. She never had any of her own until she met my father. So I'm a one generation rich bitch."

"Are you saying you're interested?"

"I'm interested. But I'll need a little time. Last time around wasn't a happy experience."

"I understand," He checked that the lane remained empty, got out of the car and began to dress.

"You see," Helen explained, "I trusted that bastard so absolutely. Mother knew he was no good from the beginning. She did everything she could to stop us marrying. And I wouldn't take any notice of her."

"I wouldn't bet on Mrs Johannsson blessing this one, either," Deardon said.

"We'll have to see. Right now, I want to get to know you better. Let's hole up somewhere for tonight. Just you and me. I want to see what you're like first thing in the morning."

"I'd like to see you first thing in the morning too. But what about Best?"

"We can get him tomorrow."

"We've no gear."

"So we'll buy a razor and a toothbrush. I've my cards."

"And your mother? She'll go spare if you just disappear, like Raisul."

"Good thinking. But if I call the office she'll tell us to come back. I know . . ." She got into the front seat, punched the numbers. "Parks?"

"Oh, thank goodness, Miss Helen. Your mother has been trying to reach you."

"Well, will you tell her I'm fine, but I am going to spend the night with a friend." She giggled, and whispered to Deardon, "That's what Raisul always says."

"Yes, Miss Helen," Parks said. "But I think you should know . . ."

"I don't want to know anything, until tomorrow. And don't try calling me back; I'm switching off." She did so.

"Your mother . . ." Deardon said.

"Is going to go even more spare. You just have to stop being afraid of her, if you're to be her son-in-law."

"Am I going to be her son-in-law?"

Helen kissed him. "It's beginning to look that way."

Joanna called the office just before six. "Anything new?"

"I don't think so," William said. "Nikky would like a word."

"Have you located Helen and Deardon?" Joanna asked.

"That's it, Mrs Johannson. Miss Helen called in this afternoon, just after you left."

"Right. Did you tell her what's happened?"

"She didn't call here, Mrs Johannsson. She called the house, apparently cut Parks off when he tried to tell her about Raisul, just said to tell you she was all right but that she was spending the night with a friend, and rang off."

Joanna stared at the phone in momentary disbelief. A friend? Colin Deardon! At any other time she'd have been laughing, at herself. What a come-uppance. Not that she had ever been going to do anything about it – or would need to, after Peter. But now, with her brother perhaps dying . . . "Call her back," she said. "Make her listen."

"That's going to be difficult, Mrs Johannsson. She's switched off the car phone."

"Shit!" Joanna commented.

"I could inform the police and ask them to look for her," Nicola suggested. "We know she went down to the New Forest."

Joanna was tempted. But sending the police after Helen was the very last thing she wanted to do; Helen existed on a knife-edge as it was – what a simile, she thought, reminded of Kelly. "Leave it," she said. "She'll come home when she's ready."

Joanna dined on hospital food, and tried to sleep; she had been given a room next to Raisul's, and was terribly aware of comings and goings throughout the night. But no alarms. She was surprised to have slept at all, was awakened at three o'clock by a nurse.

"He's speaking, Mrs Johannsson."

Joanna had only taken off her dress. She pulled this back on and went next door, where there were two doctors and the policeman.

"I've sent for the Inspector, ma'am," the constable said.

Joanna was given a face mask, and bent over the bed.

"Raisul," she said. "It's Mum."

He was breathing without the oxygen mask, slowly and evenly. "Please," he said. "You can't . . ."

She looked at the doctor. "He's reliving the last few seconds before he lost consciousness," the doctor said. "That's natural. I think we had just better let him get on with it. He won't be able to answer any questions for a while."

Joanna remained sitting beside the bed after the men had left. Raisul was restless now, moving to and fro, but too weak even to raise an arm. A nurse stayed in attendance.

Inspector McIvor arrived just before dawn.

"Has he said anything?" he asked.

"Nothing coherent."

The doctor had also come in.

"Can I ask him anything?" McIvor asked.

"I'm not sure you'll get any answers," the doctor said.

"Ye don't understand," McIvor said. "The lad was found at two o'clock yesterday afternoon. That's sixteen hours ago. Sixteen hours in which there's been no sight of the lass. Sixteen hours!"

"And still no report of any stolen car?" Joanna asked. "Even if she kept walking in a straight line for all that time, which is hardly possible, she still has to be within a thirty mile radius."

The inspector nodded. "It's my belief that she's gone to ground. The most likely thing is that she's in a house somewhere, perhaps fairly close to where the lad was found. Which means we could have some more deaths on our hands if we don't find her, quickly. The lad may just be able to give us a clue." He glanced at the doctor again, and received a nod, so he bent over Raisul. "Can ye hear me, lad. Your mother's here, and I'm a police officer. We need to know who did this to ye."

Raisul stirred. "Kelly," he said. "Oh, please, Kelly." A tear dribbled down his cheek. Joanna held his hand.

"Kelly," McIvor said. "She and you were together. Where were ye going?"

"Going," Raisul said. "Going . . ." his voice tailed away.

"Going where, lad?"

Raisul sighed. "Water," he said. "There were people by the water."

"Water?" Joanna asked.

"He was found within a few hundred yards of Loch Larn," McIvor explained. "He would have been able to see the water before he was stabbed. I mean, while he was standing up." He bent over again. "Ye say ye saw people?"

"People," Raisul said. "People!" he suddenly screamed. "Kids! Oh, God!"

"I'm afraid that has to be it for the time being," the doctor said.

McIvor stood straight and wiped his brow with his handkerchief.

"I don't like the sound of that, Mrs Johannsson. If he saw some kids by the loch, and this Kelly was going to attack them, and he tried to stop her, that would be a motive for the stabbing."

"But the children . . . if there were several of them," Joanna said.

"We don't know how many there were," McIvor pointed out. "Or what happened to them. I'm going to have that loch searched. If he says anything else, call me."

"I think the answer will be yes," Helen said, watching Deardon shave at the handbasin.

"What tipped the balance?" he asked into the mirror. "The fact that I can do it three times in a night?"

"It's not a record," she said, stretching. "But it's a useful starter."

"The fact that I don't snore?"

"You do snore."

"No one has ever told me that before."

"Probably because you didn't ask. I just think you're caring. Are you really caring, Colin Deardon?"

"I care about you, Helen Edge."

"That I like. We'd better make a move." She got out of bed. "Let's go collect Geoff Best and make sure he testifies tomorrow."

"There may be some rough stuff," Deardon said.

"That bother you?"

He grinned. "I'm looking forward to it."

"Me too," she agreed.

Joanna had nodded off, still holding Raisul's hand. She awoke with a start when her fingers were squeezed.

"Hi, Mum."

"Raisul?" She couldn't keep her voice down, and the nurse immediately came in. "He's awake."

The nurse took his temperature.

"He's strong," she commented.

"I'm hungry," Raisul said.

"I'll just connect up the drip."

"Drip?" Raisul protested. "I'd like a steak."

"You were stabbed in the stomach," Joanna said. "Don't you remember?"

A cloud past over his face. "It hurts like hell. I never thought she'd do it."

"You're talking about Kelly, right?" Joanna pressed the bell. "Get Inspector McIvor," she told the nurse. "Quickly."

"Am I under arrest?" Raisul asked.

"Not yet. Whether you are arrested or not depends on what you can tell us. Where was Kelly going?"

"Kelly," he muttered. "I never thought she'd do it. I tried to stop her . . ." his voice trailed away.

The constable had come in and was making notes.

"Tried to stop her doing what?" Joanna asked.

"Ahem," the constable remarked. "It would be best if we waited for the inspector, ma'am."

"He's my son," Joanna said. "If I want to ask him questions, I shall." The constable gulped.

The nurse came in, with the doctor.

"How's the boy?" the doctor asked.

"Hungry," Raisul said. "And she's talking about a drip."

"Well, you must understand that you received a knife wound in the stomach. Aren't you in pain?"

"Comes and goes."

The doctor nodded. "Those are the drugs. We've patched you up, but I'm afraid we can't risk putting anything into your stomach for the next few days." He checked the board. "That apart, it all looks quite good. You won't excite him, please, constable."

"*I* won't," the policeman said, giving Joanna a dirty look.

"We'll wait for the inspector," Joanna said.

By the time McIvor arrived Raisul had taken some nourishment, and was clearly feeling much better. The inspector was looking extremely hot and bothered.

"May I have a word, Mrs Johannsson?" he asked. Joanna followed him outside. "What your son said, about people and water, was right. We don't know the whole of it yet. But there were certainly people by the water. We've found two bodies."

"Oh, my God," Joanna said.

"One is a female child, the other a female adult. They were in the loch, a few feet from the bank."

Joanna swallowed. "Had they . . . ?"

"They had both been knifed to death, yes. The woman – we reckon she was the mother of the child – was killed with two thrusts of the knife. The child had its throat cut."

"My God!" Joanna said again. "Kelly?"

"Well, we can't say for certain, ma'am. We've no proof of anything. But we really are looking for a serial killer now."

"But those people . . . who were they?"

"We don't know. There was no identification. But it seems they had a car; we've found tire tracks. It also appears that there might have been some other people present. Judging by the things we've found, we're thinking in terms of a family, picnicking by the loch, set upon by . . . whoever killed them."

"A whole family? Killed by one woman?"

"As I said, ma'am, we don't yet know who killed them. But it would appear that the killer, or killers, took their car. That was twenty hours ago. She, or he, or they, could be anywhere in the United Kingdom by now. And we don't have a clue as to the make of car, or the number, or where she, or he, or they, were heading."

Joanna went back into the room.

"Raisul," she said. "Those people you saw by the loch, can you describe them?"

"Yes. It was a family. Mother and father and two children. Picnicking,"

"And they had a car?"

"Yes." Suddenly his expression changed as memory returned. "Kelly was going to take the car. She was going to kill them all and take the car . . ."

"We think she did that," Joanna said.

Raisul gazed at his mother in consternation.

"We simply have to find her, quickly," Joanna said. "Did you see the car?"

"Yes." A shadow crossed his face.

"Did you see what make it was?"

His face twisted. "She asked me something about it."

"What about it, Raisul?" McIvor was also bending over him.

"I don't remember. I don't . . . something . . ."

"And you can't remember the make of car? Was it a big car, or a little one? A van? A camper?"

"It was a family car. But I'm not sure . . ."

"A family car," McIvor said. "And she asked you something about it. There must have been something unusual for her to ask you."

"Yes," Raisul said. "I can't remember . . ."

"I think that will have to be enough for the moment," the doctor said. "He's becoming agitated. He's still very weak. He'll remember, given time."

"And meanwhile that murdering lass is running around the country," McIvor grumbled. "Ye'll be staying here, Mrs Johannsson?"

"Of course."

"Then the moment he remembers anything more, have me called."

"Well," Helen said. "Now we beard the beastie in his den." She sat beside Deardon in the front seat of the Mercedes.

He was listening to the morning news on the radio: "Police

in Scotland are still looking for a young woman, named as Kelly Johannsson" – they stared at each other – "wanted for interviewing in connection with the murder of Mrs Alice Maclain in the village of Dumrooie. Miss Johannsson may have been involved in some other serious incidents. She is described as being five feet eight inches tall, strongly built, with auburn hair and attractive features. When last seen she was driving a Renault Clio car with Scottish plates. She may be armed, and is described as dangerous. Anyone seeing this woman is requested to contact the nearest police immediately, but under no circumstances to approach her."

"Jesus," Deardon muttered.

"At least there's no mention of Raisul," Helen said. "Either she dumped him, or he dumped her."

"I'd say he's well out of it."

"And that's obviously what Parks was trying to tell me, yesterday," Helen said.

"Do you want to go home, or back to town?"

"What for? I don't know where she is. Let the police get on with it. We'll go back up to town when we've got hold of Geoff Best."

Deardon started the car and they drove back to the main road.

"He lives with a fellow."

Helen nodded. "He's AC-DC. I know that."

"What I meant was, there's two of them. Just in case he isn't keen on coming with us."

"You said you weren't scared."

"I'm not. I just don't want you getting hurt."

Helen grinned. "Chance would be a fine thing. If Indonesian pirates couldn't make it, I don't see two layabouts succeeding."

"You're the boss. It's the next on the left. You ever been here?"

Helen shook her head. "I tried to keep the relationship on a slightly higher plane."

Deardon swung off the track and down the shallow slope. In front of them was the wisp of smoke he remembered from Tuesday, and the same acrid smell of burning rubbish. "I don't think he's home. I don't see the bike."

"Well, we'll ask his friend to tell us when he's due back, or where he's gone." She got out and walked down the slope, Deardon behind her, feet quiet on the thick bed of leaves. "You wouldn't think the council would allow this."

"There are two probable answers to that, One is that they don't know he's here, and won't, until someone complains."

"Well, I certainly am going to complain. What's the other?"

"The other is that in this human rights and legal aid oriented society of ours, even if they decide that they don't want him messing up their beautiful forest, it'd probably take them months of legal debate to get an order to move him on."

"Brrr," Helen commented. They arrived at the beaten earth of the clearing, and she surveyed the caravan. "It doesn't have a door."

"Ah . . . no. I broke it down on Tuesday. On your mother's instructions."

"Can't let her loose anywhere," Helen commented. "Anyone home?" she called.

Sammy appeared in the doorway, then gazed at Colin.

"You lay a finger on me and I'll have the law on you."

"Be my guest," Deardon agreed.

"Where's Geoff?" Helen asked.

"Out."

"When is he coming back?"

"How should I know? You his floozie? He's told me about you. Good in the sack, eh?"

"Shall I hit him now, or later?" Deardon asked.

"Later will do."

"Now, you listen here," Sammy began.

"I think we'll wait," Helen decided.

"If he sees the car, he may not come back at all," Deardon pointed out.

"Good thinking. You stay here with our friend, and I'll drive the car out of sight and come back. Won't be long."

"Inside," Deardon told Sammy.

"I'm going to the police about this," Sammy complained, but he backed into the caravan, followed by the chauffeur. Helen climbed back up the slope, got into the Mercedes, backed it into the lane, and drove it out of sight of the clearing, then pulled it off the track into the midst of some bushes. She got out and surveyed the car; there were several scratches on the wings but presumably Colin would be able to get them out.

She walked back along the lane, but had not reached the caravan when she heard the roar of an engine. She stepped into the bushes, watched the motorbike turn down the slope, bumping to a stop beside the fire. There was no sound from inside the caravan; presumably Deardon had Sammy subdued.

Geoff dismounted and went to the steps. Helen followed. He heard her footsteps, and turned.

"What the shit?"

"Seems we have to drag you up to London again," she said. "Tomorrow's the big day."

"You can forget that. I've been to see my solicitor. He says your mum acted illegally in getting me to sign that paper."

"We'll let the law decide that."

"Yeah? Well, you just take yourself off before I kick you off."

Helen waited, as Sammy emerged, Deardon behind him. Geoff turned, and swallowed. "Shit!"

"That's what you're in," Helen agreed. "And you'll be in deeper if you don't co-operate. You're coming with us."

"Like hell I am. Sammy!"

Sammy reacted, and attempted to turn and butt Deardon. Deardon caught him, lifted him from the ground, and then threw him down with considerable force. Sammy rolled and set up a high-pitched wailing. "You've broken my shoulder."

Geoff was advancing, assuming what he considered appropriate poses for unarmed combat, feet stamping, arms held in front of him, hands upright. He was taken quite unawares when Helen stepped forward, seized his right wrist, ducked as she swung her hip into his, and threw him to the ground beside his friend.

"Shit!" he gasped.

"Have I broken anything of yours?" she enquired, "Get up."

Slowly Geoff pushed himself up; Sammy continued to roll on the ground, groaning.

"We are going to have the police on you," Geoff threatened. "Assault and battery, grievous bodily harm, trespass, kidnapping . . ."

"There's a notebook and pen in the car," Deardon said. "You can make a list. Just remember, try anything like running away and I really will hurt you."

Geoff climbed the slope ahead of them.

"Turn left," Helen said. "It's not far." On the lane she turned back to look at Sammy, who was now sitting up, rubbing his arm, and staring after them. Then he disappeared behind the trees as they reached the Mercedes.

"Sorry about the scratches," she said to Deardon.

"You're forgiven. Get in the back," he told Geoff. He and Helen got into the front, and he backed the Mercedes on to the lane. Then braked.

"Hello, traffic," he said.

All three of them turned to watch the Vauxhall bumping down the track behind them. It pulled to a halt, as they were blocking the way.

"Well, hi," Kelly said, looking out of the window.

Twelve

Raisul was in a deep sleep, but he woke mid-morning.

"How're you feeling?" Joanna asked.

"Fine," he lied bravely. "How long do I have to stay here?"

"Until you're strong enough to leave."

"And how long will you stay?"

"Just as long as you do. I've called down for some clothes and things. Can you remember anything more about what happened? About the car?"

"What's so important about the car?"

"Simply that it's the one Kelly is now driving. The police want to pick her up."

"What will they do to her?"

Joanna sighed. "I imagine she's going to wind up in a hospital for the criminally insane. After a long and unhappy trial. You'll have to give evidence, you know."

"I don't ever want to have to see her again."

"Snap. But it's something that has to be done."

The door was opened by the nurse, to admit McIvor, who looked even more hot and bothered than usual.

"Awake, is he? Thank God for that."

"What's happened now?" Joanna asked.

"We've found two more bodies."

"Oh, my God! Whose?"

"There's no proper identification. The killer took the man's wallet. But the bodies are those of a man and a boy, both were killed with a knife – I won't go into the details if you don't

225

mind – and we reckon they are the other half of that family picnic. They were dumped in another loch only a few miles away from the woman and daughter. Lad, if you can possibly remember anything about that car, now's the time to do it."

"Hampshire," Raisul said. "The plates were Hampshire. I can't remember the number, but it ended in EL."

"Hampshire," Joanna mused. "Geoff Best is hiding out in the New Forest."

"Who's Geoff Best?" McIvor asked

"A thug with whom we are unfortunately involved."

"Geoff Best!" Raisul exclaimed.

"What about him?"

"That's where she's going. She had this idea of hiding out with him for a few days, until things cool down."

"Geoff Best?" Joanna was incredulous. "But . . . she hit him, with that stone."

"That's what I told her," Raisul said. "But she said she'd talk him into taking her in."

"With a body like that I suppose she could do it. Especially with a stud like Geoff."

McIvor had been listening to the exchange, patiently. Now he asked, "Have you an address for this man Best?"

"No," Joanna said. "But I can find it."

"Let me get on the phone to organise things," McIvor said.

They stared at Kelly in consternation.

"You're . . ." Deardon began, getting out of the car.

Hastily Helen interrupted as she followed him: "Supposed to be in Scotland, with Raisul."

"We split," Kelly said. "Hi, Geoff. How's the head?"

Geoff had also got out. Now he put his hand up and then lowered it again.

"Just don't let that bitch near me," he said.

"Now, that's no way to speak to a lady," Kelly said. "I thought you and I might shack up together, for a day or two. I'll make it worth your while."

"Where'd you get the car?" Deardon asked, getting the message that Helen wanted to play her along until she could safely be arrested.

"I borrowed it. You guys going some place?"

"We're on our way up to London," Helen said. "Why don't you come with us? I'm sure you could do with a bath and a change."

"They're kidnapping me," Geoff shouted, choosing his side. "Call the police!"

Kelly opened her door and got out. "You serious?"

"He's an important witness in my drug case," Helen explained. "We're just making sure he's there to give evidence."

"What a hoot," Kelly commented, and watched Deardon edging sideways to get in a position to reach her. "I reckon you guys know a lot more than you're letting on." She moved with startling speed, rushing forward and throwing one arm round Helen's neck and with her other hand drawing the kitchen knife from its resting pace in the back of her jeans. "Move a muscle and I'll cut her liver out."

Deardon stopped, taken entirely by surprise. Helen had also been taken unawares, and although she didn't doubt she could cope with Kelly in a fair fight, at the moment she was too conscious of the knife penetrating her shirt to graze her flesh . . . and of the fact that Kelly had already used a knife, more than once. Geoff looked from one to the other in consternation.

"There's no way you can get away with this," Deardon said.

"I guess not. But it'll be fun trying. You with me or against me, Geoff?"

"With you," Geoff said. "Just tell me what you want me to do."

Kelly was sizing up the situation. She intended to kill both Deardon and Helen, but she knew it would not be as simple as dealing with an entirely innocent and unsuspecting family. She could kill Helen with a single thrust of the knife, but when she did that the chauffeur would launch himself at her.

"You," she said, "Deardon, make one move I don't like and your boss here gets it. Geoff, tie his hands behind his back. There's some cord in the back of the car."

Geoff opened the boot, and recoiled from the considerable blood still there from where she had stored the bodies of Clive and Robert to drive them to the next loch.

"Come on," Kelly said. "You never seen blood before?"

Geoff swallowed and took out the cord. With this he tied Deardon's wrists behind his back. Deardon was breathing very heavily, clearly seething with anxiety to do something, but he was unwilling to risk anything happening to Helen. Once his wrists were secured, Helen realised that she was the only one who could save their skins . . . and she was just as anxious to do something as he was. She gave a heavy sigh, and allowed her knees to give way. For just a moment, as she felt the prick of the knife, she had a surge of panic, but then Kelly released her.

"Jesus," she remarked. "The silly bitch has fainted."

She bent over Helen, and Helen swung both arms as hard as she could into her legs. Kelly gave a startled exclamation and fell over, the knife flying from her hand. Geoff gave a shout and ran round Deardon. Deardon stuck out his foot and Geoff tripped and landed on his hands and knees. He turned, teeth bared, and Colin kicked him on the jaw, sending him arcing backwards to strike the ground heavily.

Kelly meanwhile was reaching for the knife, but Helen got to her first, hands clasped together to swing right and left into her stepsister's face, breaking the flesh and sending her rolling over. Helen picked up the knife and ran to cut Deardon's hands free. "Look out!" he shouted.

Kelly was back on her feet, but sizing up the situation and coming to a decision. She abandoned them and ran for the Mercedes. The engine was still running; Kelly leapt behind the wheel and drove away at speed.

"Shit!" Deardon said.

Helen went to the Vauxhall, peered inside. There was no phone, and the petrol gauge was showing just about empty.

"Shit," she agreed. "We need a phone."

"You." Deardon stirred Geoff with his toe. "Where's the nearest phone?"

"How should I know," Geoff grumbled. "You've broken my jaw."

"And I'll make a better job of it if you don't behave yourself," Deardon told him.

"The bike," Helen said. "We'll use the bike. Can you ride a bike, Colin?"

"Used to own one."

"Right. Come on." They pushed Geoff into the back of the Vauxhall and drove back to the caravan.

"Oh, no," Sammy said when he saw them.

"Now listen," Helen told Geoff. "We are borrowing your bike, right?"

"That is stealing," Geoff said. "I'll have the law on you."

"Just remember that you're an accessory in the escape of a murderess," Helen said. "In addition to everything else. And we'll be back later to pick you up." She got on to the pillion of the motorbike, holding Deardon round the waist; he had already started the engine. "Let's go."

"Where?"

"The main road, for starters."

"I wish I could come with you," Raisul said.

Joanna kissed him. "I thought you never wanted to see her again? Listen, I'll be back up here just as quickly as I can."

A police car was waiting to take her to the airport. McIvor went with her, although he had now officially handed over the chase to the English police.

"We're picking up traces now we know what we're looking for," he said. "Someone answering her description and driving a Hampshire registered Vauxhall fuelled in Carlisle last night.

229

The silly attendant thought she looked familiar, but he wasn't paying too much attention."

"Do you think she drove all night?"

"I would say so. She'll know we would eventually trace the car, and she'll want to get rid of it just as soon as possible. You'll be met at Gatwick, and taken direct to this fellow's hideaway. The police are just waiting to be shown where it is." Joanna nodded, and McIvor shook hands. "I hope it all works out for you, Mrs Johannsson."

"About Raisul . . ."

"I'm afraid that's up to the Procurator Fiscal. But it's beginning to look as if he was coerced into everything he did. So . . . we'll hope for the best."

"Any word from Mrs Johannsson?" Peter Young asked Nicola as he came into the office.

"No, sir."

"What about Helen?"

"Not a thing, sir."

Peter shook his head. She was such an unreliable girl. Who he might be accumulating as a stepdaughter? Just as he would be accumulating a possible murderer as a stepson, and certainly a murderess as a stepdaughter once removed. All to share the rest of his life with Joanna. But it would be worth it.

"Well," he said, "do some telephoning. Try Caribee House to see if Miss Helen has spoken with them. Then get through to the hospital in Glasgow. Then . . ."

William came in, and needed to be put in the picture.

"What a mess," he said at last.

Nicola had been calling as instructed.

"Parks says Miss Helen did call in yesterday morning, just to say she wouldn't be home that night. But she rang off before he could tell her what was happening, and he couldn't get her back."

"Irresponsible girl," William grumbled. Peter agreed with him.

"Parks also said that Mrs Johannsson had telephoned Mrs Beckett to pack up some things and send them up to Glasgow," Nicola said.

"Looks as if she means to stay up there some time," said William.

Nicola was telephoning again; now she looked at the two men. "Mrs Johannsson has just left the hospital, to catch a plane for Gatwick."

"What on earth is she going to Gatwick for? How is Raisul?"

"Apparently much better."

William looked at Peter. "I wish to God I knew what is going on. First she sends for some additional clothes. Then she catches a plane south . . ."

"One of us should stay here," Peter said. "I'll go down to Gatwick and meet that flight. And maybe find out what's happening."

William nodded. "Okay, Nicola, you can relax."

"I was wondering, Mr Grain, if I might have the rest of the morning off. I'm feeling a little stressed, what with everything that's going on. And Mrs Johannsson won't be returning to the office before this afternoon, will she?"

"I suppose not," William said. "All right. Go home and have a lie down. But you'll be in this afternoon."

"Oh, yes, Mr Grain."

"One abandoned Mercedes," Deardon said in disgust, standing in the railway station car park with his hands on his hips. The side had been scraped to add to the scratches Helen had inflicted. Actually, he supposed they had been lucky to have caught up with the car at all. They had reached the main road, and overtaken a police car. They had flagged down and explained the situation to the two constables, who had been passed by the Mercedes fifteen minutes earlier.

"Nearly ran her in," the police driver said. "She was way over the speed limit."

"She happens to be the most wanted female in Britain, at the moment," Helen said.

"Tell me another. Now, then, riding a motorcycle without a crash helmet, both of you . . ."

"For God's sake," Helen shouted. "Run us in, if you like, but get her first. That car was driven by Kelly Johannsson."

The two policemen had exchanged glances. "You serious?"

"Of course I'm serious. We have to get her. Please."

"You can't go driving around without a crash helmet," the first policeman said. "Tell you what. Park the bike in that lay-by and come with us. We'll find her." That had seemed the best prospect. And the big black car had been easy enough to trace, as the policemen had used their radio. "Looks like you could be right," the first policeman said. "Your name Helen Edge?"

"Yes. It's my stepsister we're after."

"Well, I'd say we have her. It's an hour's ride from here by train, to London."

"If that's where she's going," Deardon pointed out.

"We'll soon find that out." They went into the station and checked with the ticket office.

"Tall, good-looking redhead?" the clerk said. "I remember her. Bought a ticket for the last train through."

"Which was?"

"The ten fifteen."

Deardon looked at his watch. The time was ten thirty. "So she'll be arriving at Victoria at eleven fifteen."

"Give or take a minute or two," said the clerk, optimistically.

"Then, as I said, we have her," said the policeman, and returned to his car to call in. "Now, what about you two?"

"We'll use the Merc," Helen said. "I assume it'll work."

Deardon had been inspecting it. "She's even left the keys in the ignition."

"Great. We'll be on our way, Constable."

"Now wait just one moment," the policeman said. "You

232

can't just drive off in somebody else's car. That vehicle was stolen."

"It was stolen from us," Helen explained, patiently. "It's my mother's car."

"Can you prove that?"

"Oh . . ." her handbag still lay on the back seat. She opened this, took out her driving licence.

"This belongs to Mrs Helen Moore. Who is Mrs Moore?"

"That's my married name."

"But you said you were Helen Edge. Can you prove this handbag belongs to you?"

"It was in the car, right?"

"Yes, but can you prove the car is yours?"

Helen attempted another tack in preference to hitting him. "Edge is my maiden name. I use them both. I prefer Edge. For God's sake, Constable . . ."

"And you say the car actually belongs to your mother, Mrs Edge?"

"Well, actually, Mrs Johannsson. Joanna Johannsson? You must have heard of her."

The constable took off his cap to scratch his head. "Your name is Moore, but you prefer Edge. And your mother's name is Johannsson, right?"

"My mother was married more than once," Helen said. "Colin!"

"I'm Mrs Johannsson's chauffeur," Deardon explained, and offered his licence. But naturally that didn't mention Joanna.

"I'm sorry," the policeman said. "But I will have to get confirmation from this Mrs Johannsson, if she does actually own this car, and if you are entitled to drive it. You'd better come with us, both of you, and I'll get hold of Mrs Johannsson."

They drove into Guildford, and Helen was allowed to use the phone, the duty sergeant at her elbow.

"Peter! Is Mum there?" she asked anxiously.

"Helen! Thank God! Where the devil have you been?"

"It's a long story. But listen, we've got ourselves involved with Kelly."

"Kelly is in Scotland."

"She's actually going to be stepping off a train in London in about ten minutes. Then she'll be arrested. I need to speak with Mum."

"I'm afraid you can't. She's on her way down from Scotland."

"What's she doing in Scotland?" she asked, and Peter explained. "Oh, Jesus. Is Raisul going to be all right?"

"It seems so. But Joanna is coming down. It's to do with tracing Kelly. I'm just leaving for Gatwick to meet her."

"That bitch," Helen said. "Stabbing Raisul. I should have hit her harder." The sergeant gave a quiet cough. "Anyway," Helen said, "what I want is for you to convince these people that Mum owns our Merc, and that Colin . . . I beg your pardon, I meant Deardon, and I are entitled to use it."

"Put someone on the line."

The sergeant took over the phone and listened, nodding gravely.

"Very good," he said when he hung up. "You can drive the car."

"Tell us how we get back to it," Helen said.

"It's in a station yard. You can catch a train back to it."

"Well, really. I would have thought the least you could do is drive us back."

"I'm sorry, Miss, but all our cars are in use. There's a train in fifteen minutes. It's a stopper on that line, but you should be back at Alresford in half an hour."

"Big deal," Helen grumbled.

"Guess what," Deardon said. "It's eleven fifteen."

"So it is," the sergeant agreed.

"Your people are supposed to be meeting the eleven fifteen from Portsmouth to Victoria. It has a wanted murderess on it. Can you find out if they've got her?"

The sergeant looked at the police driver, who had come in with them.

"That's right," the constable said. "Phoned it through myself."

The sergeant made a face, but also another telephone call. He hung up with an air of resignation. "The eleven fifteen came in a few minutes ago. There were several police officers waiting for it. But no one answering the description of Kelly Johannsson got off."

"Well, I'll be damned," the policeman said.

"When you said that train went only to London," Helen said. "Did you know that it stopped before doing so?"

"At least once," Deardon said. "She could be anywhere in the country, again."

Nicola hurried out of the office and along the street, reaching her apartment in fifteen minutes. She climbed the stairs, shut the door behind herself, and leaned against it to catch her breath. And gaze at the boxes. She had been thinking about those boxes for twenty-four hours. Several thousand pounds' worth of clothes, including the two fur coats, and lingerie out of this world. All going . . . where?

It seemed certain that the police would catch up with Kelly sooner or later. Probably today. What would happen then? All of these things would presumably be confiscated. But they had all been paid for. And no one, not even Kelly herself, Nicola was sure, would know exactly how much was here. So no one was going to miss a couple of pairs of silk knickers and a couple of bras. Then there was that super silk shirt. . . . she laid them out on the bed.

Dare she risk one of the furs? She stared at them, her tongue slowly circling her lips. She wouldn't be able to wear it for a while, of course, not until Kelly was safely put away. But just to have it in her wardrobe, and stroke it, would make her feel like a million dollars. In any event, she told herself,

Kelly owed her that, as she hadn't actually paid her a penny, nor was she likely to, now.

She selected the fox fur, smoothed it against herself, and hung it in her wardrobe. Then she put the lingerie and the blouse in their appropriate drawers. Now, she thought, as Mr William had given her the morning off, she could just lie down and have a rest, and appear back in the office as bright as a button after lunch. She took off her cardigan and skirt, hung them up together with her shirt, and stretched on the bed, to sit up again a few minutes later as there was a knock on the door.

Shit, she thought. Who could that be? She pulled on a dressing-gown, opened the door.

"Hiya," Kelly said.

"Peter!" The chartered jet had been directed to a corner of the airport, and Peter Young had been allowed on to the apron to greet Joanna as she came down the steps. Now he took her in his arms to hug her and kiss her. He was assuming possession. Well, right that minute she rather felt like being possessed. "How'd you know I was coming?"

"I called the hospital, minutes after you'd left. How's the boy?"

"Bearing up. I don't know he'll ever be able to look at a knife again without having the wobblies. There are supposed to be some policemen . . ."

"Right here, Mrs Johannsson," said the superintendent.

"I'm to take you to where we think Miss Johannsson may be hiding out."

The superintendent nodded. "There's been a change of plan. Miss Johannsson did go to the New Forest, and there had an encounter with your daughter, Mrs Moore, and your chauffeur. We've some constables down there now, sorting things out."

"You mean you've got her? Kelly?"

"Unfortunately, no. She made off in your car."

"Shit! What about Helen and Deardon? What were they

doing there, anyway? They were supposed to do that yesterday."

"I don't know about that, Mrs Johannsson. As far as I know, your daughter and the chauffeur are all right. But Miss Johannsson has disappeared again."

"In my car?"

"No, madam. We have recovered the car, from a railway station. We had assumed that Miss Johannsson had caught the train, but she was not on it when it reached Victoria. She must have got off at one of the stops along the way."

"And you have no idea where she is."

"At this moment in time, I'm afraid not."

"Then tell me where my daughter and my chauffeur are."

"I'm afraid I don't know, madam. After helping us with our inquiries, they went off to collect their, your, car. I don't know where they went after that."

"I could as well have stayed in Scotland," Joanna grumbled, gazing speculatively at the waiting jet.

"If Raisul is out of danger, I think you could do with some proper rest," Peter suggested. "You can always go back up to Glasgow tomorrow."

Joanna sighed. "I suppose you're right. But I think I should go to the office first. I've been rather out of touch the last couple of days."

Nicola backed across the room, trying to think. But Kelly, if a trifle windblown, seemed perfectly normal. She closed the door behind herself.

"You look like a frightened rabbit."

"I . . ." Nicola licked her lips.

"I know," Kelly said. "I'm wanted by the police. What a hoot. But I'm giving them a run for their money. Now, what I want are wheels. Where are yours?"

"I don't have any."

Kelly frowned at her. "You don't have an auto?"

"There's no need for one, living in London."

"Well, you'll have to get me one." Kelly went to the fridge, poured herself a glass of cider. "I needed that. But first, you can cook me some lunch, or breakfast, or whatever. Say, what are you doing home at this hour, anyway? I'm not complaining, mind. I need all the help I can get."

Nicola fussed in the kitchenette; it gave her something to do. "They gave me the morning off. Stress."

"Big deal. Stress! *You* have stress? You got any wine?"

"There's a bottle." She watched anxiously as Kelly unscrewed the foil cap.

"What are you going to do?"

"Play it by ear." Kelly poured herself a glass of the cheap wine, sipped, shuddered, sat down, and picked up the telephone.

"Mr Lustrum, please. Oh, yeah? Well you tell him it's Kelly Johannsson, and I want to speak with him, now." She grinned at Nicola. "Hi, Lustrum, Kelly . . . Yeah. . . . Don't give me any bullshit, man . . . And don't worry with where I'm calling from. Just answer a couple of questions. What do they hand out over here for a couple of killings? . . . Twenty-five year max? That's what I heard. What about remission? . . . You serious? I heard that too. You mean I could get out in ten? . . . Less? . . . Yeah. That's great. Now tell me this, if I get sent down, can that affect my inheritance? . . . Yeah . . . Yeah. That's fine . . . No, I'm not about to turn myself in. Let the bastards catch me. Just take care of my money." She replaced the phone. "What do you think of that? If we play it right, I'll be certified nuts and sent to a prison for the criminally insane. Then all I have to do is persuade the morons that I'm sane again, and they'll have to let me out. What a system. But good for me, eh? Boy, that smells good."

They sat together at the little table to eat the scrambled eggs Nicola had hastily put together. Nicola's brain was running around in circles. But all she had to do was sit it out until Kelly left, then call the police. Yet she couldn't help being curious, about the one thing that interested her most.

"What are you going to do with all this gear?"

"Yeah," Kelly said. "It's a shame, ain't it. I never wore any of it, and I guess my figure may have changed a bit by the time I come out. OK, you have it."

"Me?" Nicola cried. "You mean . . . all of it?"

"We're pretty close in size. And I never paid you anything, anyway."

"Gosh." Nicola decided against telling Kelly that she had already stolen some of the things.

"I believe in making people happy," Kelly said.

Except when you're actually killing them, Nicola thought.

"But don't forget you're working for me," Kelly said. "I'll arrange a regular payment for you."

"Gosh," Nicola said again. "Did you really stab Raisul?"

Kelly frowned. "Maybe I did. He was a wimp. You didn't really have something going for him, did you?"

Nicola bit her lip. "No, no. He was the boss's son . . ."

"And he wanted a fuck, so you gave it to him. Why not? Now, those wheels. Tell me how we get them."

"I don't know."

"You're a shitting lot of use, you know that? I'll tell you how we get them: we hire a car. In your name. You have a driving licence?"

"Well, I do, actually."

"But no automobile. You're a mixed up kid, Nikky. Let's see it." Nicola went to the desk, opened the drawer, and took out her licence. Kelly flipped it open.

"No photograph. That's great." She grinned at Nicola. "Guess what? I think you're no longer any use to me."

Joanna sat behind her desk, surveyed the accumulated mail.

"Where's Nicola?"

"She asked for the morning off," William explained. "Said she was feeling stressed out after everything that's happened. She wanted a lie down."

"*She's* feeling stressed out," Joanna commented. "I don't

think she's going to last. OK, I promised you I wouldn't fire her over her carrying-on with Raisul, but I have to have a secretary capable of holding the fort. When's she coming back?"

"This afternoon." He grinned. "We didn't expect you back before then."

"When the cat's away," Joanna said, and rifled through the pages of her diary to the telephone section. "I think we'll have her back now." She punched the numbers, waited. "Just as I thought. She isn't home. There's nothing the matter with her at all." She punched another number, waited. "OK. Now where the hell are you? Outside Basingstoke? Tell me." She listened. "So you're going back to the New Forest to pick up our friend. What makes you think he'll be there, waiting for you? All right, have a go. Then come out to the house. We need to talk. I assume Deardon is with you? Of course I want to see him as well." She looked at her watch. "I'll be out about four." She replaced the phone. William and Peter were standing in front of the desk. "I am exhausted. Would one of you gentlemen care to take me out to lunch?"

"I'm on," Peter said.

"Well, then . . ." The phone rang. Joanna picked it up.

"Mrs Johannsson? Philip Lustrum."

"Hello, Mr Lustrum. Heard from your client?"

"Half an hour ago."

"Eh?" Joanna was totally surprised. "What did she want?"

"She was checking her legal and financial position."

"I hope you gave her the works."

"I told her she was looking at a life sentence, yes. But that I would of course help her as much as I could."

"Of course," Joanna said. "Do you have any idea where she was calling from?"

"Yes. I have traced the call. It came from the flat of a Miss Nicola Outridge."

"Nicola!"

"That's right. Do you know this woman?"

"Yes," Joanna said grimly. "Have you told the police?"

"I have just done that. But I thought you might like to know as well."

"Thank you, Mr Lustrum, I'll meet them there." She replaced the phone. "We may have run her down. But Nikky didn't answer the phone. Let's get round there."

"Ah . . . just what is your plan?" William asked.

"Don't worry. The police are on their way."

"The reason Nikky didn't answer the phone is that they have both probably left."

"Maybe. But it's possible she doesn't really appreciate what she's sharing her flat with. You keep trying to get her, William. Will you come with me, Peter?" They hurried down in the lift, dashed out of the building past the eyes of the curious staff, and down into the company car park. "This is when I wish I had Deardon with me," Joanna said.

"Won't I do?"

She squeezed his hand. "I wouldn't want you to get hurt."

It was a short journey, but it took Peter several minutes to find parking. By the time they got to the apartment building a police car was waiting outside, lights flashing. "I hope you weren't blowing your hooter as well," Joanna said.

"No, madam," the sergeant said. "Mr Lustrum said he thinks the young lady is in the building."

Joanna nodded. "In my secretary's apartment. Let's go."

"Madam, this woman is described as armed and dangerous. I have called for a backup, and I think we should wait for it."

"She also happens to be my stepdaughter," Joanna pointed out. "Who a couple of days ago tried to murder my son." She went up the steps, the sergeant, his constable and Peter behind her. As they reached the door, four more constables joined them, one a woman, and all armed. Joanna rang the number of Nicola's apartment, and again, and got no reply.

The sergeant then rang the floor below, and this time a woman answered.

"Police?" she enquired. "I don't have nothing to do with them police."

241

"I'm sure you don't, madam," the sergeant said. "We just require to be let into the building."

"You got a warrant?"

"She's been watching too many TV programmes," the sergeant muttered. "No, madam, I do not have a warrant, but I can get one and it will include arresting those who have obstructed the course of justice."

By now quite a crowd had gathered behind them. The woman mumbled something, but the street door clicked open. The sergeant led the way up the stairs, and found the woman waiting on the second landing.

"Who're you looking for, anyway?" she asked.

"Miss Outridge. Do you know her?"

The woman shrugged. "Keeps to herself."

"But she's up there now?"

Another shrug. "I wouldn't know. She came in a couple of hours ago. Then I think a friend called. Then the friend left, I think. I don't spend my time listening, you know."

Just a high proportion of it, Joanna thought, and went on up the stairs. She rang Nicola's bell, but there was no response. Peter and the policemen joined her, and the sergeant tried the bell, with no more success.

"Break down the door," Joanna said.

"I'm afraid we would need a warrant to do that, madam," the sergeant said.

"Look," Joanna said. "We know she's in there, right? We know she had a visitor, who then left. That visitor can only have been Kelly, because she called her solicitor from this flat. I don't think we have time to find a magistrate and get a warrant. I'll give you the authority to break down the door. Miss Outridge is my private secretary. If there is any problem, I'll pay for the damage."

The sergeant continued to look doubtful, but he nodded to his constables. Two of them launched their shoulders at the door, which creaked, but held. The woman from the lower flat watched them, arms folded. The two policemen again heaved against the door, and this time there was a cracking sound. The third heave did it, and the door swung back, the lock shattered and half off its hinges, while two panels were cracked.

The policemen stumbled into the darkened flat – the drapes were drawn – and checked, inhaling the stale air. Joanna slid her hand along the wall and found the light switch, and they gazed at the lounge and kitchenette, the piles of scattered clothing.

"Someone seems to have come into a fortune," the sergeant remarked.

Joanna opened the bedroom door, switched on that light, and immediately recoiled. "Oh, my God!"

Peter caught her before she fell, while the sergeant pushed past her to gaze at the bed, and the young woman sprawled across it on her back, wearing only bra and knickers, and with her throat cut from ear to ear, the blood staining the sheets.

"Holy Christ," the sergeant said. "Don't touch anything," he snapped, as Joanna started forward. "You know this lady?"

"I told you, she is . . . was, my secretary." Peter was holding her arm.

"And you think this Kelly Johannsson carved her up?"

"I know she did."

"What about all these clothes?"

"Expensive," Peter commented. "I'd say they belong to Kelly."

"But she's not here. Why are they scattered about?"

"Haven't a clue."

The sergeant peered at Nicola. "And what's she doing, lying about the place in her underwear?"

"She and Kelly were lovers," Joanna said., "Do you mind if I go outside?"

"Go ahead," the sergeant said, and began telephoning.

Peter escorted Joanna down the stairs. By now all the occupants of the other flats who were at home had appeared to gawk.

"You OK?" Peter asked, when they reached the street to

243

confront an even larger crowd, being kept back by several policemen.

Joanna took great gulps of the fresh air. "I'm glad we hadn't lunched. Where is she, Peter?"

"She can't be very far. And in an hour she'll have every policeman in London looking for her."

"Thank God for that. Listen, I need to lie down."

He nodded. "I'll take you home. Parks can fix us lunch. When this is over," he said, as he joined the line of traffic, "I am going to take you away for a very long ocean cruise. And it won't be in one of our ships, either. Total relaxation will be the order of the day."

"Oh, yes," she said. "I'd like that." She leaned back and closed her eyes. Then opened them again and sat up. With her eyes shut she saw Nicola, lying there, almost peacefully, apart from the blood. "Stay with me for the afternoon, Peter. Willie can run the office."

"I'd like *that*," he said.

"And the night," she said.

Neither spoke after that. They both had sufficient on their minds. An hour after leaving London, Peter swung down the private road and they saw the gates of Caribee House in front of them. There was a strange car parked in the forecourt.

"Helen?" Peter asked.

Joanna had been half asleep. Now she sat up and shook her head.

"Helen is using the Merc." And Deardon, she thought.

Peter parked beside the strange car, got out, and tried the driver's door. "Not locked." He opened the door, checked the glove compartment. "Hired."

Joanna had also got out. Her heart was pounding. "You don't suppose . . ."

"Surely she couldn't have hired a car? She doesn't have a UK licence."

"Nicola did. Who was to know the difference?"

Peter glanced at her, then at the house, which was quiet and could have been empty. But that was as it should be, in the middle of the afternoon.

"Right," he said. "You stay here."

"Peter!" She held his arm. "That woman has already killed God knows how many people."

He grinned at her. "I'm not about to add myself to the list."

"Yes, but she's armed, and you're not. We can wait. We know Deardon and Helen are on their way. And we can telephone the police . . ."

"And meanwhile she's inside the house. Doing what?"

Joanna chewed her lip. Matilda! And Parks, and Cook and Mrs Beckett. Which of them had let Kelly into the house?

"We can't wait, Jo," Peter said.

"Then I'm coming with you. Don't argue. I'm the boss." She kissed him. "For the last time, I promise. But we'll call the police first."

He hesitated, then nodded, and punched 999.

"Emergency. Which service do you require?"

"Police."

"Police. What's the trouble?"

Joanna took the phone. "This is Joanna Johannsson, Caribee House. I wish to inform you that a wanted murderess, Miss Kelly Johannsson, is inside my house."

There was a brief hiatus. "Where are you, Mrs Johannsson?"

"I am outside the house."

"And you are certain this woman is inside?"

"Yes," Joanna said. "And she is armed."

"Right. We'll be there in ten minutes. Do not attempt to enter the house."

"Just get here," Joanna said, and replaced the phone.

"Suppose she isn't inside?" Peter asked.

"They'll probably lock me up. Let's go."

"He said to wait."

"And you've convinced me that we can't afford to." They

went up the steps. The front door was locked, so Joanna used her key, and they pushed it in, and gazed at Parks, lying on his back in the hall, the front of his morning coat soaked in blood.

"Oh, my God!" Joanna said. "How many more?"

Peter stepped over the body, left the door open, looked along the sweep of the hall to the stairs. The small parlour was on their right, and further down the double doors to the drawing-room. On their left was the billiards room, and beyond it the dining room. Beyond the stairs were the pantry and kitchen. There was not a sound.

"Upstairs," Joanna said, regaining her breath from the sight of her dead butler.

"Just let's make sure," Peter said, and opened the drawing-room doors. But the big room was empty.

"She'll be upstairs," Joanna said again.

"Doing what?"

"I'd say . . . having a bath."

"You serious?"

"It's her favourite occupation. Apart from killing people." She led the way up the stairs, moving very quietly now, led him to the Blue Room door, listened. But if the bathroom door was also closed, no sound would penetrate out here.

"What about your other servants?" Peter whispered

"There's only Mrs Beckett and Cook. Both usually do their own things in the middle of the afternoon; they'll either have gone out or be in their apartments in the wing."

"You mean they don't know what has happened to Parks?"

"I shouldn't think so, or they're dead themselves. It's Kelly we have to get, Peter, and there's not going to be a better opportunity than while she's in the bath."

"The police . . ."

"At least let's make sure she's in there."

"You want her yourself," he said. "Because of what she did to Raisul."

246

She glanced at him. "Do you blame me for that?"

He shook his head. "But I'll go first." Carefully he turned the handle, and pushed the door in, then stepped into the room. The smell of a bubble bath was strong. Joanna stepped beside him, and they gazed at the open bathroom door, the empty, but still water-filled, tub.

"Shit!" Joanna muttered.

"She heard the car engine," Peter suggested, and Kelly struck. She had been standing behind the door. Now she hurled herself forward, her dripping body scattering drops of water. Peter half-turned as she hit him, sending him stumbling sideways, a gash opened down one arm where the knife had only just missed. Joanna faced her, gazed at the bared teeth and the blazing eyes.

"Run!" Peter shouted.

In the distance they heard the wail of a police siren.

"Bitch!" Kelly snarled, "I could've had something going for you, Stepmother."

She lunged forward, and the bedroom door was again flung open.

"Joanna!" Matilda boomed. "What's going on? Why are the police coming?"

Kelly turned to face her.

"Good heavens!" Matilda exclaimed. "She has a knife."

"Run!" Joanna shouted at her sister in turn.

"Silly girl," Matilda remarked, advancing into the room.

Kelly panted, looked from sister to sister, and determined that the bigger woman was the more dangerous. She thrust at Matilda, gasped in consternation as Matilda caught her wrist with all the panache and skill of her youth, and almost threw her across the room.

"Now give me the knife," Matilda said, advancing. For Kelly had retained the knife.

"No, Tilly, no!" Joanna screamed.

"The knife," Matilda said again, bending over Kelly. Who drove her arm, and the weapon, forward. Matilda gave a grunt as the blade sank into her abdomen, and Kelly pushed herself away from her and reached her feet.

"Bitch!" Matilda said, blood soaking the front of her dress and running down her legs. But she was still moving, reached Kelly and enveloped her in a huge bearhug.

"Get away," Kelly screamed, seizing the knife and trying to withdraw it. But Matilda was still stumbling forward. The two women hit the doors to the balcony, and these opened before the impact.

"Look out!" Joanna shouted, running forward.

But Matilda and Kelly were already across the balcony, striking the rail, still fighting each other, and then going over. Joanna ran outside behind them, looked down at the drive and the two bodies lying there in a gathering pool of blood.

A police car came down the drive.

"Matilda was dead before she ever hit the ground," Dr Buckston said. "It was her weight on top of the girl that did the rest. I'm most terribly sorry, Joanna."

"She saved our lives," Joanna said.

"Strange how you never properly know people," Buckston said. "I would never have supposed she had it in her. But as you say, it was a very gallant thing to do. I must be away." He stood above Peter for a moment; he had already tended the wound and arranged a sling. "You need to take it easy for the next couple of days, Mr Young."

He left, but Sergeant Maltby remained. "The bodies are being removed now, Mrs Johannsson. Poor old Parks, eh?"

"He had no idea," Joanna said. "So many people, Sergeant. So many people."

"Yes, ma'am. A proper tragedy. There's a chief superintendent on his way. There'll have to be a proper investigation, you see. Not that you personally have anything to answer for, you understand. But I'd be obliged if you didn't go out until after he's been."

"We're not going anywhere, Sergeant,." Joanna said, and

listened to the sound of a car engine. "That's probably him now."

It was Helen, running in front of Deardon. "Mother! What's happened? The place is crawling with policemen . . ." She gazed at Maltby, who stepped outside while Joanna told her. "Aunt Tilly?" she asked. "Oh, Mum!"

"I know," Joanna said. "We'll have to get hold of the children. Helen . . ."

"I'll do it," Helen said.

Joanna sighed. "So how was your day?" she asked Deardon.

"Well, madam, it worked out very well. The police have arrested Best, on a charge of aiding and abetting a known criminal. I don't know what the outcome of that will be, but he'll certainly be appearing in court tomorrow, and Mr Sedgling is pretty sure that Helen will get away with a suspended sentence."

"Never again to be quite so stupid, I hope," Joanna said.

Helen grinned. "I don't think Colin will let me."

Joanna raised her eyebrows.

"There's something we need to tell you," Helen said.

"I already guessed."

"And?"

"I couldn't think of a son-in-law I'd rather have," Joanna said. "Especially if he's going to take you in hand." The phone was ringing. "If that's the first of the media, I'm not in."

Helen took it. "It's Uncle William."

Joanna raised her eyebrows. "He can't possibly have heard yet." She took it in the study.

"Jo? Great news."

Joanna sat down.

"I've had Lustrum on the phone. He's given up completely since hearing about Nikky's murder. He says he will no longer oppose your contest of the Will, and will support your application to be made a trustee. He even feels we may be able to have the whole thing set aside, with provision for Kelly, of course."

"With provision for Kelly," Joanna muttered.

"Jo? Are you all right?"

"Oh, I'm all right. I'm always all right." She beckoned Helen, standing in the doorway. "Helen has something to tell you."

She gave Helen the phone and went outside.

"When we've seen this superintendent," Peter said. "I think you should go to bed and have a long rest."

"When we have seen the superintendent, Peter, I am going back up to Scotland to be with Raisul. Will you come with me?"